All Alone

Twitter: @MarkEdmondson77
Facebook: Mark J. Edmondson Novelist
Instagram: mark.edmondson77

For Mum

The strongest person I've ever known

All Alone

Mark J. Edmondson

About the Author

Mark J. Edmondson is a businessman from Bolton. He now lives in Atherton, Manchester, with his wife, Maggi and grandson, Joe. As well as writing, Mark likes to read, walk, play and coach football, and is also a lover of animals and nature, and even wild camping.

All Alone is the first book in the Whitford Stories series.

Oliver

1

Whitford had everything every other town had; a church, a primary school, a secondary school, a bus and train station, a library, and a retail park that had suddenly appeared as if by magic several years earlier. There was an industrial park on the outskirts with several factories where most of the town worked; those who didn't commute to Manchester to make a living. But the industrial park was hidden away, only accessed by a long road leading off the carriageway where if you blinked you missed it. So the town still appeared scenic to anyone passing through, with all the huge industrial buildings out of view.

Apart from the council estate on the east side which was mainly flats and bungalows, most of the town had semi-detached houses with front gardens and low bricked walls. The more expensive houses were situated on the main road that led through the town. These houses were only affordable to the likes of doctors, politicians and professional footballers. Because of this 'millionaires' row', as people referred to it, Whitford had a reputation of being a more sought-after area. Even though there were only twelve houses that fit that description, the rest all being more affordable family homes, and just one or two in between.

The population was around eight thousand, which didn't quite mean that everyone knew everyone, but it seemed as though most of the people who lived there were all connected one way or another, either by their kids going to the same school, or by working in the factories or the stores at the retail park.

There was some truth in the fact that it was a close-knit community. The church was still a regular meeting place for many, although numbers in the congregation had dwindled over the years. And the local football and cricket teams were another way of everyone coming together, gathering for the weekly games, standing on the side-lines and catching up on the local gossip. And the players from the older teams would of course go for a drink in one of the two pubs in the town, or the bar at the cricket ground, or even the small public house at the bowling club. There was always something going on. If not a sports event, there would be a spring fair, or a bring and buy sale at the community hall. Whitford was too big to be referred to as a village, but there was certainly a village feel to the place.

Oliver Derwent, aged ten, lived in Whitford with his mum. He was drawing a picture at the desk in his bedroom with the charcoal pencils his mum had bought him the previous week. The picture was of the tractor he could see in the distance through the window. It was parked in the field behind the farmhouse further along the lane. It was quite a way from where he was, but he could just about see it well enough to draw a reasonably accurate picture.

The sun shone through the window creating a diagonal shadow across the page. This didn't bother him, or distract him. He was enjoying the warmth on his right forearm as he gently moved the pencil over the paper. His left arm felt a little cooler as it rested in the shade.

He could hear his mum pacing around the house, getting ready to go out shopping, but despite that, and the chirping noises from the birds speaking to each other in their own language as they did every morning outside his window, Oliver was fully focused on his drawing. He always preferred to draw in pencil or charcoal. His teacher, Mrs Wheaton, was always telling him to add some colour to his work, saying things like, '*That would look nice if it was a little brighter,*' or '*Why don't you at least colour the sky in blue?*'. But he had no intentions of doing so. He liked his drawings just the way they were. All the shades of black and grey would allow him to tell the story just fine. He didn't need colour. And he couldn't imagine ever changing the way he created his works of art. He didn't draw for other people's approval. He drew for himself and himself alone. Although it did make him a little happier when his mum said she liked them. But even if she didn't say anything about his pictures, he would still continue to draw. This was how he liked to spend most of his time; in fact, almost all of his time. He would stop to eat, or drink, or watch the occasional cartoon on television, but other than that, drawing was what he loved to do.

Over the last couple of years, his mum had been asked to go into school because of the drawings Oliver had created. She'd had to go in at least five or six times.

Oliver didn't understand what the problem was. People sometimes die, so why couldn't he draw a picture of a dead person? And the drawing of the graveyard was his best work yet. He'd spent hours getting the shading just right on that one, just for Mrs Wheaton to phone his mum again, asking her to go into school for another meeting.

He really didn't understand. And he really didn't know what there was to discuss. He just enjoyed drawing, and he drew whatever he wanted. He didn't care if the drawings weren't to other people's taste, he just had to do it. Once he'd seen something he wanted to draw, whether it was something real in front of him, or something that had jumped into his mind's eye, he couldn't not draw it. It was like an itch he had to scratch and it wouldn't go away until he'd seen it on paper. It didn't bother him too much if it didn't turn out how he'd wanted, or how he'd imagined it to be. He just had to see the finished product in front of him before he could relax and move on to the next project. If a thought or an idea popped into his head while he was at school, he would think about it all day and run home as fast as he could once the school day had ended. Unless he was lucky enough to have had one of these images climb into his brain on a day when there was an art lesson. If that was the case, he would work on the drawing at school until it was finished. Even if it meant him missing his breaktime. And he'd much rather stay inside and draw than run around outside with the other kids. He preferred the gentle sound of the pencil sliding across the paper to the annoying noise of the other kids all running around, screaming and shouting.

Oliver lived in a bungalow next to Hunter's Farm. It felt like they were living in the countryside to him and his mum. It was surrounded by fields, and there was a small forest at the back that led through to the town centre via a nature trail that passed the pond everyone called *the bucket.* Oliver didn't know why it was called that, and he didn't know if it was its real name or just a nickname the locals gave it. And it was certainly bigger than a bucket. It was a little bigger than the large swimming pool he went to in the town with school.

He used to like going to the bucket, feeding the ducks while he sat on one of the benches next to the water, or maybe having a picnic on the grass. But this was something he hadn't done for a long time. Not since his dad had left.

Oliver briefly glanced up from his picture as his mum walked into the room. She was dressed in her red skirt and white blouse, her hair and make-up as perfect as ever. She would always spend a lot of time getting ready, and she always looked nice by the time she left the house. But Oliver didn't like it when she wore skirts like that one. Whenever she dressed in her more colourful clothes, people would stare; usually men, but he'd sometimes witnessed other women looking her up and down with a disapproving expression on their faces. Occasionally men would shout things to her or even whistle. His mum didn't seem to like it. She would always tut or shake her head while walking away. But she still dressed that way. Her clothes were always bright and colourful. He felt as though this always gave her unwanted attention of some sort.

Oliver really didn't like it when people would do this to her. He'd thought on many occasions about telling them off. But he didn't think they would listen to him. Maybe when he was older, he could tell them to cut it out, and maybe they would listen. After all, they had no right treating his mum that way.

'OK, sweetheart, I'm off to the supermarket. Are you sure you don't want to come?' she said, standing at the side of him with her hand on his shoulder.

'I'll stay,' he said, still drawing.

His mum leaned over and kissed him on the top of his head before looking at the picture. 'That's nice, Ollie. You like the charcoal pencils then?'

He nodded as he carried on shading.

The smell of his mum's perfume was overpowering. He wanted to cough, but he fought it, not wanting to offend her like he did a few weeks earlier. The smell was very nice, but whenever she'd only just sprayed it, it would always smell much stronger, and it would tickle the back of his throat. He could still smell it on her when she'd arrive back from her shopping trip, but by then it wouldn't be as strong.

'You're not going to...'

Oliver interrupted by sticking the pencil into the noisy electric pencil sharpener that was fastened to his desk.

His mum started again. 'You're not going to draw a dead body under the tractor, are you?'

Oliver shook his head before pointing to the tractor outside.

His mum leaned over him to look into the distance. 'Excellent. It's very good,' she said, looking back at the half-finished picture.

'Thanks.'

'You're getting better and better. One day you'll be a famous artist.'

After a brief silence as she watched him draw, she said, 'See, if you had a games console, that would distract you and you wouldn't be as good.'

Oliver had asked for a games console for the last two Christmases and birthdays. He knew they were expensive, and he knew this was something his mum couldn't afford. But everyone else had one, so he thought he should have one too. He did have one a few years ago that stopped working, but he'd heard they'd changed a bit since then. Deep down, he wondered if he did actually want something like that. Just because it was all everyone ever talked about at school didn't mean it would be something he would enjoy.

Drawing was his passion, and he didn't really want anything to get in the way of that. And the games console he had when his dad still lived with them – as great as it was to play with another person like his mum or dad – he found that he became bored of it when playing on his own. He knew the new consoles would've been much better by now, even though it was only a few years ago. But he still wasn't sure it was what he wanted. Asking for one just felt like the right thing to do. He wondered if he should tell his mum he wasn't that bothered, just in case she was putting money aside, trying to save up. That money would be better used on other things, like decent food instead of the cheap stuff she would normally buy. And she'd talked about needing new windows for the bungalow before now. He didn't know what was wrong with the ones they had. Although he had noticed the wood crumbling a little on the outside frame of his bedroom.

From the corner of his eye, he watched his mum pick up the unopened pack of coloured pencils from his desk. 'I see these were a waste of money,' she said.

He smiled and carried on with his shading.

'Right, I'm going. Is there anything you want?' she said as she walked away.

'Chocolate,' he said.

'I know that,' she answered, then turned back to him. 'You be good.'

'OK.'

'I'll be back in twenty minutes,' she said as she left the room.

'Mum!' Oliver shouted.

She poked her head around the door.

'I heard voices this morning.'

She suddenly looked a little flustered, as though he'd asked her something he shouldn't. 'Voices?'

'Yes. It was really early. The sun was up, but I think it was only about six o'clock. It sounded like a man talking.'

'Oh... err... that was just the television. I fell asleep on the sofa last night so the TV was still on when I woke up.'

'OK,' Oliver said.

After a moment's silence, she said, 'Twenty minutes, OK?', smiling once more.

Shortly after, he heard his mum go through the door in the kitchen that led to outside, and then she locked it. Oliver then heard the car making its usual grinding sounds before it finally started. It then fell quieter and quieter as his mum drove the car down the lane until he could no longer hear it.

The bungalow was on the outskirts of Whitford. It was a long way from anywhere else in the town as it was built on the land of Hunter's Farm. It stood at the bottom of the long and dusty gravel road that led from the carriageway. The farmhouse was about fifty metres away. Oliver occasionally had to walk past the farm to go to school, usually when his mum's car wasn't working.

He didn't like the farm. Mostly because of the huge German Shepherd who went by the name of Kaiser; Oliver was terrified of him. Kaiser was mostly black with the odd patch of brown on his chest. He always had a trail of spit hanging from the corners of his mouth, and he had one white eye. Oliver didn't know if he'd been injured at some point in his life or if he was born that way. But he looked all the more menacing for it; a menacing image Oliver had seen in many of his nightmares. He was a vicious dog, and he would run at Oliver barking and snarling whenever he walked by. He hadn't bitten him as of yet because the farmer would always shout him back before he did. But Oliver always wondered what would happen if the farmer wasn't there one day. Was Kaiser's bark worse than his bite? Or would he sink his teeth into the back of his neck as he tried to run away?

Oliver didn't like the farmer much either. His name was Len Hunter, and he was horrible. He was a bit younger than his mum, and he was thin and pale with messy hair. Oliver especially didn't like his eyes. He didn't know what it was about them, but they looked evil to him. He also looked at Oliver's mum in the way he didn't like, just like all the other men did; only worse. Mr Hunter would put his hands on his hips and make a groaning sound as he looked her up and down. Oliver didn't like people doing that. He understood that his mum was pretty. She had long dark, wavy hair, and he'd heard people say she had curves to die for, whatever that meant. Usually, it was a woman who would say that to her, which his mum didn't seem to mind. But it was when men stared at her that she wasn't happy, and neither was Oliver. Which is why he didn't want to go to the supermarket. He'd rather stay at home and draw.

18

He looked at the clock on his bedroom wall. This was something he did often, especially when his mum had gone out. He didn't mind being left alone, but he was always a little anxious. He was much happier when she was home. The clock read thirteen minutes past eleven, so if his mum was back within twenty minutes, then she should be home by eleven thirty-three, he thought. But he knew she wouldn't be. It was going to be at least an hour. It always was.

2

'Finished,' Oliver said, the sound of his own voice breaking the deathly silence of the room.

He pulled some pieces of sticky-tape off the roll, cutting each piece by pulling it against the serrated metal edge of the holder, and then carefully placed them in each corner of the paper. Once he'd made his way across the bedroom, he climbed onto his bed, and stuck it to the wall with all the others. There was a space between the picture of Kaiser – which, he admitted to his mum, didn't look much like him – and the picture of a ghostly figure he'd drawn making its way along one of the school corridors. He'd created that picture while at school and it had caused another spot of bother. The head teacher, Mr Grimes, had walked into the classroom to talk to Mrs Wheaton. He stopped talking to her when he saw Oliver's artwork, and told him how much he liked it. But when he noticed the faint outline of the figure of a man dressed in baggy robes, looking like the Grim Reaper – except carrying a wooden staff instead of a scythe – the compliments suddenly stopped and he and Mrs Wheaton walked away and had a private discussion. His mum was called into school yet again.

Oliver looked at the clock on his bedroom wall, on the opposite side to all his pictures. It was eleven forty-five. She was already twelve minutes late. He rolled his eyes and wandered through to the kitchen. Once there, he took a chair out from under the kitchen table, dragged it over to the cupboards and climbed onto it so he could reach the snacks.

He took out a couple of chocolate bars, then closed the cupboard door before putting the chair back. As long as he put the wrappers in the bin and pushed them down a little, his mum wouldn't know he'd eaten two. It was the perfect crime.

He ate in front of the television as he watched cartoons. Although he didn't like being left alone for too long, he hoped his mum would be out longer than usual. If she started making dinner as soon as she got back, he knew he wouldn't be able to finish the meal, not after eating two chocolate bars. But if she was another half an hour or so, he thought there would be more chance of him managing to eat it all.

She didn't like it when he wasted food. And he understood why. Money was tight and it was a waste for her to buy and cook food for him just for it to end up in the bin, as she'd told him many times before.

It was always about this time on a Saturday when his dad would get out of bed. He'd worked hard all week, so on Saturdays he would sleep in until dinner, and on Sundays he would get up earlier to work on the house or the garden, or to take Oliver and his mum out somewhere.

It was almost two years since his dad left without saying goodbye. Oliver was only eight at the time. He was very sad when he'd first left, but not nearly as sad as his mum was. She'd cried and cried every night for weeks. Oliver cried too, but as much as he missed his dad, and was upset that he'd gone, he only ever cried when he saw his mum crying. There was something about how sad she looked and the expression on her face that caused him to shed tears too. He still missed his dad, and hoped he would come back one day. Even now, whenever there was a knock at the door, or when his mum returned from a shopping trip, he hoped for a split second that it was his dad coming back home. But so far, his wish hadn't been granted.

He'd asked his mum several times why his dad left, and more importantly, where he'd gone. But she would tell him she didn't know, or she would change the subject and not really answer him properly. She would always kiss and hug Oliver whenever he mentioned his dad, but she definitely didn't like talking about him.

There were several photos of his dad on top of the chest of drawers in Oliver's bedroom, but his mum took all the ones from the living room walls down, and packed them away. He presumed it upset her to look at them. He didn't understand why. Oliver missed his dad like crazy, but he always felt better whenever he looked at the photos. He'd also attempted a couple of drawings of his dad, but they didn't really look like him, a bit like his attempt at drawing Kaiser. Pictures of people and animals – in fact, all living things – never quite came out as he imagined. But still objects and scenery were very easy. Trees, gravestones, cars, tractors, hills, fields, houses, and even ghostly figures; they were all easy. People's faces and animals weren't his speciality. But that didn't mean he wouldn't keep trying.

3

It was now twelve-fifty. His mum had been gone for an hour and thirty-seven minutes. She would usually have been back by now, but there was the odd occasion where she'd taken longer, presumably if she'd bumped into someone she knew and was chatting to them. He pushed aside the blinds and looked through the living room window. The long dirt track was empty. On a sunny day like today, when his mum or anyone else drove their car along the dusty, gravel road, the clouds of dust would hover in the air for a while, almost like smoke. But the air was clear.

Oliver went into his bedroom and sat at his desk once more. He took a fresh piece of paper from the top drawer, then picked up the charcoal pencil and thought about what to draw next. This was the most exciting time for him. He loved looking at a blank sheet, wondering what it could turn into. He loved the drawing process, but his heart always skipped a little as he looked at a new page. He could only imagine what story would be told by the time he'd finished the picture. There was something magical about taking a piece of paper and turning it into something that deserved to be taped to his bedroom wall.

Oliver also found numbers fascinating. Especially times. He would always try to work out how long something would take in his head. Counting the minutes of his mum's shopping trips were a regular thing. But he'd also work out to the minute how long he'd be asleep before the alarm clock at the side of his bed would wake him. He would do this before he went to bed, and after he'd woken up.

He'd gone to bed around nine-thirty the previous night, which was early for a Friday night, but his mum said she was tired and he should get an early night. He didn't understand why he had to go to bed early just because his mum was tired, but he didn't question her. Nine-thirty to seven-thirty was exactly ten hours, if he ignored being woken around six to the sound of the television in the living room.

Even at weekends he would set his alarm. He didn't want to waste time staying in bed. He wanted to get up and start the day so he could move onto his next drawing, or finish any half-done pictures.

His fascination with numbers would spread into his drawing hobby too. He had three separate folders in his cupboard. One had a hundred pictures in it, one had a hundred and forty and the other had one hundred and eighty. His mum bought him a bigger folder each time he filled the last. With the three folders and the thirty-four pictures on the wall, that made a total of four hundred and fifty-four pictures... so far.

He would cringe a little at the older pictures in the first folder, and the second wasn't much better. But he would never throw them away. They were his creations. And he also liked to see the quality of his drawing getting better as he drew more and more. Once his wall was full, he would ask his mum for another folder. He'd maybe ask her for an even bigger one this time, and then all the pictures from the wall would be put away once more, leaving the wall as another blank canvas, waiting for his new creations.

Oliver pushed his pencil into the pencil sharpener. He knew his mum hated the noise it made; he didn't like the noise himself for that matter. His dad had brought it home from work, and apparently, there were quieter ones available, but Oliver liked this one. Maybe because his dad gave it to him, and he remembered watching him fix it to the desk with screws. Or maybe it was because it sharpened pencils to a very fine point, which was helpful when drawing fine lines. No other pencil sharpener he'd used before had ever been as good, so he wanted to keep this one, regardless of the noise it made.

Before he could put pencil to paper, he heard a car in the distance.

He jumped off his seat and ran through to the kitchen. Once he was there, he opened the tall cupboard next to the kitchen door, pushed the mop and broom to one side and then climbed in before pulling the door closed on himself.

The previous week when his mum returned from her shopping trip, he'd hidden crouched down behind the door. He always enjoyed scaring her like that. She wasn't best pleased last week as she dropped a bag of shopping when he jumped out, grabbing her ankle as she walked in with the bags. But nothing was broken, so she eventually saw the funny side.

He waited quietly in the dark, hearing nothing but his own breathing, which was more rapid than usual as he felt the excitement of the game.

He waited.

He stood in the dark cupboard for a good couple of minutes. When nothing happened, he opened the door and poked his head out, listening for the sound of his mum's car. He couldn't hear any movement from outside of the bungalow. He couldn't hear anything at all.

Oliver climbed out of the cupboard, fighting with the falling mop handle as he pushed it back inside before closing the door, and walked back through to his bedroom to look through the window.

The car wasn't there.

He made his way to the living room and looked through that window. There was no car on the lane, but there was a cloud of dust hovering in the air. Oliver presumed it must've been a car from the farm.

He looked at the clock, did the maths in his head once more, and then shrugged and went back into his bedroom to begin his next masterpiece.

4

Oliver didn't have many friends at school. In fact, he didn't really have any friends at all. Although his teacher would always seat everyone in groups of four or five, Oliver would always sit farthest away from the others. There would be three or four kids sat around one side of the table and he would sit in the opposite corner. He would've preferred to sit on his own really, but Mrs Wheaton wouldn't allow it. He didn't see the problem. But on one of the many times his mum was asked to go into school, Mrs Wheaton must've discussed this with her, because she asked him that night why he didn't have any friends. Oliver had never given it any thought before. It's not like he didn't join in with the lessons. If Mrs Wheaton asked the class a question, Oliver would put his hand up if he knew the answer. If it was a maths question, Mrs Wheaton would sometimes say, *Anyone except Oliver.* At first, he was offended by this, but she explained after class one day that it was a compliment because he was better at maths than everyone else, and so he had to give the other children a chance. Oliver understood.

Although he didn't have any friends, he didn't mind talking to other children in the classroom, or in the playground. He just would've liked to have a desk to himself, and he preferred to get his head down and get on with his work rather than chatting to the other kids or messing about like some of the others would. For some reason, this, just like his choice of drawings, seemed to cause more discussions amongst the adults.

He didn't understand why they couldn't just leave him alone. Everything he did seemed to cause a meeting between the teachers and his mum. He was happy at school. There was no need to keep talking about these things; he was perfectly fine. He did wonder sometimes if it was something to do with his dad. He didn't recall one of these meetings ever happening before his dad left home. So maybe it was something to do with him.

His mum had asked Oliver several times if he wanted a friend to come to tea one night. Or even a weekend sleepover. But Oliver always said no. He didn't see the point. Why would he want someone in his bedroom, messing things up and more importantly, interrupting his drawing? He said this whenever she brought it up and eventually, she stopped asking. He was quite happy on his own. And he liked all his toys and ornaments arranged in a certain way. He didn't like it when his mum moved things while dusting, so he wouldn't be happy if anyone else moved them.

This was another reason he wished he could sit on his own in the classroom. Before every lesson began, he would take out his pencils and pens, erasers, and all the other items from his pencil case, and lay them out neatly on his desk. If anyone was sat next to him, they would most likely disturb his arrangement. And he really wouldn't like that. He wouldn't be able to concentrate.

Now, as he sat at the desk in his bedroom, he was *in the zone* with the picture he was drawing. His mum would sometimes say that when she'd been shouting for him and he hadn't heard her. He didn't know why he couldn't hear her; drawing didn't make much noise. It was as though he was focused on the picture so much, he blocked out everything else in the world. She used to joke that he wouldn't notice if the house was on fire while he was engrossed in one of his pictures. But he hoped that was an exaggeration.

The picture he was doing now was of a tree, with a boy sat underneath it with his knees up and his arms wrapped around them with his head down.

He knew that by the time he'd finished, the entire piece of paper would be covered by charcoal as he would shade all the way to the edges. The scene was becoming dark, definitely a night-time scene. Although people weren't his speciality, this one was turning out OK because you couldn't see the boy's face. And it wasn't based on a real person so it didn't matter what he looked like.

Occasionally, he would give the pictures a name. This one he called *The Lost Boy*, writing the title in the bottom right-hand corner. He knew this was where he should be signing his name, but he never did that. He preferred the title to go there instead.

A while later, after taping the picture to the wall, he looked at the clock. It was two-twenty. Mum was late.

Very late. It was eleven-thirty when she'd left the house. It took him a moment to work it out, but it was three hours, seven minutes since she'd left. It wasn't unusual for her to be later than she'd promised, but not this late. Something was wrong.

He looked through the window. Still no car. He wandered around the house, wondering if she was playing a trick on him. But he really didn't think she would hide for so long.

He took the key from the hook next to the kitchen door and unlocked it before stepping out onto the gravel.

He felt the warmth spread across his body as he held his hand up to shield his eyes from the sun.

He then walked around the outside of the house so he could see further along the lane that led to the main road. The long, winding and dusty lane had hedges each side that stood about the same height as him, separating the lane from the fields either side. Oliver could just see over the hedges and into the distance where the farm was, but he couldn't quite see the main road.

There was nothing on the lane; no cars, no people, and no dust-clouds.

He contemplated going to the farm to ask Mr Hunter for help, but he didn't want to risk getting bitten by Kaiser, and he didn't know if Mr Hunter would help him anyway.

He'd tried to speak to Oliver quite a few times, usually about the farm, or the weather, just general chit chat. But his mum had told him to stay away from the farm. Although Oliver wasn't sure if that was because of Mr

Hunter or because of Kaiser. Mr Hunter had occasionally spoken to him, but he really didn't enjoy being in his company. There was something about him he just didn't like.

Oliver stood for a moment, pondering what to do. Then he went back inside the bungalow and closed the door behind him before locking it and returning the key to the hook.

5

He stood in the kitchen wondering what to do next. He thought about what the other kids from school would do if they were in this situation. Most of them would probably be so engrossed in their game consoles that they wouldn't even notice their mums hadn't come home. But he decided he had to do something. Something constructive rather than just sitting around and worrying. After all, worrying wasn't going to help him. So, he decided to do what anyone else would do in this situation; build a fort. If he was on his own in the house, he needed to protect himself, and a fort would be a good place to hide. He thought his mum might shout at him for making a mess of the living room once she was home, but he didn't mind that. At least she'd be home.

The living room reached from the front of the house, all the way to the back where glass sliding doors led to the back garden which overlooked the forest. Although it was all one room, his mum referred to that end as the dining room. At the living room end there was a two-seater sofa and an armchair, both facing the small television, and a coffee table in the centre of the room. Other than that, and the small table against the wall with a lamp on top, there was nothing else in there. At the dining room end, there was a table with four chairs. It was light-wood and matched the coffee table in the living room.

One at a time, he dragged the four dining room chairs into the living room and placed them in a square up against the wall. He had to move the small table with the lamp to make room.

Next, he went into his mum's room. Her bed was bigger than his, so the cover would make a much better roof than his would.

Back in the living room, he dragged the cover and lifted it over the four chairs to create the roof and walls. He tucked the sides under the legs of the chairs so the roof wasn't sinking in the middle. He then realised he should've left the table with the lamp where it was, so he pulled the chair away from the wall and slid the table along so it was inside the arrangement of chairs. He then put the chair back in place so the table and the lamp were now inside his fort.

After he'd finished pulling the cover into place, he climbed inside and sat on the floor and felt his way in the dark to the lamp and turned it on. It was quite a good little place to hide, but it wasn't very comfortable so he climbed back out and went to his bedroom and removed the cover off his bed. He dragged it through to the living room where he folded it over three times before sliding it along the floor and into the fort. Now he was finished.

He sat inside, leaning his back against the wall next to the table. He wasn't sure what to do while he was in there, but he felt safe.

A rumble in his stomach told him he was hungry again, so he left the fort and went to the kitchen.

He looked through all the cupboards, but there weren't many things he knew how to cook. He'd made beans on toast before now, and he'd even fried eggs, with his mum's supervision. But he thought the easiest thing was to get some cereal, so he poured himself a bowl of cornflakes, and took it back to the safety of the fort.

He felt as though the fort should have a name. *Derwent Towers,* was his first thought. But that was a bit of a mouthful. Maybe he'd just call it *the bunker.* Yes... that would do for now.

6

Pulling the cover to one side, Oliver looked at the clock on the living room wall. It was three twenty-five. It took him a couple of seconds to work out that his mum had been gone for four hours and twelve minutes.

He'd taken his paper and charcoal into the bunker and finished yet another drawing. This one was of his bunker, only in the picture it was outside in a field, covered with leaves and branches – and that gave him an idea.

He went through to the kitchen and unlocked the door. His feet crunched on the gravel as he walked around to the back of the house and to the small, wooded area at the bottom of the garden. There was no garden fence separating the property from the woods, just a grass lawn that turned to dry mud at the bottom near the entrance of the woods. He reached the opening and walked through. The cool air hit him as he stepped into the shade of the trees, and his stomach flipped a little at being in the woods on his own, and also at leaving the house empty. He wondered briefly if his mum would've returned by the time he got back. If so, she would be wondering where he was. So he knew he had to move quickly.

Oliver started gathering branches from the forest floor. When he had as many as he could carry, he set off back to the house, the sharp twigs stabbing his bare arms as he went.

Once back inside the bungalow, he stood them vertically against the bed cover to try to camouflage the bunker. When he stood back to admire his work, he realised he would need a lot more.

After making several trips back and forth, and fighting with the trees as he had to break some twigs and branches off of them, Oliver stood back and admired his creation. The bunker looked like something he'd seen on television at some time or other. He couldn't remember what the programme was, but he remembered a man making a shelter for the night in a forest somewhere. The man didn't have a bed cover, or a table with a lamp inside, but it was still similar to what he'd seen. And Oliver was very happy with it.

The foraging and carrying the branches to the bunker had worked up an appetite, even though it wasn't long since he'd eaten his cereal. He went into the kitchen and made himself a ham and tomato sandwich. It didn't look as good as when his mum made him sandwiches; the butter wasn't all the way to the edges, even though he'd tried his best to do so, and there were lumps in places across the bread. And the slices of tomato were ragged and a lot thicker than usual. But it would keep him going until his mum came home.

He looked at the clock on the wall. It was four-fifteen.

Five hours and two minutes.

As he climbed into the bunker with his sandwich and a glass of milk, he began to feel a little scared for the first time. His mum would never leave him on his own for this amount of time. He was beginning to wonder if something had happened. Even if it was her stupid old car breaking down, she could've walked home by now.

He ate his sandwich, drank his milk, and then lay down in his comfy new den.

He decided not to let himself worry too much as of yet. Surely, she'd be back soon and then he'd find out what had delayed her. He closed his eyes and tried to just enjoy the time in his bunker. Moments later, he drifted off to sleep.

7

Oliver opened his eyes, only to realise he was in the dark. He knew he'd left the lamp on, so why was it dark? He stretched a little before climbing out of the bunker. As he got out and stood in the living room, he realised the room wasn't as bright as it was before.

He ran over to press the light switch on the wall. Nothing happened. He presumed the meter must've run out. This happened a lot since the electric company changed the meter to one where his mum had to use a card to pay for electricity at the shop or petrol station. Whenever the power cut out, she'd have to nip out to get more electricity put onto the card. Once home, and the card had been slotted into the meter and the red button was pressed, the power would be back on.

Oliver remembered last winter, maybe around February time, when the power went off one evening and his mum didn't have any money until the next day. So they lit a few candles and cuddled up on the sofa to keep warm. He could tell his mum was a little upset about it, but Oliver enjoyed it. He found it exciting, and a little creepy, being in the house in complete darkness. And taking a candle with him when he went to use the bathroom was something his mum said people had to do all the time many years ago. Although he was scared, and cold, he would always remember that night as being a special one.

Sleeping with his mum, trying to keep warm by cuddling up to her, with just his cold face above the covers was a memory he'd never forget.

But now, in the house on his own, he wondered how he would cope without power. At least it was summer, he thought.

'Mum,' he said.

Nothing.

He didn't think she'd be home. Surely, he would've heard her. But he wanted to shout to make sure.

He walked into the kitchen.

'Mum,' he said a little louder.

Still nothing.

He then checked both the bedrooms. The bungalow was empty.

He looked through his bedroom window. Her car still wasn't there and it was getting dark.

The clock said eight-forty. He did the maths in his head. *Nine hours and twenty-seven minutes.*

Something was seriously wrong.

Oliver sat on the floor and wrapped his arms around his legs, just like the lost boy in his picture.

After building the den, he'd started to enjoy the adventure of being left on his own. But now, he just wanted his mum back. For the first time in a long time, Oliver began to cry. At that moment, he missed his mum, he missed his dad, and he even wished he'd agreed to have a friend stay over once in a while. Maybe if he had friends close by, there was a chance one of them would pay a visit.

At least he could've asked them for help, maybe get their parents to look for his mum. But as it was, he had nobody in the world he could turn to.

After a few minutes of crying, Oliver got up from the floor and wiped the tears from his eyes with his sleeve. He then decided it was time for him to act. He couldn't just sit there waiting for something to happen. That wouldn't get him anywhere. The time for feeling sorry for himself needed to come to an end. He had to make something happen.

After running through to the kitchen, he took his coat off the hook on the wall, put it on and then rummaged through the kitchen drawers for a weapon. He didn't want to take a knife, but he needed something to defend himself with.

He looked in the bottom drawer, the one where his mum kept a few tools. There was a hammer, but as he picked it up, he realised it was quite heavy. He then noticed a smaller hammer, almost like a miniature version of the first one. He picked it up and swung it through the air. Even though it was small, it was still heavy and quite hard to control.

He then turned it around and held it by the metal end. Somehow it was easier to swing that way. He gently swung it at the kitchen work top. Even though the handle was covered with rubber, it still made an almighty bang. That would put anyone to sleep if he caught them right with it. Certainly, the metal end would do more damage, but he wouldn't be able to control it as well as if he held it the right way round. Plus, he didn't really want to harm anything or anyone. He just wanted to protect himself.

He took the key from the hook, unlocked, then opened the door, and he walked outside into the cool, spring-evening air.

It was almost fully dark by now, but he didn't know if his mum owned a torch or not. She always used candles whenever the power went out. And even if she did own a torch, he didn't know where it was. He hadn't noticed one in the drawer he'd just taken the hammer from. So he'd have to rely on the light from the moon to see where he was going. Luckily the sky was clear, so he could see reasonably well.

He headed along the dirt track towards the main road. He knew he'd have to pass the entrance road to the farm, but he hoped that Kaiser was asleep at this time of night. He walked slowly. He couldn't hear anything but his own footsteps, and the sound of his own breaths. He tried to breathe more quietly, but he couldn't. His heart was racing and his pulse was thrashing in his ears. He heard the occasional noise in the distance, like the hoot of an owl, which wasn't unusual living close to the woods. And a few other noises that the forest behind the house would normally unleash. But other than that, and the gentle hum of cars in the distance, the air was silent.

A sudden, loud screaming noise came from behind him that made him jump. He held his breath, but then he realised what it was. He'd heard the noise before, from when he and his mum would sit out late in their garden. It was the scream of a vixen fox. That was what his mum said anyway. It was a horrible screeching sound that made his stomach turn. But at least it sounded a long way away.

After a few more minutes of walking along the track, he arrived at the turning to the farm.

Oliver was briefly tempted to turn right and knock on Mr Hunter's door. But he knew he'd have to get past Kaiser first, so instead, he decided it was best to carry on towards the road.

His heart bounced around his chest as he walked along the track. He could hear the occasional car driving by on the road, but he was still a long way from it yet.

Now he'd passed the farm entrance, he couldn't help but turn around to look behind him every few seconds. Kaiser was a noisy German Shepherd. Oliver knew he wouldn't just appear without barking and growling first. But he still couldn't help but check every few minutes to make sure he wasn't being followed. If Kaiser was to chase him, he would need as much of a head start as possible.

Oliver made his way closer to the road, still holding the hammer at the metal end. The hedges that flanked either side of the track came to an end which meant he could now see into the fields. For some reason, this made him feel a little better. He wasn't quite as scared now, probably because he had more of a view around him. When he was on the track where the hedges were, for all he knew, something could've been watching him, waiting to jump out at any moment. He was slightly less frightened now he could see all around, and it was slightly brighter with the glow of the street lights.

Finally, he arrived at the road that led into the town to the right. It wasn't a motorway, but cars were allowed to drive much faster than they were on roads around town. Because of this, his mum told him never to attempt crossing it. If he headed left along the road, there was an exit that led to the housing estate where his school was, probably about a mile away. The opposite side of the road was lined by trees which hid the fields from view. And there was the occasional lamppost that lit up a small area around each pole, but they didn't fully light up the road.

Now what?

He looked both ways, he couldn't see his mum's car. He half-expected to see it abandoned at the side of the road, having broken down, which it had done on many occasions. But there was no sign of it.

Oliver just stood there. He'd made it this far, when he didn't think he'd have the nerve; not at this time of night. But now he'd reached the road, he didn't know what to do.

Should he wave at cars to try and stop them? Should he keep walking and head into town? Should he head left towards the housing estate? He didn't know.

He just stood there watching the cars go by, becoming more and more nervous. He realised if somebody in a car saw him on his own, they might stop. But what if it wasn't a nice person that stopped? What if it was someone who wanted to kidnap him? The more he thought about it, the more he thought he'd be safer on his own at home. He really wanted to see his mum again. But he didn't want anything bad to happen to him. And surely, she'd be home sooner or later. She wouldn't purposely leave him on his own.

He saw the driver of a white car turn his head and look straight at him as he drove by. It was only for a split second, but Oliver could see the confusion on his face. The man probably wondered why a young boy was out on his own in the dark.

Oliver turned and ran along the track, heading back towards home. He didn't want anyone to stop and talk to him. He just wanted to wait on his own for his mum to return.

As he got closer to the farm turning, he slowed down. He didn't want Kaiser hearing his footsteps on the gravel. Although the farm was quite a distance from the road, at night and with no other noises, Kaiser might hear him.

As he reached the turning, he stopped and wondered if he should go and ask Mr Hunter if he'd seen his mum. But Oliver really didn't like him, and neither did his mum. Maybe he wasn't as bad as they thought he was. And maybe Kaiser was inside the house, rather than outside wandering free.

Oliver had never seen him at night, but he'd never been this far from his own house at night, certainly not on foot anyway.

He started to walk along the track towards the farm. He swung the hammer a couple of times, just to get the feel of it once more. He hoped he wouldn't have to use it.

He reached the area where all the vehicles were. There was a four-by-four car, a tractor – but not the one he drew a picture of – and a lot of equipment, including wheelbarrows, barrels, tools, and a digger that was parked next to a stack of hay bales.

As he got closer to the house, he heard shouting. He thought it was Mr Hunter but he wasn't sure.

He stopped moving so he could hear properly.

'What the hell do you want me to do?' the voice shouted.

Oliver decided to turn back. He sounded as though he was in a really bad mood. He was grumpy anyway, but he sounded really annoyed so Oliver decided to head back to the bungalow.

He walked a little faster than he should've done, not wanting to disturb Kaiser, but he didn't want Mr Hunter to see him. Especially if he was in a bad mood.

A sudden deafening noise made Oliver's heart stop.

It was Kaiser barking.

Oliver didn't turn to look; he just bolted into a sprint and ran as fast as he could towards home.

He almost felt his bladder lose control, and a sickness build up in his stomach he had to try hard to keep down as he ran. He wanted to look behind him but he knew that would cost him valuable seconds, so he threw his head back and ran as fast as he could.

The barking grew louder and louder, the sound of the dog's four paws hitting the gravel, almost sounded like rain on a car roof.

He could feel Kaiser's presence getting closer and closer until the animal was right behind him. But he had to keep going.

As he got closer to his house, he realised as he felt Kaiser getting closer that he wasn't going to outrun him. He had to think fast. He really didn't want to know what it would feel like to have Kaiser's teeth sink into his flesh.

After making the decision, Oliver slowed to a stop and quickly looked over his shoulder, making sure he had a good grip on the metal end of the hammer.

As he turned, he saw Kaiser lunging, front paws off the ground. Even though it was dark, Oliver could still see the dog's white fangs making their way towards him, his evil eyes focused on him, the creepy white eye the most obvious.

He spun the hammer, still holding it as tight as he could. As it spun through the air, the rubber handle hit Kaiser – who was in mid-flight – hard across the mouth, sending his head to one side.

The dog still clattered into him with the momentum of the chase, but quickly turned away after landing back on the ground, he then circled the area, shaking his head and whimpering.

'Kaiser!'

Oliver jumped into the hedges to hide.

Mr Hunter had obviously heard him barking and come out to see what was happening. Kaiser trotted back towards his house, shaking his head once more before running to his master.

'What's going on?' Oliver heard him ask Kaiser.

Oliver crouched against the sharp prickles of the hedges, holding his breath, still trying hard not to pee or vomit while offering a thank you to God that dogs couldn't talk.

Moments later, he heard Mr Hunter close the door.

Oliver took a deep breath. He was overcome with relief. He was relieved that he'd survived an attack from Kaiser, and also thankful that he'd managed to avoid being seen by Mr Hunter.

Still holding the hammer that had saved his life, he dragged himself along the ground, trying to get out of the hedge without scratching himself any more than necessary.

He felt as though he was covered in cuts. He couldn't see, but he thought his summer jacket must've been torn in several places.

He slowly walked back to the house.

As he got there, he noticed the door was open. For a split second he expected his mum to appear in the doorway, asking him where he'd been. But that didn't happen. He knew he must've left the door open. Also, if his mum was home, she would've passed him on the track, and her car would've been there, and, she would've put the electricity back on.

Oliver walked inside, closed the door, he then locked it. He'd decided to accept the fact that his mum wasn't coming home that night. He had to prepare for a night on his own.

8

Oliver fumbled through the dark to get a candle from one of the kitchen drawers. After finding one, he lit it with the lighter that was also kept in the same drawer, then carefully walked through to the living room and set it down on top of the coffee table.

It was quite a wide candle, so he didn't think he needed a plate. Once he'd placed it on the wooden surface of the table, he looked around the room. Although he was a little scared, it felt quite nice to him, lit only by the single flame from the centre of the room. There were shadows cast in all directions by the flicker, which played tricks with his mind as he kept checking over his shoulder, making sure he was still all alone.

After making himself a glass of orange cordial in the kitchen, he went back through to the living room and sat on the sofa while he rehydrated himself after the mission he'd just survived.

He was still feeling the rush of the chase. His heart had slowed considerably, but he still felt the adrenaline from his near-death experience. Kaiser got what he deserved. Oliver hadn't done anything wrong, but he insisted on chasing him and trying to bite him. Maybe he'll think twice about it in future.

In the candlelight, Oliver could only just make out the clock on the wall. It said twenty past nine. He decided that he wouldn't bother working out how long his mum had been gone for anymore. It wouldn't make a difference now anyway. She hadn't come home. That was the top and bottom of it. She would normally be gone for an hour or so – even though she always said twenty minutes – and she'd been gone all day. There was no doubt in his mind that something awful had happened.

He couldn't believe that his dad would leave him, even though he had. But there was no way on earth his mum would. She wouldn't leave him and not come back, especially leaving him on his own. If she had to go away, like his dad had, she surely would've left him with a baby sitter rather than leave him on his own in the house. He knew with all certainty that something must've happened. Something bad.

He wished they still had a house phone. His mum had a pay as you go mobile phone, but she couldn't afford to buy Oliver one. And they hadn't had a landline phone since a year or so after his dad left. There were a lot of things they couldn't have since his dad had gone. The cordial he was drinking was the horrible one that he didn't really like. Most of the food they ate was the cheaper brands that didn't taste as nice as the household names, and they hadn't been on holiday in the last two years. He was also wearing clothes he was pretty sure were second-hand, possibly from a charity shop. He remembered new clothes used to come with labels on that his mum would cut off with a pair of scissors. But in the last year or so, they never had labels attached. And they felt a little different too.

Clothes with labels would always feel a little stiff until they'd been worn. But the clothes without labels always felt softer, like they'd already been washed.

Another reason they didn't have a landline was because of the man who kept calling the house over and over again. Oliver didn't know why, or what he wanted, but he knew it scared his mum because he remembered her phoning the police.

She would scream and shout down the phone at the man whenever he called. Oliver didn't really understand why he did this, and his mum never told him what he'd said to her. But he knew it upset her because she would always cry after she'd slammed the phone down, and her hands would shake.

Oliver answered the phone to him once. The man's voice was creepy; low and husky. And he was breathing heavily, like he was holding the phone too close to his mouth.

Put that bitch on the phone was what he'd said to Oliver. When Oliver asked him what he meant, the man screamed *Now!* at the top of his voice, which hurt Oliver's ear and caused him to pull the receiver away quickly.

That was one of the times his mum phoned the police. After that, she unplugged the phone and put it away. Whoever it was mustn't have had her mobile number because they never rang again. Whether the police found him and made him stop, or the man just gave up, Oliver didn't know. But that was the end of it; as far as he knew, anyway.

Oliver understood why he couldn't have his own mobile phone. His mum had explained to him that the household bills used to be covered by two incomes when his dad was there. But now, since he'd left, there was only one income to keep the roof over their heads.

Oliver said he'd get a weekend job to help out; delivering papers, or milk, or something like that, but his mum told him he wasn't old enough. As soon as he *was* old enough, he would definitely be getting a job. He wanted to help his mum. And he'd really like to buy the better food and snacks from the supermarket; not just for himself, but for his mum too.

Oliver didn't want his own mobile phone to ring anyone but his mum. Many of the other kids in his class had one. And Oliver did think they looked pretty cool. But he'd only use it to phone his mum when she was out shopping. He wouldn't call anyone else. It would've been very useful now. But he wasn't interested in all the features the other kids in school talked about; WhatsApp, TikTok and Facebook and all those things. He didn't really understand what those things were. He felt a little left out when they were discussing things they'd seen on YouTube, or the latest games like Fortnite, but these were things that didn't really interest him. He just wanted a phone to hold in his hand, and to ring his mum whenever he wanted.

His mum had apologised many times for him not having things like a phone or a new console or computer. But the truth was, if he did ever get lots of money from somewhere, he would just give it to his mum; maybe after buying himself an easel and a bigger drawing pad.

He didn't really know how he could suddenly have lots of money; maybe by selling a drawing, or maybe even his dad sending him some. That would be nice. Although he'd prefer him to come back rather than just send money.

As he sat there in the candlelit living room, a noise suddenly came from somewhere that stopped him from breathing. It was a low grumbling noise, like the noise his belly would make when he'd missed his dinner or breakfast. Only much louder. It seemed to bounce off the walls from all directions. He couldn't tell what it was, or where it had come from, but he'd definitely heard it.

He froze waiting for more noises, but they didn't come. He leaned forward and gently placed the glass of cordial onto the coffee table next to the candle. He knew he hadn't imagined the noise, but he couldn't decide what it could be.

He listened.

He looked around the room. The television certainly couldn't make any noise while the power was off, and there was nothing else in the living room. He could see through to the dining room area. It was darker in there but he could still see the table legs, and there was nothing hiding underneath.

He looked over to the bunker. The four dining room chairs he'd used to make the den still stood in the same place. Even though he couldn't see them because of the cover draped over them, and the cover was now mostly hidden by branches and leaves, he knew they were in the same place.

He wondered if the noise came from inside the bunker. But if it did, what was it? He waited for more noises as he sat still. Nothing.

Oliver began to wonder if he'd imagined the noise. Moments earlier, he was certain he'd heard it. But as the minutes went by, he began to wonder if it was possibly in his head.

It had been a stressful day. Maybe it was his mind playing tricks on him, because of what had happened with Kaiser.

It could've even been his own belly rumbling. He hadn't eaten as much as he normally would. His mum would've made his dinner; maybe ravioli on toast, or a cheese and pickle sandwich followed by a bag of crisps. And his evening meal on a Saturday would normally be something fancier than his week-night meals. Maybe spaghetti bolognaise or lasagne, or even a shepherd's pie. All he'd eaten today was a bowl of cereal, two chocolate bars and a ham and tomato sandwich. So it could've been his own belly rumbling, but he really didn't think so. He certainly didn't think that when it happened. Something made the noise. It hadn't happened a second time, but he knew he still had to check the bunker.

He stood up and stepped very slowly over to the pile of branches and leaves. He wondered if he could've brought some weird kind of creature or insect into the house within all the twigs and shrubbery.

The noise suddenly happened again. It did come from the bunker, there was no doubt. He jumped back and onto the sofa. The grumble went on for longer than it did the first time. He sat still, legs up and his arms wrapped around them once more.

Oliver had never been so scared. He couldn't move, even though he knew he should run through to his bedroom and slam the door shut. Or maybe even the bathroom. At least the bathroom door had a lock, and there was a water supply in case he was stuck in there for a long time. But he couldn't move.

The candle on the coffee table was the only light in the whole bungalow. And not only did he not want the candle to go out by picking it up with his shaking hands, but he also didn't want to turn his back on whatever it was that made that noise. He didn't know what to do. He thought about a weapon. The small hammer he'd introduced to Kaiser's mouth was on the worktop in the kitchen. Maybe that would give him the confidence to at least look in the bunker to see what it was.

With a rush of blood, Oliver jumped off the sofa and ran through to the kitchen.

He was barely able to see in the dark open-plan room, but he could see enough to grab the hammer. Again, he took it by the head end, and then walked back through to the living room.

He walked over to the bunker and stood in front of it. The candle was still burning behind him. He wondered if he'd be able to see whatever it was when he pulled back the bed cover, but he didn't want to hold the candle and the hammer. He had to be ready for whatever it was.

I really wish my mum was here, he thought, as he took another step forward and leaned down slightly, with the hammer in his right hand, held high ready for action.

He gently peeled back the cover with his left hand and looked inside.

He struggled to hold back a scream as he saw two eyes in the dark, shining with the reflection from the candlelight.

The split second of fear at what Oliver could see was accompanied by a loud yelping noise from whatever it was.

At first, he thought it was Kaiser, but it wasn't as big as him, and Kaiser had never made a yelping noise before. It almost sounded like a bird, maybe a crow, but the eyes weren't positioned like a bird's eyes would be. They were both on the front of its face, more like a dog or a cat, and they looked straight at Oliver when he pulled back the cover.

Oliver dropped the hammer and ran as fast as he could to his bedroom, bumping into the door frame as he made his way through. Once there he threw himself to the floor and scrambled underneath his bed, pushing his way between the boxes of toys that were under there.

He then pulled the boxes back towards him as he tried his best to hide from whatever lurked in the bunker. He didn't hear it follow him, but he wanted to make sure if it did, it didn't find him; whatever it was. He shivered with fear as he lay underneath his bed, but he didn't move. He just stayed where he was and prayed for daylight, and also, for his mum to come back home. And more than anything, he really wished he'd closed the bedroom door.

9

Sunday 2nd May

Oliver opened his eyes. He'd slept reasonably well considering he was on the floor underneath his bed. The carpet beneath the bed felt a little thicker than it did in the rest of the room, so it wasn't too uncomfortable. Although he would've much preferred to have slept in his bed. But after an hour, or maybe two, of lying there terrified of whatever it was he'd seen in the bunker, he'd somehow managed to drift off. After all, he'd had an exhausting day.

He could tell it was morning because he could now see the boxes that were in front of him beneath the bed – when he'd first clambered under, he couldn't see a thing.

He was thirsty, and he was bursting for the bathroom. His first thought was that he should stay where he was, hiding from the creature, but he couldn't. He had to move. As well as needing the bathroom, he also felt the pang of curiosity at what the creature was. Although he was terrified last night, he thought he might not be quite so scared now it was daylight. And he needed to know what it was so he could decide on the best way of dealing with it.

He crawled out from underneath the bed. His back and shoulders ached from sleeping face down on the floor, so he stretched before stepping towards the bedroom door, which was still open from when he'd ran through to get away from whatever it was.

He felt stupid for not taking the time to close it, even though all rational thought had left him once he saw the glow of the eyes staring back at him.

He tiptoed through to the bathroom. After peeing, he flushed the chain and then ran the cold tap and put his mouth underneath, trying to take in as much water as he could while making as little noise as possible. He then went through to the living room where the bunker was. He picked up the hammer from the floor and stood there contemplating his next move. He didn't quite feel fully awake, coming around from what was certainly a strange night; in fact, an altogether strange twenty-four hours. His mum hadn't come home, the power had gone off, he'd had a run-in with Kaiser and then he'd heard noises from a creature that had taken over his bunker. By now he was questioning himself once more, and wondering if he'd imagined the noises. But then he thought of the ghostly eyes that looked back at him as he peeked into the bunker. He wasn't imagining them. Not unless the whole thing was a dream.

A sudden rustling sound from the bunker made his heart jump, and he turned and ran back to his bedroom, but this time still holding his hammer. Just like the previous night, he threw himself to the floor and scrambled underneath his bed. He lay still, trying not to breathe too loudly.

The mattress cover hung over the gap under the bed, but he could still see a few inches underneath it. The sun was hitting the beige carpet. As he stared at the bedroom floor, he wondered if he'd have to spend all day there, just like he'd spent all night there, which was why his back ached so much.

Moments later, he held his breath as he heard a very quiet noise, he was pretty sure were footsteps on his bedroom carpet. As he listened, four black paws came into view. They walked past his bed as he lay, trying not to make a sound. He thought it was a dog, but he wasn't sure. The animal, whatever it was, was only small, bigger than a domestic cat, but much smaller than a German Shepherd. After it pottered around for a few seconds, it turned and left the room.

Oliver climbed out from under the bed as quietly as he could, still holding the hammer by the metal end.

The animal had obviously come into the house the previous evening after he'd left the door open when he headed for the road in search of his mum.

Oliver was terrified, but he realised that if he could hold off an attack from Kaiser, a huge German Shepherd, then surely he could defend himself against whatever this animal was.

He walked through to the hall, and as he reached the entrance to the living room, the creature suddenly appeared in his mum's bedroom doorway. Oliver froze, and held his breath once more as he stared at the animal.

It was a fox.

The fox stared back at Oliver with its head down and eyes looking upwards, tail moving very slowly from side to side.

Oliver wasn't quite as scared now he knew what the animal was.

He stood in awe at such a beautiful creature. It stayed there, looking right at him, still with its head pointing downwards, and its nose up, one paw in front of the other as it had stopped mid-stride. The beautiful orange-brown fur looked soft; its black ears raised as its bushy tail pointed downwards to the ground.

Although his drawings of living things were never accurate, he knew he'd be attempting a picture of this wonderful creature at some point.

Oliver – slightly more confident, not only because now he knew what he was dealing with, but also because the fox hadn't immediately attacked him – decided to try and speak to it.

'Hello,' he said in a soft voice.

The word had barely left his lips when the fox bolted into a sprint and shot into the living room.

Oliver ran through to follow it. He reached the living room just in time to see the end of its bushy tail disappear into the bunker. He didn't know what to do. Should he feed it? Should he go in after it? Should he open the door and wait for it to leave? He didn't know. All he knew was that he needn't have slept all night under his bed, thinking there was a monster in his house, when all along, it was just a fox.

61

He went into the kitchen to look for some food. There were a couple of pieces of ham left in the fridge; the fridge that was no longer cold, and starting to smell a little.

He grabbed the ham and walked over to the bunker, talking to the fox as to not surprise it. 'Just bringing you some food, Mr Fox.'

He pulled the cover up slowly and draped it on the top of the bunker. Some of the branches fell, but not enough to scare the fox.

'Here, try some of this,' he said, dropping the ham onto the floor.

Oliver went and sat on the sofa. He could see the fox huddled at the back of the bunker, staring back at him.

After a few minutes of staring, the fox looked at the pieces of wafer-thin ham on the carpet in the opening of the bunker.

It didn't move, and neither did Oliver.

'Come on,' he said. 'You'll like it.'

Oliver then noticed the candle on the coffee table, only it wasn't candle shaped anymore. He sat forward to examine the wax that had fallen into a flat pile with a small amount hanging over the edge in a drip that looked like an icicle hanging from a gutter. There was also a small white disc on the carpet.

He touched it. It felt hard and cold. The wax on the table felt the same, only there were ripples in the pile that still felt smooth, but with much more texture than the disc on the carpet.

The pile of wax might be easy to break off the table, but he was sure the carpet would be ruined. He wondered if his mum would be annoyed at him. He knew she couldn't afford a new carpet. He thought that maybe he could move the sofa back a little and then do the same with the table so it would be covered.

His mum had spoken about them having to move to a council house. Oliver wouldn't mind too much if that was what they had to do. At least they'd never have to see Mr Hunter and Kaiser again. But he knew his mum loved the bungalow.

She loved the fact that they felt as though they were living in the countryside, even though they were only a mile or so from the town. When they sat in the back garden on the summer evenings, all they could see was the forest and the clear skies above. His mum would be upset if they had to move, and if they did have to, then his mum would certainly be angry at him damaging the carpet. He wondered if it would stop someone from wanting to buy the house, and his mum wouldn't be happy about having to replace it.

The fox took a step forward. It looked up at Oliver, he presumed to make sure he didn't move, which he didn't.

It then took another step forward.

'Go on,' Oliver said quietly. 'It's OK.'

The fox had one last look at him before grabbing the ham and taking it back into the bunker.

For the first time since eleven-thirteen the previous day, Oliver smiled.

10

After running himself a bath, Oliver stripped off his clothes, put them in the washing basket – wondering if his mum was ever going to come back and wash them – and walked back into the living room with just a towel around his waist.

'I'm going for a bath,' he said to the fox that was still cowering within the safety of the bunker. 'I'm going to leave the door open, and I want you gone by the time I come back, OK?'

The fox looked to Oliver as though it had listened to every word, but it didn't answer.

Oliver walked through to the kitchen, unlocked the door, and pulled it wide open.

He stepped outside barefoot and as he walked across the gravel, he felt the warmth with every step, as well as the gravel digging into the soles of his feet. He put his hand up to shield his eyes from the morning sun.

His mum's car wasn't parked at the side of the house where it normally was, but he felt the need to see along the lane once more. He gingerly walked along the track. As he passed the corner of the bungalow, the track came into sight, and there was no car there, just like there wasn't the night before.

Oliver was still confused, as well as concerned at what might have happened to his mum. If it was her stupid car breaking down, she would've been home by now, but he also realised that if she'd had an accident, maybe even if she'd ended up in hospital, the hospital or the police would have come and checked on him by now. If she'd died, a thought that brought a tear to his eye, somebody surely would've come to tell him the news. And he wouldn't be allowed to live on his own. He knew that much at least. He briefly tried to imagine what would happen if his mum had died. Where would he go? And who would he live with? He didn't know.

He continued to search his brain for a logical answer to what could've happened. The only scenario Oliver could think of that made any sense was that she'd maybe come off the road in her car, and nobody had found her yet.

If she didn't come back soon, he knew he was going to have to venture further from the house, and the dirt track, and go looking for her.

He turned and hopped along the gravel and went back inside, leaving the door open for the fox. He then went to the bathroom to have his bath, locking the bathroom door in case of any unwelcome visitors.

He placed one foot into the water and almost screamed. It was freezing cold. He felt deflated as he realised that the power being off must stop the hot water from working too. He turned the tap off, and then tried the tap on the sink. After a moment of the water running, it still felt cold, so he turned it off.

Oliver pondered what to do. It wasn't a huge problem for him to smell a little if he was living on his own. But he didn't like the idea of that, and he also didn't want his mum to think he hadn't coped when she came back. If she came back. At some point or other, Oliver was going to have to be around people, and if he smelled or wore dirty clothes, this wouldn't make his mum look good in their eyes. He had to stay clean.

He removed his towel.

He felt the water with his hand. It was unbelievably cold. Not as cold as the tap water was in winter, but still far too cold for a bath. He left his hand in the water, and after a moment or two, his hand got used to it.

He thought that if this was the case, then his whole body would get used to it too.

He took a deep breath and stepped into the bath.

The cold water on his feet caused a high-pitched screaming sound; a sound he didn't know he was capable of making.

He counted to three and then plunged himself down in the water.

He screamed again as his body hit the water.

There was no time for relaxing. He wouldn't be lying back and soothing his troubles away like he usually would. Oliver just grabbed the bottle of shower gel – the cheap one, not the brand his mum used to buy him – and squeezed it into his hands before rubbing it all over his head and body. Once he was covered, he lay back into the water to rinse himself all over.

Still making noises he'd never heard himself make before, he took out the plug and climbed out of the bath.

After wrapping himself in a towel, he sat on the lid of the toilet as he waited for the shivering to stop.

Once Oliver had warmed up a little, brushed his teeth, and been to his bedroom to put some fresh clothes on, he went through to the kitchen and closed and locked the door.

He poured himself a glass of cordial and then went to see if the fox had gone.

He walked over to the bunker and looked inside by gently peeling back the cover; it was empty. This made him smile. It would've been pretty cool to have a pet fox, but he knew letting it out was the right thing to do.

He sat on the sofa, wishing he could watch cartoons again. But instead, he thought about starting another picture. As he tried to decide what his next picture should be, there was a knock at the door. It startled him so much that he spilled his cordial. He fleetingly thought about how much more damage he could do to the living room carpet before his mum came home. First the candle wax, and now his drink. And she probably wouldn't be happy at the branches resting on the carpet in front of the bunker. But at that moment, he didn't care. What he did care about was who was at the door.

He put his glass down on the table, then scrambled into the bunker as fast as he could, pulling the cover down so it felt a little safer.

There was more knocking.

He wondered who it could be, and if he should answer or not. It could be someone with news about his mum, or someone looking for his mum. Maybe they'd found the car.

His mum had always told him never to answer the door when he was in the house on his own, especially if it was Mr Hunter from the farm. She really didn't like him for some reason or other. But either way, Oliver had no intentions of opening the door, to him or anyone else who might call by.

He listened for more knocks, but they never came.

He held his breath as he listened. When he heard footsteps on the gravel, he shot out from the bunker and ran to the kitchen window. Through the gaps in the blinds, he saw a man standing next to a car parked outside the house. It was a white BMW; a very new-looking car. The type of car he knew his mum could never afford.

The man looked about the same age as his mum, maybe slightly older. He leaned on the car roof as he held his phone to his ear. He had dark hair, neatly styled, and the tidiest beard Oliver had ever seen. He was also tanned, as though he'd just returned from a holiday abroad. Not that Oliver had ever been abroad, but he'd seen his teachers and some of the other kids at school when they came back from trips away.

Oliver tried hard not to make the blinds move as he watched the man through the window. He really didn't want to give away that someone was inside the house.

He listened hard as the man held the phone to his ear. Finally, he said, 'Look, Louise, can you please give me a call. I just want to talk to you.' He then hung up before getting back in the car and driving away along the dusty dirt track, sending clouds of dust into the air.

Who was he? And how did he know Oliver's mum? He must know her; he'd said her name. And presumably he had her phone number. She didn't just give that to anyone.

Oliver partly regretted not answering the door. But his mum obviously wasn't answering her phone to him, so maybe he had made the right decision. This man was trying to get in touch with his mum, and for some reason she wasn't answering. Why? Maybe she was trying to get away from him. Maybe she was trying to get away from Oliver. Was that it? Had she left him?

He'd briefly thought of that earlier, but didn't even want to consider it a possibility. Was there a chance his mum might've left him, just like his dad had done two years earlier? Was that possible? And if so, was there something wrong with him for this to happen? Was it the creepy, grey pictures he liked to draw? Was it the fact that he didn't want any friends and was happy on his own? Was it because he preferred to draw rather than play computer games like all the other kids?

Oliver knew these things made him a little different to everyone else, but he didn't care. But did his mum and dad care? Did they care so much as to move away and leave him on his own? Is that what was happening? Had his mum left him to go looking for his dad? Was that another possibility?

He ran through to his mum's bedroom. As he walked in, he was hit with a horrible smell. A smell he'd never smelled before. He covered his nose as he looked around, trying hard not to be sick. It was overpowering. The large double bed was against the wall with space either side. The dressing table was in one corner, with the wardrobes in the opposite corner.

He wandered around the room and saw what was making the awful smell. In the corner of the room there was a pile of what he could only presume was fox poo. It wasn't a big pile – he'd seen bigger from Kaiser – but the smell was awful. He ran out of the room, trying to hold his breath as he went through to the kitchen for some kitchen roll. He wrapped a tea-towel around his face and tried to tie it at the back of his head, but he couldn't, so he took a bigger towel from the kitchen drawer. He managed to tie this one, covering his nose and mouth.

Oliver went back into the bedroom and opened the window before kneeling down at the disgusting pile in the corner. He put the kitchen roll over it and squeezed as he picked it up. He couldn't help but heave and cough as the smell made its way through the towel and into his lungs; he felt as though he could taste it as he breathed in the smell.

Holding the fox poo at arm's length, he went through to the bathroom and dropped it, with the kitchen roll, into the toilet and flushed it away. He washed his hands thoroughly, using the antibacterial soap from the dispenser.

After putting the towel back into the kitchen, he searched the cupboards for an air freshener. Once he'd found one, he went into his mum's room and sprayed, holding the trigger for almost a minute to try to get rid of the disgusting smell.

When he'd finished spraying and had put the air freshener back in the cupboard, he went to the living room and finished his cordial, gulping it down as fast as he could, trying hard to remove the taste from his mouth.

Once the glass was empty, he felt ready to return to his original quest, which was to check if his mum had taken any of her belongings.

He went back into his mum's bedroom, the room that smelled like a strange mixture of fox faeces and air freshener, and opened the drawer at the side of her bed. It was full of his mum's underwear.

In the bigger drawers next to the wardrobe there were jeans and trousers, all neatly folded, and again, the drawer was full.

He opened the wardrobe door. It was split into two sections with a shelf across the middle. There were clothes hung on rails in both sections – more trousers, tops, blouses, dresses, coats and again, all full. If his mum had moved out, surely she would've taken at least some of her clothes.

He was just about to close the wardrobe door when something caught his eye through the gaps in the blouses. He pushed them to one side, sliding them along the rail, and focused his eyes on something he'd never seen before. It was a box. A wooden box made from dark red wood.

He slid it out from underneath the hanging clothes. It felt smooth, as though it had been varnished, and as he brought it closer to him, he noticed two things. One, how heavy it was, and two, there was a metal badge on top of it. The badge, or maybe it was a plaque, had his dad's name engraved onto it in fancy lettering.

It read,

Michael Derwent

Oliver didn't understand. The box was very well made, and it looked to Oliver like a miniature piece of furniture. But whatever it was, he wondered why his dad hadn't taken it with him. If he'd gone to the trouble of buying something so nice, why would he leave it behind? He must have paid to have his name engraved on it too, unless it was a gift from someone.

Oliver took the box out of the wardrobe, almost dropping it as the weight of it surprised him, and rested it on his mum's bed. He stared at it for a moment, still wondering what it was. He then decided to open it. He wondered if it had something valuable inside, or maybe even money. Perhaps his mum didn't know his dad had left it behind. He had to open it. He needed to open it. He was sure his dad wouldn't mind, and he didn't think his mum would either.

He pulled at the lid, but it didn't move, so he pulled harder, but still nothing. Even when he wrapped his arm around the top and pulled as hard as he could, the lid still wouldn't come off.

He looked to see if there was a lock or a catch you had to undo, but there wasn't. After trying once more to open it, he gave up and stroked the box gently with his fingers. The smooth wood felt nice. He tried to think what his dad would keep in such a fancy box. But he guessed he'd have to wait until his mum came home before he could find out. If she knew, she would tell him. If not, they would have to try to open it together.

He lifted the heavy box and slid it back into the wardrobe, then closed the door and went to the kitchen to make himself something to eat.

11

Oliver noticed the milk had started to taste a little funny as he tried to eat his cereal. After only a few mouthfuls he poured it away and took an apple from the fruit bowl instead.

Just before he bit into it, he remembered listening to some of the kids in his class talking about an interesting game with an apple and a pack of cards. Although he was hungry, he felt an overwhelming urge to try it.

He placed the apple in the middle of the coffee table, ignoring the pile of wax that he still needed to try and scrape off, and went into his room to get the pack of cards he knew were in his top drawer. Back in the living room, he stood under the archway that separated the living room from the dining area.

After opening the pack of cards, he discarded the box onto the floor, and took the top card and held it between his thumb and forefinger. He didn't even turn it over to see which card it was. For this game it didn't matter.

He focused on the apple. Then, with a quick flick of his wrist, he threw the card across the room.

Unfortunately, it spun off towards the bunker and went nowhere near the apple, so he tried again. Still nowhere near. By the time he'd thrown ten or so, he finally managed to hit the apple, but it didn't stick into it. He'd heard the other kids in school say that they had managed to do it, so it couldn't be too hard to do. He kept trying and trying, and although he managed to get the hang of hitting the apple almost every time, it just bounced off onto the carpet. Minutes later, his hands were empty and the cards were all over the floor. Undeterred, he scooped them all up and went back to the archway to try again. Only this time, he crouched a little as he threw, putting much more effort into the power of his throw. His arm was aching, but he wasn't going to stop until he'd succeeded. Again, the first few missed, and although the next ten or so were closer, with most of them hitting the apple, none of them stuck in. As he worked his way through the pack, he got closer and closer as more and more cards hit the target. He even started to see little dents appear in the apple's skin. Once he was finally down to the last card, he'd decided he didn't want to go through the whole pack again, not yet anyway. His arm was aching and he was still hungry. But he still didn't want to accept defeat. He knew if he missed, he'd be trying it again later that day, or maybe after a snack, but he wouldn't be giving up until he'd managed to complete the challenge.

He closed his eyes and took a deep breath and pictured the card sticking into the apple. He'd seen a few martial arts movies, so he knew he had to focus and channel his energy and only think positive thoughts. There was no room for negativity in this game.

One more deep breath and he opened his eyes, stared sternly at the apple and put all his strength into spinning the last card from the pack across the room towards it.

To his amazement, the corner of the card stuck into the side of the apple, which rocked a little but stayed on top of the table. Oliver couldn't believe it.

He jumped up and down with his hands in the air. He was starting to think it wasn't possible, but he'd just proved it was.

'Yes!' he shouted.

He wasn't a fan of sports, but he imagined this was how footballers felt when they scored a goal. He'd sat with his dad when he used to watch football matches. Sometimes he would shout 'Yes!' and jump up and down, screaming at the top of his voice. He didn't know why he cheered more for some goals than the others, but he loved seeing his dad so happy. His face changed from a stern, lifeless expression to one of overwhelming joy whenever his team scored a goal. That was how Oliver felt right now as he grabbed the apple with the card – which he could now see was the seven of clubs – still sticking out of it, and thrust it above his head.

He stopped cheering as he continued to think about how his dad would cheer and shout at the football. The more he thought about it, the more he realised that that was one of the few situations he'd ever see his dad happy. He hadn't clicked on that before. Oliver remembered playing with his dad, and having fun with him, but mostly, he just remembered him sitting quietly and not really speaking. His team winning at football must've meant a lot to him.

12

Oliver could never understand why his dad would sometimes be happy and other times be so miserable. He almost felt as though he had two dads. Some days he would greet Oliver by picking him up and throwing his arms around him. Other times he would just put his hand on Oliver's head as he walked past.

Oliver learned not to disturb him when he was in the bedroom. Whenever he'd gone in to see his dad in there, he would just be lying on the bed, fully clothed, staring up at the ceiling. Oliver would ask him what he was doing, and he'd just get a one-word answer like, *Nothing*, or *Resting*. Occasionally he would put his arm around Oliver if he climbed up onto the bed and lay next to him. But the last time he did that, his dad had tears in his eyes. Oliver wondered if he'd done something to upset him. He'd asked if he was OK, but that time, he didn't answer. His dad just hugged him tighter than he'd ever hugged him before. Oliver wondered now if that was the last time it had happened before he left, but he couldn't remember.

Every now and then, Oliver's mum would come to him and whisper something along the lines of, *Go and give your dad a big hug.* Oliver didn't know why, but he did it anyway. He couldn't remember his dad ever shouting at him for anything. In fact, he couldn't remember his dad ever being annoyed at all. There were some fun times. If he was in a good mood, he would play with Oliver and play-fight, throwing him around on the sofa, or tickling him until he screamed with laughter. He would also take him on long walks through the woods. Sometimes the walks would go on for so long that his dad would have to carry him on his back all the way home. The motion of his dad moving up and down with every footstep as Oliver rested his head on the back of his neck had more often than not sent him to sleep.

Oliver could never understand why his dad left. He was always kind to him, and he was always kind to his mum. He heard them laughing sometimes when he was in bed trying to sleep. And he witnessed them hugging on a daily basis, and he would always kiss his mum when he went off to work, and he would do the same when he got home. Oliver never heard them arguing and he never saw them ignoring each other. The only thing he could think of that would cause a problem was the fact that his dad would sometimes be sad, and lie on the bed. Oliver didn't know why he did this, but he seemed to do it a lot, especially around the time he left.

Oliver loved his mum, and he loved the time they spent together. She would regularly ask him to sit and watch a film with her, or play board games like Monopoly or Yahtzee. At first, he would roll his eyes as she dragged him away from his drawings, but he always enjoyed whatever activity she'd planned for them.

The only thing he refused to do was go for a walk through the woods with her. He used to love everything about a woodland walk; the scenery, the smells, the wildlife, the feeling of being away from the towns and all the houses. He also loved it when they came across horses. His dad would pick him up so he could reach them as he stroked their noses from the other side of the fence.

Oliver always said no when his mum asked him to go for a walk in the woods because he knew it wouldn't be the same without his dad. Every day, Oliver would think about him, wondering if he'd ever come back. But the box he'd left behind in his mum's wardrobe looked expensive. Surely he'd want to come back for it at some point. This made Oliver a little more confident about his return, but as time went by, he was feeling less and less confident about his mum coming back.

13

Four chocolate bars was too many. Oliver knew that, but he still took them and a glass of cordial into the bunker. He left the cover up so the light could get through. The lamp inside the den was useless with no electricity, but he saw no need to remove it. And the little table was handy to rest his chocolate bars on.

His mum always told him if he ate too much chocolate, he'd be climbing the walls. And that was what he wanted now. Not to climb the walls, but to have enough energy to embark upon a mission, a mission to go and find his mum.

Oliver wanted to go early enough to make sure he had enough time to get back before it went dark. He certainly didn't want to have another run-in with Kaiser, so he knew he'd have to be alert, and he definitely didn't want Mr Hunter to see him. His mum said never to answer the door to him if she wasn't home, and she probably wouldn't want him to know Oliver was all alone. He had to make sure Mr Hunter didn't see him.

After eating three of the four chocolate bars, and feeling a little sick rather than energised, he climbed out of the bunker. He finished the last mouthful of cordial before putting the glass down on the coffee table, next to the other empty glass. As he walked towards the kitchen door, he heard footsteps – slow footsteps in the gravel outside the house

Oliver went to the window, looked through the blinds and almost brought back all the chocolate he'd eaten when he saw Mr Hunter walking up the track heading towards the bungalow.

Oliver hurried towards the bunker, leaping over the coffee table like a stuntman before jumping inside and pulling the cover down.

He tried his best to hold his breath as he gently pulled the bed cover to one side so he could peer through the gap at the living room window.

There was no knocking, but he heard a noise that could've been the sound of the kitchen door handle, but he wasn't sure. He knew for a fact the door was locked. He would never leave it unlocked. Yes, he'd left it wide open when he ventured down the lane, which allowed the fox to enter the house. And he left it open when he had a freezing cold bath, allowing the fox to leave, but he would usually lock the door when home alone, even before his mum went missing.

Suddenly, Mr Hunter's head and shoulders appeared in the living room window, his hand on the glass to shield the sun as he looked through. He seemed to look all around the room before finally focusing his eyes on the bunker.

Oliver still felt sick. He was sure that Mr Hunter couldn't see him. But if he couldn't, why would he stare for so long? Mr Hunter then smiled, which made Oliver's heart jump around his chest. Had he seen him? Or was he just smiling at the bunker? Seconds felt like hours as Mr

81

Hunter continued to stare through the window. Finally, he gave a short laugh and stepped away, shaking his head.

Oliver started to breathe once more as he listened to the footsteps become quieter and quieter until finally, they were quiet enough for Oliver to leave the bunker and run to the window in time to watch Mr Hunter walk away along the lane.

Oliver didn't know what he wanted. And he didn't know what Mr Hunter would do if he told him about his mum not coming home. Would he help him look for her? Would he call the police? Or would he kidnap him and make him work on the farm? He might even make him share a dog bed with Kaiser. Or tie him up somewhere. He didn't know. He'd spoken to him before about Oliver having a job there when he was old enough, but his mum had said no.

He really didn't know what Mr Hunter could've wanted. But what he did know, was that he was glad he'd gone.

14

It was almost two o'clock; nearly twenty-seven hours since Oliver's mum left the house. He was running out of ideas as to what had happened. Although he was filled with energy for the mission ahead, his mind was exhausted at going through the possible scenarios for why she hadn't come home. He had thought she might have left him behind, just like his dad had, but after searching her bedroom and finding all her clothes still there, he knew that wasn't the case. His mum had unquestionably meant to come straight home from the trip to the supermarket. Something had to have happened to stop her from doing so.

He put on his summer jacket. It might've been warm outside, but Oliver didn't know how long he was going to be, so he had to be prepared.

He had a quick drink of water, straight from the tap, and then unlocked the kitchen door, took the key out and stepped outside into the sunshine.

Before he could turn to lock it, he was surprised to see he had a visitor. Standing not too far from him, by the hedges, was the fox.

Oliver stayed perfectly still, expecting it to turn and run away, but it didn't. It just stood there watching him, almost like a pet dog might do.

'What do you want?' Oliver asked.

The fox didn't answer, but it did take a step closer to him.

'Are you wanting some more ham? If you are, I've none left.'

The fox took one more step towards him and then stood still, looking up at Oliver with the expression of a pet dog. It certainly didn't look aggressive in any way. Oliver was convinced it'd come back for more food, but he had no intentions of letting it back in the house, not after the mess it'd made in his mum's room. Oliver could still remember the smell, and knew he would for a long time.

After thinking for a moment while looking at the soft gentle features of the fox, he decided to give in and feed him. 'Stay there,' he said, and went back inside the house.

He searched the fridge for something to feed the fox, but everything in there was starting to smell funny. He closed the door and checked the cupboards. He couldn't find anything meat related that he thought would be suitable, but there was a can of tuna. His mum liked tuna, but Oliver couldn't stand it. To be fair, he'd never tried it. The smell was enough to put him off. But he thought the fox might like it.

He grabbed the tin opener from the drawer and clipped it to the edge of the can, then he squeezed the handles together as hard as he could and spun the lever. Each turn rotated the can a little, leaking the smelly, oily liquid onto the counter top. It knocked him a little sick, but he didn't mind too much as he wasn't the one eating it. After the can had gone all the way around, he held it upside-down over the sink to drain some of the liquid away. He then tried to remove the lid.

Although he could see gaps in the rim, the lid stayed fully attached. He tried harder and harder to remove it, but it wouldn't budge, especially with his fingers being slippery from the oil. He took one of the large knives from the rack. His mum wouldn't let him use any of them when she was there. But she wasn't there to stop him now.

He enjoyed helping his mum when she was cooking. She wouldn't let him do anything too difficult, but she had shown him how to use the tin opener, and she taught him to always cut away from yourself when using a knife, even though she'd never actually let him use one yet.

Now, he slotted the point of the knife into one of the gaps in the can and pushed away from himself as hard as he could.

Eventually, the knife cut through the small piece of metal that was keeping the can closed. The knife flew onto the floor and the thought that he could've lost one of his fingers entered Oliver's head, but after a quick count, he realised he'd got away without hurting himself.

He checked the can all the way around, squeezing it as he turned. But there were still a few parts where the tin opener hadn't cut all the way through the metal properly, so he picked up the knife once more and cut another nodule. The knife didn't fall this time, but he did drop the can. Oliver decided against using the knife for the last two parts that needed separating. If he cut himself, there was nobody there to help him. So, he squeezed the can to create a gap in the lid, and then pushed two of his fingers through and into the disgusting contents before pulling the lid as hard as he could. Finally, it snapped open, splashing some of the liquid onto the floor.

He ran to the door to see if the fox was still there. To his surprise, it had walked over to the doorstep. It shot back as Oliver opened the door, but only a little.

Oliver crouched down and held the can out towards the fox. It looked a little nervous, but it lifted its nose, sniffing the air frantically as it turned its head slightly from side to side, then it took a step closer as Oliver held the can out. His fingers felt slimy from the oil, but he still managed to keep hold of the can.

'Come on,' he said. 'It's OK.'

It took another step closer, reaching to sniff the aroma that was obviously more enticing to the fox than it was to Oliver. It took a couple of licks, barely lifting any tuna from the can before stepping back and looking around, then it reached its long, black snout forwards and really started to tuck in to the food. It was amazing. Oliver wondered if anyone else had ever fed a wild fox like this before. He was uncomfortable as he knelt there, but he tried not to move as he didn't want to scare away his new friend. He tried his best to ignore the discomfort as he didn't want the moment to end. He was pretty sure none of the other kids at school had ever done anything like this. He was also pretty sure Mr Hunter, or the man with the white BMW had never done anything like this either. And he couldn't wait to tell his mum he'd hand-fed a wild fox.

This was the happiest he'd been in a long time. He couldn't help but smile. He thought that if this fox was now his friend, he'd better give it a name. He searched his brain for a moment, trying to think of a name, preferably beginning with *f*.

'Franky,' he said.

He nodded to the fox as it continued to eat from the tin. 'Yes. Your name from now on is Franky.'

He didn't know a lot about animals, but he knew enough to know that feeding a wild fox like this must be unusual. Wild animals didn't trust humans enough to get this close to them. He wondered if it could actually be someone's pet. Or maybe it had been rescued at some point and released back into the wild. He'd seen that happen on some of the television programmes his mum watched. That would certainly explain why Franky was so confident around him.

As he enjoyed the magical moment, Oliver suddenly felt an uncomfortable, stinging sensation in his fingers. It was at that point that he noticed the blood running from his hand.

15

The half-eaten can of tuna hit the ground as Oliver dropped it and ran inside the bungalow as fast as his legs would take him.

He felt sick and woozy at the sight of blood, especially his own, but there was nobody to help him. He had to be strong and assertive, so he took the tea-towel from the worktop. Just before he applied it to the cut, he stopped and decided to get a clean one from the drawer; the other one had juice from the can of tuna on it, and he thought that might make it sting even more.

He pressed the light-blue towel onto his shaking fingers. There was so much blood, he couldn't see where the cut was. The dark red liquid had spread across his hand as it mixed with the oil from the can of tuna.

The towel soaked up a lot of the blood, but his hand was still red, especially within the wrinkles of his skin.

He went to the sink and rinsed his hand under the cold tap. Then the pain really kicked in.

As he turned his hand over, he saw two cuts on the backs of his index and middle fingers. He must've cut himself when he slotted his fingers into the can to force the lid open.

For some reason he hadn't felt the pain straight away. But now it hurt. It really hurt. As the cold water ran over the cuts, it not only stung, but the force of the flow opened two small flaps of skin, one on each finger. As he saw them open under the cold waterfall from the tap, everything suddenly went black.

16

Oliver was awoken by three things; the cool spring breeze making its way through the open kitchen door and moving the hair on his forehead, the strange feeling in his fingers as his hand rocked back and forth in a rhythmic motion, and the sound of running water. All three sensations felt strange to him, as he couldn't remember where he was.

He opened his eyes and stared at the ceiling. His head ached, and he felt sick, as the kitchen ceiling – blurred at first – gradually came into focus. He lay there, fighting the urge to roll over and vomit onto the floor. After a few seconds, he then remembered what had happened and how he came to be lying on the kitchen floor. He knew why he was there, but what he didn't know was why his hand was rocking back and forth.

He turned his head slightly, still trying to keep the chocolate bars he'd eaten earlier inside him, and saw Franky. There was no fear at being so close to a wild fox, that had already passed and he knew the animal wouldn't attack him, not without being provoked at least. But as he focused on the fox, he realised why his hand was moving. Franky was licking the blood from the cuts on his fingers.

'Ahh!' he shouted. Without thinking, he quickly sat up and shuffled backwards until his back hit the kitchen cupboards.

Franky jumped backwards too, but then stood looking at him while licking his lips as though he'd just finished eating some delicious meal.

Oliver looked at his fingers. He was tempted to pull back the flaps of the cuts to see how bad they were, but he didn't. He knew he had to clean the wounds once more. Fox saliva, especially from a fox that had just been eating tuna, couldn't be a good thing to get into a cut.

He pulled himself up and put his hand under the cold tap, only this time, he didn't look. Instead, he turned and looked at the fox as he rested his head on his own shoulder, still trying hard to come around from the nausea he was feeling.

Franky sat down and began to lick one of his front paws, obviously still comfortable in Oliver's company. He briefly wondered if Franky liked the taste of human blood, or if he was actually trying to help him.

After he'd rinsed his fingers, he dried them on the towel. The bleeding had stopped, so he thought he'd better seal the cuts by putting a plaster on each one.

He searched in the cupboard under the sink. Although the medications and tablets were kept in a high cupboard he couldn't reach without a chair, he knew his mum kept the first-aid box where he could reach it. He opened the container and found a small box of plasters. It wasn't easy applying them to his right hand, but after a small struggle, he managed to do it.

Once he'd leaned over the sink and had a quick drink of water from the tap, he started to feel a little better.

After turning the tap off, he looked at Franky, wondering if he was thirsty. He grabbed a cereal bowl, filled it with water and put it on the floor near him. Franky bared his teeth and growled a little as Oliver got close to him.

'Oi, grumpy,' he said. 'I'm giving you a drink, you ungrateful shit.'

Oliver was shocked as the word left his lips. He'd never used bad language before, but for some reason, it felt right to do so. After all, he was the man of the house now. And he'd been left alone by his mum, so really, at that particular moment, Oliver was the head of the household. There was nobody there to tell him off for it. He would've been happy if his mum suddenly appeared to shout at him, but sadly that didn't happen.

Franky leaned forwards and took several laps from the bowl, still looking up at Oliver as he did.

Oliver was sure now that his earlier idea of the fox being a rescue animal at some point was true, because Franky, although obviously still a little on edge around him, was surprisingly accepting of Oliver. He'd been locked in the house the previous day, and yet, because he'd been fed some sliced ham, he'd decided to come back.

After a few more laps from the bowl, he turned and trotted through the open door.

'You're welcome,' Oliver said, sarcastically.

Still feeling a little dizzy, and shaky – possibly through fainting, possibly because the energy from the chocolate he'd eaten was wearing off – Oliver decided to make himself something to eat. He knew he still had to go ahead with his mission, but he had to make sure he was ready. He couldn't leave the bungalow until he'd fully recovered.

As he opened the door to the fridge, the smell that was getting worse each time he looked in there hit him, so he shut it again.

Everything in the cupboards needed his mum's help in making. But then he saw the little microwavable tubs of beans. That would give him all the energy he needed.

He peeled back the plastic lid and opened the microwave, but then he remembered the power was off making the microwave and cooker useless. Even though he presumed the cooker was electric, he turned the knob to try to bring one of the rings to life. Nothing. And he needed to eat before he could leave the house. He had a long walk ahead of him.

After a moment of thinking, he came up with a solution. He took three candles from the drawer. This time, he stood them all on a plate, to make sure he didn't create a messy wax puddle like he had in the living room. After lighting each one with the lighter, he took a metal saucepan from the bottom cupboard, emptied the beans in and then held the pan over the candles.

He wasn't sure if this was going to work, but he thought it was worth a try. It almost felt as though he was cooking over a campfire, but not quite as much fun as he imagined that to be.

After a few minutes, his arm was aching, so he rested the pan on one of the cooker rings before gently picking up the plate of candles and putting them onto the floor. He opened the tall cupboard where the cleaning equipment was, took out the plastic bucket, turned it over and then sat down next to the plate as he held the pan of beans over the flames once more.

He waited. And waited, his arms aching as he tried to hold the pan still. The pain in his fingers made it even more difficult, but he kept it as still as he could, until eventually, he saw a bubble burst in the sauce as the beans started to cook. Taking the pan with him, he went to the kitchen drawer to grab a spoon. He then went back and sat on the bucket once more and stirred the beans as he held them over the flames. They weren't cooking as fast as they would on the cooker, but after another five minutes or so, they were finally ready to eat.

After blowing out the candles, he ate the beans with a spoon straight from the pan. They weren't fully cooked, and in places they were barely warm, but he ate them anyway. He didn't want to light the candles again, so he just ate them as they were.

When he was finished, he put the saucepan in the sink and filled it with water, and a squirt of washing up liquid, and then put his jacket on, at last ready for his mission.

He wondered if he should take a weapon. Maybe the little hammer, he thought. Or maybe even a knife? After a moment, he decided on the hammer. After all, it'd helped him once already. And if Kaiser attacked him again, he would prefer to hit him across the mouth once more rather than stab him. He knew that was something he couldn't bring himself to do unless he absolutely had to. And he hoped this wouldn't be the case.

He tucked the hammer into his trouser pocket, head end sticking out at the top, with his jacket hanging down to conceal it. He was ready.

17

As Oliver walked past the farm, his heart dropped as Mr Hunter came through his front door. Oliver was quite a way from him along the track, but the sight of him still filled him with dread.

Mr Hunter had a large dog bowl in his hand as Kaiser sat patiently in front of him. He stopped and stood still to watch Oliver walk by.

Oliver wished he'd ducked behind the hedges as soon as he'd seen him, but it was too late now, so he just kept walking, trying hard not to look back, but every time the urge to turn his head came over him, he saw Mr Hunter still watching him. The look on his face was almost a smile, but not quite. It was more of a smirk. He leaned to put the bowl on the ground, and as Kaiser started eating, Oliver walked a little faster. He was relieved, as he knew Kaiser wouldn't leave a bowl of food to come and attack him. But he didn't like the way Mr Hunter just stood there watching him as he walked along the track. Oliver tried his best to keep his eyes on the ground in front of him, but he couldn't help but look back at him once more. Mr Hunter put his hands on his hips, and seemed to give a short laugh. Was he being smug, or maybe pitiful, like he was looking down on Oliver, or even laughing at him? Whatever it was, Oliver didn't like it. And he was glad he'd locked the door to the bungalow. Mr Hunter had visited his house once already. Why? He didn't know. He didn't even knock. Was he thinking of robbing the place? If he did, Oliver would have no choice but to tell the police. Living there on his own was hard, but if the house was to be broken into, that would make things much worse. He already had to cope without electricity. But if all his belongings were stolen, he didn't know what he'd do. Especially if they took his drawings or his pencils.

As he reached the end of the track where the busy main road was, he turned right and walked along the grass at the side of the road, heading towards the town.

He saw a pole on the opposite side of the road that said fifty. He knew cars drove faster on this road, but he'd never taken much notice of the speed limit. He'd never had to walk towards the town that way before so it'd never been an issue. He wasn't sure how fast fifty was, but he remembered there were signs outside of his school that had the number ten on them, so he presumed fifty was pretty fast. The cars did seem to pass him at quite a speed, and they were much noisier than when cars had passed him near the school.

Although the sun was beating down on him, and he was getting hotter and hotter as he walked, he still felt a surge of energy as he walked towards the town. He could see people in cars looking at him as they went by, much like the man in the white car the previous night. Even though he only saw them for a split second before they were gone, he saw the looks of confusion on their faces. Most likely because he was only young, and out on his own. Or maybe it was because the road didn't have a pavement so people didn't normally walk alongside it. Maybe people weren't allowed to walk at the side of this road, and maybe that was why there wasn't a pathway, but he had no choice other than to keep going.

After ten minutes or so of walking, he came to a dead end. As the road went over the canal, the side he was walking on led to a brick wall where the bridge was. He had to somehow cross the road to get to the grass verge on the other side so he could continue his journey.

He stood there for what seemed like forever, waiting for a gap in the traffic. One car beeped at him, even though he hadn't stepped into the road. Oliver presumed he was annoyed at him just for attempting to cross.

As he looked right, the traffic at the roundabout that wasn't too far from him had stopped as the lights must've been on red. There were still cars coming from the left, but he stepped out onto the road and walked half way across. After another three cars went by, he saw a gap and ran across the road as fast as he could. He wasn't quite all the way across when a car came flying along the road. It missed him by a couple of seconds, but that didn't stop the driver from beeping loudly on his horn and shouting some swear words through his window. Oliver couldn't hear every word. The blast of the horn had drowned most of them out. But he didn't really care. He just wanted to carry on with his journey.

He walked along the grass and down the hill to the large and complicated roundabout. There were five exits and at least two lanes on the road for each one. Oliver found the layout confusing, but rather than risk getting beeped at or shouted at, again, he used the crossings properly and pressed the buttons, then waited for the beeps and the flashing green man to tell him when to cross.

Eventually, after three separate crossings, he made his way into the supermarket carpark. His mission to get there safely was complete, but suddenly he felt overwhelmed as he looked around at the huge carpark. There were hundreds of cars, and lots of people walking around. He really didn't know where to start.

Whenever he'd been to the supermarket with his mum, she always parked on the opposite side to where he was now. He thought that was the best place to start, so he walked alongside the parked cars and made his way there, checking each car as he went.

As he walked through the carpark, a car suddenly moved forwards and hit him on the leg, hard. The hammer, still concealed in his pocket, gave him a dead leg where the bumper hit him. The car jerked and stopped as soon as it made contact. But the pain in his right thigh burned.

The driver's door opened and an older man with white fluffy short hair and silver-rimmed glasses got out. 'I'm so sorry,' the old man said. 'Are you OK?' he asked as Oliver limped away.

'It's OK,' Oliver said, and did his best to carry on walking, but the old man chased him.

'Wait,' he said. 'I want to check you're OK.'

He caught up with Oliver and put a hand on his shoulder, gently stopping him from leaving.

'I didn't see you. I'm really sorry,' he said, looking directly at Oliver's face.

'Really, it's fine. It was my fault,' Oliver said, still holding his right thigh, and staring at the ground.

'It wasn't your fault, it was mine. My reactions aren't what they were.'

Oliver glanced up to see the man had a genuine look of concern on his face, and he didn't want him to feel bad. But he also just wanted to leave so he could get on with his mission.

'Where's your mum?' the man asked.

Good question, Oliver thought.

'She's parked over there,' he said, pointing to the other side of the carpark.

'I'll come and tell her what happened,' he said.

'No!' Oliver barked.

'Why not?'

Oliver had to think fast. 'Because she'll tell me off for it. It happened a few weeks ago and she told me to be more careful.'

The man seemed to weigh things up a little. Finally, he said, 'OK.'

Oliver felt relieved that he'd managed to convince the man that he could leave him be. 'Honestly it's fine. Sorry for not looking where I was going.'

'You've nothing to be sorry for,' the man said. 'It was all my fault.' He put his hand on Oliver's shoulder once more in a very gentle way. 'You take care,' he said softly.

'I will.'

With that, Oliver walked away, trying hard not to limp so he didn't make the man feel any worse than he already did.

He carried on walking through the carpark looking for his mum's car, being more careful, especially if he heard any of the engines running.

As he got closer to the supermarket, he saw that almost every space was taken, making it much harder to find her car.

He spent the next twenty minutes or so wandering around the huge carpark and was just about to give up when he finally spotted it.

It wasn't anywhere near the side he first checked. It was tucked away in the far left-hand corner of the carpark.

He ran over and peered through the window, hands against the glass to shield the reflection. It was his mum's car. Not only was it the right make, model and colour, it also had the tree air freshener hanging from the mirror. There could be a few cars with the same air freshener, but he also recognised her sunglasses in the gap between the two front seats.

He tried all of the doors, which were locked. And there was no sign of any problems; no new dents, or anything different about the car. And there was no blood anywhere.

He didn't know why he was thinking about blood. But he knew something had to have happened, so he was glad to eliminate the possibility of her being murdered in her car, as far-fetched as that was.

'What are you up to?'

Oliver held his breath as he spun around to see a policeman getting out of his car and walking over to him. He panicked and even thought about running, but the police officer must've guessed what he was thinking and said, 'Don't you dare,' pointing at Oliver as he stepped towards him.

Oliver froze.

The officer looked about the same age as his mum. He was slim, with dark hair. He didn't have his hat on, but he was in uniform. Oliver presumed he'd left his hat in the car.

The driver's front door was open and there was another officer in the passenger seat, a lady. Oliver couldn't see her properly because of the reflection on the windscreen. He was annoyed at himself for not realising a police car was parked there. Especially as he felt as though he'd looked at every car in the car park. It was parked in a space like all the other cars, but he still should've noticed. But then he realised he had nothing to be scared of. He hadn't done anything wrong, and the police officer could help him find his mum. Oliver realised he was being defensive, and he had no reason to be. This policeman coming over to him was the best thing that could've happened. He could finally get some help.

'Now, I'll ask you again,' the officer said. 'What are you up to?'

Oliver swallowed hard and then said, 'I'm looking for my mum. This is her car.'

This was true, but it was very unlikely she'd be coming back to the car within the next ten minutes or so.

The officer leaned his head to one side and frowned a little. He obviously didn't believe him. 'I saw you try all the handles. Why would you do that if you're waiting for your mum?'

Oliver thought for a second before saying, 'I don't know where she is.'

He knew that didn't really answer the question, but he was still nervous about being asked questions by a police officer. Even though he seemed like a nice police officer. Oliver didn't really like talking to anyone, so he hoped he would let him go as quickly as possible.

'Why have you come outside and not brought the keys with you?' He then turned back to the police car and shouted, 'Ally... do a plate-check.'

Oliver saw the woman in the car nod, although he still couldn't see her face properly.

'I live down the road. I didn't come with my mum.'

'OK,' the officer said. 'Where do you live?'

'The bungalow next to Hunter's farm.'

He raised his eyebrows. 'Oh yes. I know that house. My friend used to live there when we were kids, many years ago. It's a nice little house. How long have you lived there?'

'All my life,' he said.

'Well, you're very lucky. It must be like living in the countryside there, all those fields and being next to the farm. Seems like heaven to me.'

Oliver thought he wouldn't think that if he had to live with the fear of Len Hunter and Kaiser every day, but he didn't say anything.

'What's your mum's name?' the officer asked.

'Louise Derwent.'

The officer turned to his colleague and repeated, 'Louise Derwent?'

'Spot on,' the lady-officer said.

'Hang on a minute,' the officer said, turning back to face Oliver. 'You said your mum is inside, and you've come to meet her?'

'Yes, but...'

'And you live at Hunter's farm?' His tone had changed from being friendly to suddenly being annoyed.

'Yes,' Oliver answered nervously.

'I think I need to speak to your mum,' he said, sounding very stern now.

'Why?' Oliver asked.

'How old are you?'

'Ten,' he said.

The officer put his hands on his hips and shook his head.

Oliver felt as though he'd said something wrong, but he didn't know what.

'I definitely need to have a little chat with your mum. She shouldn't be letting you walk along that carriageway

104

on your own. It's dangerous for an adult, never mind a ten-year-old. And you would've had to cross at some point.'

Oliver was just about to tell him what had happened, and the fact he'd been living on his own for the last two days. But if he was so unhappy at the thought of Oliver walking to the supermarket on his own, he certainly wouldn't be happy at his mum leaving him alone for all that time. And he certainly didn't want to get her into trouble.

Oliver thought he might be better keeping the story to himself.

The officer leaned forwards with his hands on his thighs, his head was now the same height as Oliver's.

'Now, what's your name?' he asked.

'Oliver.'

'Nice to meet you,' he said, offering his hand to be shaken. 'I'm PC Haines.'

Oliver shook it, but he winced at the pain in his fingers.

The officer looked at the two fingers that had plasters on them. 'What've you done?'

'I err... I cut myself on a tin can.'

'Oh,' he said. Then he seemed to go into deep thought. He didn't seem happy at the cuts on his fingers either. After a moment he finally said, 'We need to go in the supermarket and find your mum. Come on.'

As they started to walk, a voice came through the radio that was attached to his jacket. It was a crackly, inaudible sentence that Oliver couldn't make out, but PC Haines obviously heard it. His demeanour changed as he stopped and turned to look at the other officer who was still in the car.

PC Haines bent down and put his hands on Oliver's shoulders. 'OK, listen,' he said, looking him directly in the eye.

Oliver suddenly became more scared, but he wasn't sure why. He tried his best to look away from him. Even though he seemed like a nice man, he still didn't like being so close to him.

'You go inside the supermarket, and tell the security staff, who will be just inside the door, that you've lost your mum. OK?'

Oliver nodded, briefly looking back at him.

'Make sure you do,' the officer shouted over his shoulder as he ran back to his car and got in.

The blue lights came on as the car made its way from the car park.

Once it'd got through the traffic of the car park, Oliver saw it speed up as the sirens came on and it shot through the town.

Oliver didn't know what had happened, but whatever it was, it was more important than him.

He couldn't decide if he should've told the officer about his mum not coming home or not. He definitely didn't look happy at the fact Oliver had crossed the road – or carriageway as PC Haines called it – by himself. He didn't want her to get into trouble. Maybe it was for the best that the policeman and his partner had been called away.

Oliver wondered what they'd been called to. It was serious whatever it was. The policeman's face had changed from being reasonably happy, to suddenly looking a little nervous or flustered, and he seemed to be in a mad rush.

After leaning against his mum's car for a minute, wondering what to do next, he thought maybe he should do as the officer said, and made his way through the car park, to the hustle and bustle of the entrance to the supermarket. The sliding doors were permanently open as people wandered in and out. As he walked through the doors, side-stepping a few supermarket trolleys being pushed by people who were more focused on reading their receipts than watching where they were going, he saw a lady behind a small, but high desk to his right.

Oliver walked over to her. She looked a little older than his mum, and had short blonde hair, and lots of makeup, and was dressed in black pants and a black jacket with a badge that said *Security*. As Oliver stood at the side of her, he could see she was staring at a monitor. He leaned around and peeked at the screen that showed a constantly moving scene of people entering and leaving the supermarket from a camera that must've been above the doors.

'Can I help you, love?' she said.

Oliver was nervous. He didn't like talking to strangers anyway, but after the conversation with PC Haines, he really didn't want to get his mum into trouble. But the policeman had told him to ask inside for his mum, and although Oliver didn't think she would still be inside the supermarket after all this time, he still thought it was worth finding out.

'I can't find my mum.'

Her face softened. She tilted her head to one side and said, 'Aww. Don't worry. We'll find her for you.'

Oliver doubted that.

The lady got up from her seat and put her hand on his back. 'Come on.'

She walked him over to the counter with a sign above it that said *Customer Services.*

'Hi Jan,' the security guard said to the woman behind the counter.

'Who's this?' Jan asked. She was an older lady, possibly in her sixties. She had a welcoming smile that made Oliver feel safe.

'This young man has lost his mum.'

'Oh dear,' Jan said, reaching for the microphone. 'What's her name?'

'Louise Derwent,' he answered.

'OK,' she said. She then pressed the little black button at the base of the microphone stand in front of her. *'Customer announcement, can Louise Derwent please make her way to Customer Services; Louise Derwent to Customer Services. Thank you.'*

The security guard then said, 'He can come and sit with me while we wait.'

'No problem,' Jan said.

After five minutes of sitting on a seat behind the security desk, it was quite obvious that Oliver's mum wasn't in the supermarket. He wondered if he should tell the lady that he'd been living on his own. But it still bothered Oliver when he thought about the police officer's reaction to him crossing the carriageway.

He didn't think she'd left him alone on purpose, but supposing something had just happened and she was now on her way home; she could get into trouble. He decided he wasn't going to risk it.

'I'll go and get her to ask again,' the security guard said. 'Maybe your mum didn't hear it the first time. You wait here.'

As the security guard walked over to the Customer Services desk, Oliver decided it was time to leave.

He jumped off his seat and ran through the supermarket doors, not bothering to look behind him to see if either of the two ladies had noticed.

He ran as fast as he could through the car park, being careful not to get hit by any more cars.

Once he'd negotiated all the crossings, and reached the carriageway, he took a breath and leaned up against a tree that was set back from the road.

He didn't want any more adults to approach him, and he didn't want to get beeped at by any more bad-tempered drivers, so he set off walking along the grass verge until there was a reasonable gap in the traffic. Once he thought it was safe, he crossed the road and headed home, feeling disappointed with himself – he'd failed on his mission. And he didn't know what to do next. But he also wondered if in his absence, his mum had gone back home.

18

Going all the way to the supermarket felt like a complete waste of time to Oliver. All he'd got for his efforts was a bruise on his right leg, although he hadn't yet looked, but it certainly felt painful to the touch.

He now knew for sure that his mum had made it to the supermarket, but for some reason or other, she'd disappeared before coming home.

The situation didn't make sense. Why would she go to the supermarket, but leave her car there? And if the car had broken down, surely she would've taken a taxi home. Could she still be in the supermarket somewhere? He wondered if maybe she was locked in one of the bathrooms.

Oliver started to regret not waiting there and letting the staff help him. But he'd panicked at the thought of his mum getting into trouble for leaving him on his own. Something had to have happened for her not to have come home by now. She wouldn't have left him on his own, not on purpose. But where was she? He felt as though he needed to make some notes listing the timeline of events, like they did on the detective shows his mum would sometimes watch. He needed to see things clearly to try to understand what might've happened.

He'd managed to walk by the turning to the farm without being seen by Mr Hunter or Kaiser. He felt relieved as he walked up to the kitchen door, unlocked it and walked inside.

As he took his first steps into the kitchen, he saw something on the floor that he recognised. It looked like a credit card, but it wasn't. As he picked it up, he realised straight away what it was. He'd seen it many times. It was the electric card, the card his mum had to take to the supermarket, shop or petrol station to pay for the power for the bungalow.

As he stepped forward, the card in his hand, he noticed there was water everywhere. A large puddle had made its way along the tiled floor and further into the kitchen. Luckily the card had been on the mat and not in the water, so he hoped it still worked. He closed and locked the door.

'Mum!' he shouted.

He ran around the house looking for her.

'Mum!' he shouted again. 'Are you home?'

After running from room to room, checking everywhere in the house, he was left disappointed. His bedroom, and his mum's bedroom looked the same as before he left. The kitchen still had the glasses and plates in the sink. The first-aid box was still on the side. In the living room, the melted candlewax was still draped over the edge of the coffee table, and the bunker was still there, positioned against the wall.

He felt deflated.

Why would his mum post the card through the door but not come back in the house? And where had the water come from? He really didn't understand.

After taking the mop and bucket from the tall cupboard, he mopped the kitchen floor as he pondered over what might have happened. Had she maybe come back home, but lost her keys and so posted the card so he could have the electric on if he came back before she did? If so, she could be out looking for him now. If that was the case, then surely, she would come back home soon. He didn't know. He just wanted his mum back home with him, where she belonged.

He couldn't figure out where the water had come from. Was there a leak somewhere? Had he spilled some water when he'd washed the cuts on his fingers? If he had, it was a lot of water. And he hadn't noticed before he left. After all, he was lay on the kitchen floor.

He leaned the mop up against the kitchen counter and walked into the living room. All he could do at that very moment was crawl into the bunker, lie down on the bed cover, and cry.

He felt deflated. He felt defeated. And he was running out of ideas of what to do, as well as ideas of what might've happened. He'd never felt so exhausted.

After ten minutes or so of uncontrollable sobbing, he drifted off to sleep.

He didn't know how long he'd slept for; it felt like about an hour, but it could've been longer. He stared into the dark and began to run the situation through his mind once more. He wasn't sure why, but he'd woken up feeling a little better. He wasn't sure if it was the sleeping or the

113

crying that had helped, but either way, he was now feeling more positive, and decided it was time to get organised.

He climbed out of the bunker and stretched.

He then took the electric card to the meter which was in the cupboard in the corner of the kitchen. He knelt down on the floor and inserted the card.

The LED display said there was ten pounds on it. He pressed the red button to deposit the funds into the meter. His mum had shown him how to do it before; possibly because the meter was so low down it was hard for her to reach. Or maybe because she knew she'd be leaving him alone to fend for himself one day. He didn't know.

He heard the power come back on. There was a humming noise coming from the fridge. After closing the cupboard, and placing the card on the worktop, he went over to the fridge and opened it.

The light came on, but the smell that hit him was overpowering. It was like a sour milk and bad egg smell. Not as bad as the smell from his mum's bedroom after Franky had been in there, but it was still quite horrible.

He closed the door, knowing that later on, he'd have to throw everything away, and maybe even go back to the supermarket for some food. He'd have to search the house for money first. He had a piggy bank with four pounds and fifty-seven pence in it. Maybe that would buy him a couple of things. Most likely milk and bread. But he'd have to make sure the security guard and the lady at the counter didn't see him. He wondered if he went at a different time, they might not be working there. After all, it was a twenty-four-hour supermarket. They couldn't work every day. Or maybe he could just go to one of the smaller shops or even the petrol station.

He went into his bedroom and found his whiteboard and dry-wipe marker pen. It was only a small whiteboard, just twice the size of an A4 piece of paper, but it should suffice for the job in hand.

Back in the living room, Oliver wiped the job list his mum had written for him a few days earlier – all of which he'd completed – off the board with his sleeve.

He then placed it on the coffee table and began to go over things in his mind; the time his mum left to go shopping, when the man with the BMW called around and knocked on the door, the car being left at the supermarket.

He didn't have much to go on, but he had to try and work out what had happened, so he started to write,

Saturday May 1st

Mum left for the supermarket at 11·13am

Said she'd be twenty minutes

Power goes out at 9·00pm ish...

Sunday May 2nd

BMW man knocked on door at 10·30am ish...

Mr Hunter comes to house at 1·45pm

Car still at supermarket – no sign of mum

Electric card posted while gone

Water on floor

115

He wasn't sure if all the times were correct, but he knew he wasn't far off with his estimates.

He stood in front of the board, looking closely at the list. He thought that writing the events down would help him try to figure out what had happened. But unfortunately, it hadn't.

With his hands on his hips, he stared at the board. 'Well that's got me a lot closer,' he said.

19

The smell was so bad, he had to tie a towel around his face again as he emptied the contents of the fridge into a bin bag. Even though the power was back on, it was too late for most of the food that was in there. It felt like a waste, throwing it away. But at least the fridge wasn't full.

His mum always went shopping on a Saturday morning, and she had to be careful what she bought and always checked the dates on everything. She couldn't afford to throw food away, so she planned out meals for the whole week before setting off to the supermarket with the list; the list she would usually stick to and only ever deviate from if Oliver was with her and had spotted something he fancied, either for a meal or just a snack, or some nice new paper maybe.

After the fridge was empty – apart from the butter and a few other things like ketchup and mustard that he thought might be OK – he tied the bin bag and took it to the outside bin.

He had a quick look around for Franky, but there was no sign of him. Oliver had no intentions of letting him back into the house, but it would be nice to see him again. He also looked over to the farm to see if he could see Kaiser or Mr Hunter, but he couldn't see either of them.

Once back inside, still with the towel around his face, he sprayed bleach into the fridge, then wiped all the shelves as best he could, using a wet dishcloth. Even though he still had plasters on his fingers, the water stung the cuts, but he fought through the pain and carried on.

Once the fridge was clean – not as clean as his mum would make it, but good enough for now – he decided to clean the rest of the house.

He hadn't drawn a picture for a while, and thought it wouldn't be too long before he was sat at his desk again, creating another masterpiece. But for now, he thought that if he was living on his own, he needed to be more of a man and look after the house. He wasn't planning on doing any DIY or decorating, but he could at least keep it as clean and tidy as it usually was. Partly so he felt as comfortable as he could being in the house on his own, but also in case his mum came home. It would be nice if she came home to a tidy house and he could show her how well he'd coped.

He gathered all the glasses, plates and bowls he'd been using, and put them into the sink, ran the tap and squirted some washing up liquid into the stream of water. Once he'd cleaned and rinsed them, he set them to dry on the draining rack.

The bunker was his next port of call – he removed the chocolate wrappers, as well as straightening out the bed cover, almost like he was making his bed. He put the pack of cards away, and set to work on the melted candlewax that was hanging over the edge of the table.

He got himself a sharp knife and slid it under the wax puddle. As it separated from the wood, the long, solid drip stayed in one piece as it broke away. The structure was amazing. It reminded him of icicles he'd seen hanging from the roof in winter.

There was still a solid disc on the carpet about the size of a pound coin, but the wax from the table came away easily, just leaving a white dusty mark behind. He was about to take it to the bin outside, but he couldn't bring himself to throw it away. It was a work of art. He turned it around, looking at all the ripples and creases in the hardened flow of wax. Instead of throwing it away, he rested it on the kitchen worktop to show his mum. He knew he'd probably have a go at drawing it too.

Back in the living room, he tried to pick up the small puddle of wax from the carpet, but he couldn't. It was stuck. He took hold of the knife and tried sliding the blade underneath. It had worked for the wax on the table, but it wasn't working on the carpet. After pondering for a moment or two, Oliver decided to try the hammer. He had mixed feelings about the little hammer. It'd saved his life when Kaiser tried to kill him, but when the car had hit him, it dug into his thigh giving him the dead leg of all dead legs. He knew it would've hurt anyway, but he was sure it'd hurt more because of the hammer in his pocket.

He knelt down in front of the disc of wax that was fixed firmly to the carpet and swung the hammer, hitting it right in the centre. It cracked across the middle so he swung again, and again. After hitting it several times, he then started to break bits away with his fingers. Some of the pieces he pulled away brought up fibres from the

119

carpet, but he kept pulling regardless of that. By the time he'd finished, the wax was gone, but there was a circular dent in the carpet with a tinge of white, just like the stain on the coffee table, but it still looked better than before.

Once he'd thrown all the wax pieces away – apart from the sculpture he was keeping to show his mum – he took out the vacuum cleaner, and continued to do a proper job of making the house clean and tidy.

The bunker was still there, covered by branches and leaves. But other than that, the room looked pretty OK, ready for his mum coming home. He hoped with all his heart that that would be before he had to spend another night on his own.

20

The clock on the living room wall said eight-forty-five. He'd eaten a full tin of ravioli that he'd prepared in the microwave, and not by holding a pan over three lit candles. He'd washed up and put away the bowl and the cutlery.

He wondered if his mum would be annoyed about the bunker being there, but at least the rest of the house was tidy.

Oliver thought about going to bed.

It was now thirty-three hours and thirty-two minutes since his mum had left the house to go shopping. It was looking more and more like he was about to spend another night on his own.

He still couldn't understand why she would post the electric card but not come into the house, or if she had lost her key, at least wait outside the bungalow. It just didn't make sense.

He briefly wondered whether it had been on the floor the whole time. Maybe she'd dropped it before she went shopping. But he didn't think that was likely. He'd been in the kitchen many times and he hadn't seen it. He'd also been in and out of the door several times so it must've been posted. And there had been ten pounds added to the card. It really didn't make sense. And why was there water on the floor? It was quite a lot of water, but the floor was dry now, so it wasn't a leaking pipe. And it hadn't rained in ages.

His head hurt again from thinking about it, so he decided he'd get some fresh air. Outside, he locked the door behind him, put the key in his pocket and walked around to the back garden. The sun was setting on the clear springtime evening, and the sky glowed a deep orange that hovered over the forest and the fields. It looked amazing. Oliver briefly thought about drawing a picture of the scenery before him, but he didn't know how a sunset would look in grey and black.

He made his way along the grass to the bottom of the garden. He didn't really want to go into the woods. He hadn't gone very far into them since his dad left, but he especially didn't want to go in there now because it was getting dark. Being on his own in the house was scary enough, but being on his own in the woods at night would be terrifying.

At the mouth of the woods, he looked through the gap in the trees, wondering if Franky would show his face. It would be nice to see him again, but he had no intentions of feeding him. Not only because the last time had left him with cuts on his fingers that were still stinging, but also because of the possibility of running out of food. Foxes were capable of hunting and foraging for something to eat. If Oliver ran out of food, he didn't know what he'd do.

He'd tried climbing the tree at the bottom of the garden before, but his mum made him stop when he got to the height of the gutters on the bungalow. Oliver knew he could get higher. And there was nobody there to stop him now.

Without giving it a second thought, he reached up and grabbed the first branch and pulled himself up. Once his feet were on the first bough, he took a deep breath before climbing to the next. The cuts on his fingers hurt with each grasp of a branch, but he tried his best to ignore the pain and keep going.

Once he'd got to the place level with the gutter, he stopped and looked around. He remembered this part of the tree from the last time he climbed it. There was a protruding branch that he could sit on without having to crouch too much from the branches above. But he wasn't going to sit down; he wanted to go further, so he climbed and climbed, making his way towards the top of the tree.

As he got near to the top, the branches started to get thinner and thinner so eventually, he had to stop. He held on tight as he looked around at the view. It was wonderful.

He stepped back down some of the way so he could sit on a firm branch he thought would support his weight. He held on tight as he positioned himself into the area that looked like the perfect place to sit, almost as if Mother Nature had created it just for him. Once comfortable, he relaxed his grip and looked around at the view.

He was above the height of the roof of the bungalow. He could see the carriageway and Hunter's Farm. Behind him, if he looked over his shoulder, he could see the woodland. To the left, in the distance he could see the housing estate where his primary school was. After searching, and squinting a little, he finally spotted the school building, and the football field behind it.

He turned and looked over the top of Hunter's Farm and he could see the retail park in the distance where the supermarket was.

Although it wasn't in his head to climb the tree to look for his mum, now he was there, he did wonder if it was possible to see her. He shuddered as he pictured her dead body in one of the fields in his mind's eye. He couldn't imagine what he'd do if he did see her lifeless body lying there. He would have no choice but to ask for help if that was to happen. Maybe even from Mr Hunter. He hoped it wouldn't come to that. As well as the fact that he really didn't want to ask him for help, he especially didn't want anyone to know his mum had abandoned him, and think anything bad about her. And whatever reason she had for leaving him, he knew it must've been important. It would be best to wait for her return rather than tell anyone what had happened.

The sun was low to his right, behind the farm. He decided to stay at the top of the tree and watch the sunset. Although he hated Mr Hunter, and he really didn't like Kaiser, the view of the farm and the fields made for a beautiful scene, especially from where he was, and especially for the time of the evening he'd chosen to climb the tree. He just sat there, enjoying the view in the fading light. The peaceful and serene setting was incredible. He could understand why his mum would try so hard to keep this house, although she would certainly never have climbed the tree to see the scenery, it was still an amazing place to live. Oliver didn't always appreciate it, but he did appreciate the fact that they were away from other people and maybe from now on, he'd enjoy the scenery just as much. He would certainly appreciate his mum more from now on. And he would most likely say yes to trips to the supermarket, and maybe even to a walk in the woods.

21

Oliver was the happiest he'd been over the last two days as he sat high up in the tree watching the sun go down. He'd been stressed, and scared throughout the ordeal, but even though he was high off the ground, and knew very well if he slipped, he'd most likely fall to his death, he felt safer where he was right now; much safer than he'd felt in the house on his own since his mum had left.

He looked over to Hunter's farm again. From the height he was at, he would be able to see if Mr Hunter or the man with the BMW came back and knocked on the door. He also thought they wouldn't see him there. After all, you don't look up at a tree and expect to see a ten-year-old sitting there enjoying the view. He also thought he would be hidden by the leaves. He wasn't exactly dressed in army camouflage, but his clothes surely weren't bright enough to grab attention from the ground.

As much as he was enjoying the view, and as happy and safe as he felt, he knew it was time to climb back down. The sun had fallen into the ground in the distance where the sky was still reasonably bright with a mixture of orange and red, and fading into a dark blue everywhere else. He knew within the hour it would be completely dark. He was surprisingly comfortable and he briefly considered sleeping in the tree. But he didn't think he would be able to drift off to sleep for the fear of falling off the branch he was sat on, and most likely hitting every other on the way down.

After enjoying one last peaceful moment while soaking in the amazing views, Oliver started to climb down the tree. But before he'd made it past the first branch, he stopped.

In the ever-growing darkness, he noticed a set of headlights making their way along the track towards the bungalow. With the lights pointing towards him, he could just about see the silhouette of the car, but he couldn't see the colour, and certainly not the make; not that he knew one car from another anyway. But this car looked as though it could be his mums.

He hoped with all his heart that it was. He'd experienced two days on his own, and he'd survived with a few stories to tell. But he was now ready to get back to normal. He really didn't want to be on his own for another night.

He watched as the car reached the turning to the farm, hoping it would drive past and head towards the bungalow.

'Please, please, please, please, please, please, please,' he said over and over again, and sure enough, it passed the turning.

'Yes,' he said quietly to himself. But as the car approached, he saw that it wasn't the same shape as his mum's car. There was a rectangular box on the roof, and the car was white.

As it drew closer, he felt deflated, but also anxious as he saw that not only was it not his mum's car, it was actually a police car.

Why would a police car come to the bungalow? Had somebody called them after seeing him in the tree? If that was the case it could only be Mr Hunter. Unless maybe someone saw him through a telescope. Either way, he wasn't climbing down from the tree until he knew why they were there.

There were two police officers in the car, and they both climbed out after parking outside the kitchen door. The driver was a man, and the passenger was a woman. Oliver couldn't see them properly in the fading light, but as the man knocked on the door, he realised who it was. It was PC Haines from the supermarket carpark. He wondered why he'd come to the bungalow. When he'd spoken to him, he seemed annoyed at his mum letting him walk along the carriageway on his own, which was why he didn't tell him she'd gone missing. He wondered if he should climb down the tree and tell them what had happened. But he really didn't want his mum to get into trouble. And she could come home at any time.

Oliver watched as they waited for an answer. He of course knew that nobody would answer the door, and there were no lights on inside so they must realise that the bungalow was empty.

'I'll check round the back,' the woman said, and walked around the back of the bungalow, stopping briefly to look through Oliver's bedroom window on her way past. She then went to the patio doors at the back, pressing the edge of her hands onto the glass so she could see. She shrugged to herself and rejoined PC Haines.

'Empty,' she said.

PC Haines stroked his chin. Oliver froze as he watched him as he looked all around the garden, but luckily, he didn't look up.

'Well, we'll try again tomorrow,' he said, walking back towards the car.

As Oliver watched them drive away, he thought that they must've come to check on him after he'd ran away from the supermarket. Maybe the security guard reported him for disappearing after she'd told him to stay put. Or perhaps PC Haines wanted to teach Oliver's mum about road safety. He didn't really know, and he didn't understand why they would go to so much trouble. He just hoped his mum would return before they came back tomorrow.

Once the car had reached the end of the lane and turned onto the carriageway, Oliver started his descent down the tree. He felt nervous as he made his way down, and was extra careful of where he put each hand and each foot. He thought maybe it was because the ground was in his eyeline as he climbed down that was making him feel this way – on his way up, he was fully focused on the branches.

Once he got to the bottom branch, he leapt from the tree, landing on the ground feet first, quickly followed by the palms of his hands. He stood up straight, dusted his hands off and headed along the grass back to the bungalow. At the kitchen door, he felt in his pocket for the key and felt a sudden bolt of fear as his hand went into an empty pocket. His other pocket was empty too. His hands that had felt too dry after climbing the tree suddenly felt moist as the reality of the situation kicked in. Not only had he been left alone, but he'd now locked himself out of his home.

He tried the door handle, knowing full well it would be locked. He then walked back towards the tree, searching the ground as he did, hoping to see the reflection of the shiny metal key as it lay in the grass. But he saw no such thing.

He spent the next few moments retracing his steps, but it wasn't there. He'd only walked from the door to the tree at the bottom of the garden. He knew it couldn't be far. But as the night was drawing in, and it was falling darker and darker, he was really starting to panic.

He combed the grass on his hands and knees, then crawled towards the tree, searching every stone, pebble and blade of grass.

Nothing.

He did this a couple more times before he finally accepted the fact that he wasn't going to find it in the dark, and realised he had to start thinking about a plan of action for the night. He could sleep on the grass in the open air, but although the weather had been nice the last couple of days, he knew it would be cold at night. It was getting pretty cool already.

He could wander over to Mr Hunter's farmhouse. Not to knock on the door, but maybe one of his vehicles might be unlocked. But to do that, he would have to get there without disturbing Kaiser.

Oliver also knew that farmers tend to start work early, and he couldn't guarantee waking up before Mr Hunter did. The thought of being woken first thing in the morning by Mr Hunter opening the tractor door and finding him there filled Oliver with dread.

He wandered around the outside of the bungalow trying all the windows and doors. All of them were locked.

He checked his pockets again, but they were as empty as they had been the previous five times he'd checked.

The darkness was closing in and Oliver had to decide what to do.

He began to walk along the track towards the farm, even more scared now than he was the previous night because he didn't have his trusty little hammer with him. But he knew in his heart that he wouldn't be going far enough to alert Kaiser. At the bottom of the lane that turned towards the farm, Oliver stopped.

He wasn't intending to knock on Mr Hunter's door. And he didn't want to get savaged by Kaiser. He just wanted to weigh up his options by looking at the farm a little closer. The farmhouse was obviously not an option. And although there were several vehicles outside of the house, he really didn't want to risk getting caught.

Behind the farmhouse, slightly to the left, there was a huge outbuilding; a barn, he thought. He wondered if there was a way of getting to it without letting Kaiser hear or see him.

He walked a little further along the track, terrified at the thought of the dog chasing him again.

He looked around for a weapon, but there was nothing other than a few twigs on the ground. As he reached the first vehicle, a type of pickup truck, he began to feel even more scared. His legs felt weak and he couldn't control his breathing. All he could hear were the noisy breaths making their way in and out of his lungs as his chest expanded and contracted. If he could hear himself breathing so loudly, then maybe Kaiser could hear him too.

There was a noise. It sounded like shouting, only it wasn't as loud as the last time he'd heard it. Almost like it was further away. Oliver wondered if Mr Hunter was always in a bad mood. He didn't want to antagonise him and put him in an even worse mood, by him catching him on his land. Oliver crouched behind the pickup truck and waited for the shouting to stop.

After a moment of silence, he started shuffling his way along the grass behind the truck. Oliver was determined to get to the barn, but he knew he was risking his life by doing so. If Kaiser heard him, he would have no chance of escape. But he had to try to find somewhere to sleep for the night. It was already getting cold, and there wasn't much light. He was running out of time.

He passed a pile of bricks, and a wheelbarrow, then he came to a pile of hay bales all wrapped in black plastic.

The huge round shapes were stacked two-high and there were around ten of them. Rather than risk being spotted, he made his way around the back of them, squeezing his way through the tight gap between the bails and the hedges.

As he got to the other side, he froze. He wasn't far from the house, but what he saw almost made him faint with fear.

A dog kennel.

The wooden box had a roof and a hole in the front. A hole big enough for a dog like Kaiser. It was dark inside the kennel, but Oliver knew the chances were Kaiser was inside.

He didn't know what to do. Should he sneak his way past and hope not to wake him? Should he give up and find somewhere else to go?

There was a pile of wood just to his left.

He bent down and picked up a piece about the length of his arm. The cuts on his fingers stung as he gripped his hand around the wood, but that didn't bother him at that moment. What bothered him was the chance he could wake up the sleeping monster.

He heard a noise and was pretty sure it came from inside the kennel. It sounded like a crying sound, only very short, and no sooner had it started, it stopped. Maybe a yawn, or maybe a wheeze, but he wasn't sure. What he was sure about though was the fact that if he woke Kaiser, he would be dead before Mr Hunter came out and called him to heel.

He wondered why he was doing this. He wanted to find somewhere to sleep for the night so he could try to find the key tomorrow. But was a good night's sleep really worth risking dying for? He decided to turn back.

So he'd be awake all night. So he'd be tired the next day. So what. It wasn't like he'd be going to school.

He walked away slowly, trying hard not to disturb Kaiser as he climbed back around the hay bales. But as he passed the pickup truck, the piece of wood he was still carrying banged against the side of the truck. The noise wasn't too loud, but it could've been loud enough.

Without thinking, he shot into a sprint, dropping the stick as he ran faster than he'd ever ran before.

Kaiser started barking, but Oliver didn't turn to look. He just put his head down and ran as fast as he could back towards the bungalow.

After a few seconds, the barking stopped, but Oliver still didn't turn around. He just kept going until he got to the bungalow, then he ran around the back before slamming his back against the wall.

After a moment of struggling to get his breath back, he peered around the corner of the wall to see if he was safe.

To his relief, there was no Kaiser. He hadn't followed him.

He'd survived yet another ordeal with the vicious farm-dog. But he knew sooner or later, if he kept going back there, Kaiser would eventually get lucky.

22

Oliver sat on the ground with his back against the wall for what felt like an eternity, but it was actually more like half an hour or so. He was cold, he was tired and now that it was fully dark, he was terrified.

The sky was cloudless, so the moon and the stars stopped the night from being completely black, and his eyes had slowly adjusted as the light had faded. The cuts on his fingers were still hurting, and he was feeling weak. He needed to change the plasters, but on the list of things that were important, that was quite low down. He needed to find somewhere to sleep for the night.

He got up from the cold ground, too cold to stay where he was. He was only dressed in tracksuit bottoms and a tee shirt. Even pulling his arms inside the tee shirt and folding them across his belly didn't keep him warm, although it did help a little.

He stepped over the grass towards the tree at the bottom of the garden and knelt down, feeling around for the key once more, but it was to no avail. He considered breaking a window to get inside, but he knew that as soon as the sun came up, he'd be able to find the key. He hadn't gone very far, so it had to be in the garden somewhere.

He walked towards the opening to the woods at the bottom of the garden. It *was* totally black as he stepped through the gap in the trees, but he thought it might be warmer under the shelter of leaves and branches rather than staying out in the open air.

He couldn't see where he was going, but he continued to walk forwards regardless. The soft ground sank beneath his feet as he walked deeper into the woodland. He'd only travelled a short distance from the mouth of the woods, but he was still terrified at how dark it was. For all he knew, there could be any kind of creature in there, or even a person.

There weren't any noises, other than the gentle breeze and the slow sway of the trees. But he knew that a lot of animals were nocturnal, and they would be about to start their night-time routines. He'd heard lots of noises through his bedroom window over the years, especially in spring and summer. He knew he was taking a risk by heading into the woods, but he had to try to get warm, one way or another.

As he stretched his hands out in front of him, he felt the bark of a tree. He then slowly felt his way down to the bottom.

The soft, mossy ground surrounding the tree felt nothing like his comfortable bed cover, the one that was now lying unused inside the bunker in the living room. But it would have to do. He dug his fingers into the ground and pulled the moss and leaves away from the tree. His fingers hurt once more as he did this, but he fought past the pain and carried on digging. He felt his way around the tree, collecting more and more of the dry moss. Once he had a reasonable pile, he felt his way over to the next tree and did the same again, then brought it over and added it to the rest.

He lay down next to the pile he'd made and wriggled on the ground until he felt comfortable, or as comfortable as he could be, lying in the woods in almost complete darkness.

He then reached to the side and with both hands, lifted the moss and the grass and spread it across his body. After he'd covered himself as best he could, he tucked his arms into his tee shirt again, and waited, hoping to warm up very soon.

As Oliver lay there, shivering, he was suddenly aware of all the noises from the woods, noises he hadn't noticed while trying to make a bed. He hoped the foxes wouldn't start screaming. That was a noise he still hated, even since becoming friends with Franky. Being alone in the woods at night, he couldn't think of any worse noise to come echoing through the trees.

He wondered if Franky would pay him a visit. And if he did, would he lie next to him and help keep him warm? He doubted it; that was the kind of thing that would happen in a Disney film, not in real life.

He lay there, terrified, shivering and wishing for sleep. The events of the last two days spun through his mind as he tried his best to relax and slow his heart rate. He was still no closer to coming up with a good explanation for his mum not coming home. Even though he'd played every single thing that had happened since eleven-thirteen the day before through his mind, he just couldn't understand it. Would he ever find out what had happened, or was this how he was going to live the rest of his life?

He shivered, partly through fear, and partly because of how cold it was. His body and arms had started to warm up a little, but his face felt like ice. The noises he could hear, the rustling, the hooting of an owl in the distance, and the occasional snap or movement of a twig or branch scared him into staying absolutely still. Even if an animal came close, he knew he wouldn't be able to move. He was rigid with the fear of what was around him in the blackness. It felt as though the dark was touching him as he lay, frozen to the spot. Eventually, after lying shivering for what felt like hours, he finally drifted off to sleep.

23

Monday 3rd May

The sky was a little brighter as Oliver slowly opened his eyes. He didn't think the sun was up as of yet, but it must've been on its way because he could see the leaves as they moved gently in the springtime breeze. It was still a little dark, but when he'd entered the woods the night before, he hadn't been able to see a thing. Now he could see everything.

He heard a gentle shuffling noise to his left. It didn't sound far away, and although he felt a little scared of what it might be, he felt he had no choice but to slowly turn his head to look.

It was a rabbit; a young grey rabbit.

Oliver's fear was instantly replaced by pleasure and appreciation at the sight of such a beautiful creature. He would've liked to have stroked it, but he knew it would most likely run away as soon as it saw him, so he watched it chewing the weeds for a few minutes.

His back was aching, and his fingers were still stinging, yet he couldn't help but try and block this from his mind as he watched the cute little creature go about its morning routine.

Suddenly, the rabbit stood on its back legs and looked around, sniffing the air. It looked a little startled. Oliver hadn't moved or made a sound, so he didn't understand why. It then shot off into the woods at top speed.

Oliver tried to get up, but his aching back wouldn't let him. When he finally did sit up and brush all the moss and grass off himself, he stretched and gave a yawn. As he struggled to his feet, he realised what had scared the rabbit. A familiar face came towards him from the direction of the bungalow. It was Franky.

'Oh, it's you,' Oliver said.

Franky walked over to him.

'It's no good turning up now. Where were you during the night when I was freezing cold and scared?'

Franky ignored the reprimand and stepped closer, sniffing the air as he did.

'I haven't got any food,' he said. 'I've been locked out all night.'

Oliver made his way towards the house, stretching once more as he walked.

Franky jumped aside to let him pass.

Once Oliver had left the woods, he went over to the tree and wandered around the area beneath, looking for the key.

Within a minute of looking, he saw it. It was on its side in a little dip in the grass right at the base of the trunk. It was almost a hole within the root formation. He couldn't believe how easily he'd found it now, when the night before he'd spent so long searching. If only he'd put his fingers underneath the roots, he'd have found it and avoided having to spend the night in the woods.

Oliver was annoyed, and his back still ached, but he was also relieved. He limped over to the bungalow and put the key in the kitchen door and stepped inside of the house. As he went to close the door, he saw that Franky had followed him and was stood in the doorway looking at him.

'I'm sorry, Franky, but I'm not feeding you. You'll have to go and fend for yourself.'

He felt a little bad for closing the door on the fox, but he really didn't want to have to clean up after him again. And he had to look after himself first before helping the local wildlife. He hadn't properly checked the cupboards as of yet to see how long the supplies would last. This was something he should do today. But until he did, Franky would have to feed himself.

Oliver locked the door, made a glass of cordial, drank it all in one go, and then ran a bath.

Once in the bath, he lay back and relaxed and hoped the hot water would sooth his aches and pains. He hadn't had anywhere near enough sleep, so he knew he could fall asleep at any moment, and he really didn't want to do that while lying in the bath. As he lowered his hands into the water, his fingers stung, even more than they had been already. The plasters were now dirty and falling loose in places. He began to peel them off, thinking it would be better to clean the cuts in the bath before replacing the plasters with clean ones.

As he peeled away the first plaster from his index finger, he felt a sudden wave of sickness come over him.

Last time he'd looked, the back of his finger had a small, but deep cut just above the first knuckle. Now, it looked like something from a horror film. It was swollen, and the area around the cut was much fatter than the rest of the finger – the skin looked stretched like it was going to burst. And although the skin around the cut was white, the actual cut oozed a green and white substance that he'd never seen before. That was when the smell hit him.

It was repulsive. Even worse than the smell Franky had left in his mum's bedroom. He really thought he was going to be sick. He looked away as he pushed his hand below the surface of the water. The pain was immense, but whatever was wrong with the cuts, surely soapy water had to help.

As he lifted his hand back out of the water, he peeled the plaster off his middle finger. That too looked horrific, with gunge oozing from the cut.

He put his hand back into the water and shook it as hard as he could, screaming as the sting grew into a burning sensation.

He put his left elbow on the edge of the bath and rested his head on his left hand. He didn't want to look at his wound again, and thought that the longer he left his fingers under the water, the better. He didn't know what to do. They had obviously become infected, either from the can of tuna, or from the fox licking the cuts as they dripped with blood.

Suddenly, he didn't think of Franky as a friend anymore. It wasn't the fox's fault as such, but at that moment, as two of his fingers felt as though they were on fire, he really wished he'd never bothered to feed him.

He tried his best to wash himself all over.

The shower gel caused a fresh wave of pain in his fingers, but he fought through it, aware that they needed to be cleaned. He didn't know just how badly infected the cuts could get, but the thought of losing his fingers popped into his head. He really didn't want that. Obviously, he would never want to lose any part of his body, but losing his fingers could keep him from drawing, and that was unthinkable.

After he'd got out of the bath, he went to the kitchen and dried his hands with kitchen towel as he stood there naked and wet.

He then wrapped two new plasters around his infected fingers, trying to block out the pain as he pulled them as tight as possible. He wasn't sure if this was the right thing to do, but it felt like it could be a way to try and stop the infection from getting any worse.

In his bedroom, after getting dressed, he sat on his bed. The clock on the wall said ten past seven. He tried to think of what day it was. His mum left to go shopping on Saturday, he'd spent that day and all Sunday on his own, so it was now Monday.

Oliver suddenly thought of a way he could bring an end to the situation.

24

Oliver didn't want to get his mum in trouble, which was why he hadn't told the police officer at the supermarket what had happened, and had hidden from him when he came to the house. But enough was enough.

She'd been gone for almost two full days by now, and it wasn't looking as though she was coming home. Whatever had happened to her, Oliver knew he needed help. He'd managed to keep himself alive, but the cuts on his fingers needed medical attention. And he needed a decent meal. There were still things in the cupboard he could eat. There was at least another pack of microwavable beans and he'd seen another tin of ravioli in there somewhere. But even if he tried his best to carry on living alone, eventually the food, and the power, would run out. And the four pounds fifty-seven pence he had in his piggy bank wouldn't go very far.

He'd made his decision.

He was going to school.

25

Oliver didn't think it was necessary to change into his school uniform, although he did briefly contemplate doing so.

He couldn't see the day being a normal school day for him. Surely once he'd told Mrs Wheaton that he'd been on his own all weekend, because his mum had disappeared, she would... well, he didn't know what she would do. Maybe she would phone the police. Maybe she'd phone the hospital. He didn't know. But she certainly wouldn't make him sit through a maths lesson, or whatever the first lesson of the day would be. This was something he would usually know, but he couldn't be bothered to think about it at that very moment. Either way, he wouldn't be taking part.

He wondered if Mrs Wheaton would believe his story or not. But she'd know his mum wouldn't let him go to school without wearing his uniform. And if she still didn't believe him, then he only had to show her the cuts on his fingers.

He could still smell the awful stink of the cuts, or whatever the gooey stuff was that was causing the smell. It wasn't as bad as when he removed the plasters in the bath, but he could still smell it.

His house was only a mile or so from his primary school, so he knew it wouldn't take him long to get there.

After locking the door, he walked slowly down the track, keeping an eye out for Kaiser.

He hadn't had any breakfast and so he felt as though he didn't have the energy to run from him again. Luckily, Oliver didn't see Kaiser, and more importantly, Kaiser didn't see him.

As he reached the carriageway, he turned left. Although there was no footpath when he turned right to go to the supermarket, turning left did lead onto a pavement, so it was much safer.

After walking for a while, he reached the passageway that headed away from the road and into the estate. Once through it, he turned right and headed in the direction of the school.

It was at that point that Oliver realised he hadn't seen any other kids.

When the weather was nice and his mum felt like walking, or on days when her car wasn't working, they usually saw loads of people walking to school.

Oliver looked up at the bright blue sky and thought that today would have been one of those days when they'd walk the route together.

He would give anything for his mum to come back home. Why hadn't she? He had no idea if she was ever going to come home again. If she had disappeared altogether, what would happen to him? He'd heard about kids living in care homes or foster care. Was that what was going to happen to him? Would he have to leave the bungalow and live with another family? He really wished for his mum, and his dad, to come home. At that moment, he would settle for either.

Mrs Wheaton would know what to do. He trusted her to help him. One way or another, he was going to get the help he needed. After all, this couldn't be his life forever. The situation had to end one way or another.

He walked along the empty street towards the school. As he got closer, he could see that the blue gates at the front were locked. He didn't know why, so he continued to walk towards them. Once he'd got there, he looked all around. The gates were definitely locked. He might've arrived too early, but it felt strange that there was nobody around.

He looked at the houses opposite the school. He couldn't see anybody. Outside the school at that time on a Monday morning would normally be chaos. There would be kids and parents rushing around and cars would be either fighting for a parking space, or just stopping in the middle of the road so the kids could jump out. But today, nothing.

As he waited in front of the school, weighing up his options, he noticed two boys walking towards him. He couldn't remember ever talking to them, but he recognised them. They were two or three years older than him and had left primary school and gone on to secondary.

As they walked past, the tallest one said, 'Bank Holiday, stupid.'

'What?' Oliver said.

147

'I said, it's the May Day Bank Holiday. The school is shut.'

Oliver tried his best to hide his disappointment. He thought quickly to try to save face. 'Oh, I know,' he said. 'I'm just meeting a friend.'

'Oh yeah?' the second boy said. 'Admit it, you've got your days wrong.'

'No, look,' he said, opening his jacket to prove he wasn't in uniform.

By this point the two boys had already lost interest and walked past him, moving on to the next subject in their conversation.

Oliver felt foolish, but he also felt deflated. He didn't know what to do. Should he knock on a random door and ask for help? If he did, how would he know he'd chosen a house with a nice, honest person living there who would help him. His mum always told him not to talk to strangers. Maybe she was right.

His thoughts then went to the electric card. If his mum had managed to get back to the house to post it, then surely, she could turn up again at some point. She might even be there now.

Oliver clicked on an important piece of information. Information that needed writing on the whiteboard once he got home. If his mum had managed to pay for electricity on the card, then that meant she'd done the shopping. She'd been into the supermarket and she'd left. If this was the case, then where was all the food she'd bought? Where was his favourite cereal? Where was the chocolate he'd asked for, and all the other things they were running low on?

She must've left the supermarket before she went missing. Maybe her car didn't start. And for some reason or other, she didn't manage the journey home with the shopping bags.

He was exhausted, and he was starting to feel a little ill. He'd felt weak ever since waking up in the forest, but now he was starting to feel sick. Maybe it was through the lack of sleep, or maybe because of the infection in his fingers. He didn't know. But he did know that he had to find the energy to walk home and endure yet another day on his own.

The fact that his mum must've finished her shopping made him feel as though he was getting ever closer to solving the mystery. But he didn't see any way of it having a happy ending.

His shoulders dropped as he started on the long walk back home.

He was hot, tired and scared. But if it was the May Day Bank Holiday, then schools would be open the following day. So, all he had to do was keep himself alive for another twenty-four hours, and then he could get the help he needed, from the people he trusted.

Just one more day.

26

The pillow felt good as his face landed into it. It took all his efforts to turn his head just a little to the right so he could breathe. He'd felt more and more queasy as he walked home. Although it was only a mile or so, it felt a lot longer as he staggered back and forth throughout his journey. He was so glad to be on his bed. The cover was inside the bunker, but there was still a pillow on his bed. It was uncomfortably flat, but he didn't care. He was still really worried about the whole situation, and he still needed to write on the whiteboard that his mum must've finished her shopping before her disappearance. But that had to wait. What he needed was sleep. He didn't know how much sleep he'd had in the forest the previous night, but he couldn't imagine it would be more than three hours or so.

His brain grew tired of thinking and he drifted off into a very deep sleep.

The supermarket was crowded with more people than he'd ever seen in any of his previous trips there with his mum. Oliver just stood there, looking around at everyone. Although the place was crowded, there was a perfect circle of space all around him that none of the shoppers walked into. They all dashed by at top speed, as if they were buying emergency stocks before a war started, or maybe even a storm that was predicted to knock out the power and destroy buildings.

Oliver was scared, but he also found watching everyone rush by hypnotic.

He then noticed a figure in the distance. The figure stood out because although everyone else was dashing around and panic buying, this figure seemed to move in slow motion.

It was Mrs Wheaton.

As she strolled around the supermarket, quite a distance away from him, she turned her head and looked straight at Oliver. This made his heart bounce a little.

He waved, but she gave a little smile and shook her head before walking out of view and into the crowd of people.

As Oliver stood in the circle, people still rushing past, he saw his mum and dad suddenly appear. They were holding hands and – like Mrs Wheaton – they were walking slowly. They too turned to look at Oliver, but no sooner had they looked straight at him, they turned away and carried on their journey into the crowded supermarket.

Oliver wanted to run after them, but just as he was about to leave the safety of the circle, he saw two men standing completely still, looking straight at him. One was the BMW man, and the other was Mr Hunter. They both had angry expressions on their faces, and although that scared Oliver, he was even more scared as he noticed Kaiser sat at Mr Hunter's feet.

151

Seconds felt like hours as the two men stared at him, almost snarling. Oliver didn't know what to do.

The BMW man turned to Mr Hunter and said something, but Oliver couldn't read his lips or hear him over the noise of the crowded supermarket.

Mr Hunter nodded, still staring at Oliver. Whatever BMW man had just said, Mr Hunter agreed with it.

The two men moved in slow motion, as everyone else rushed around at top speed.

Mr Hunter bent down and tapped Kaiser on the shoulder, causing the dog to stand. Mr Hunter then pointed towards Oliver and shouted something to Kaiser. It must have been a command, because Kaiser shot forward, towards Oliver, still in slow motion, but definitely running. All four paws left the ground before the German Shepherd planted hard on the solid floor of the supermarket. The motion repeated as the dog grew closer and closer.

Oliver felt glued to the spot in the centre of the circle that everyone else was still walking around. People dashed in front of Kaiser, some pushing trolleys, some holding baskets, but none of them seemed to notice the vicious dog running, mouth open to reveal white fangs and pink gums, tongue flailing from the right side of his mouth, his eyes – one black and one white – fixed firmly on Oliver.

Suddenly, Kaiser seemed to go from running in slow motion to top speed and he jumped, leaving the ground, leaping towards Oliver's face.

Oliver knew there was nothing he could do...

He screamed as he quickly sat up on his bed. He frantically looked around wondering where Kaiser had landed, then realised he was in his bedroom. In his confused state, he checked himself over, looking for any signs of teeth marks, or scratches, but of course there were none. Although relieved, he thought it would take him a while to forget such a vivid dream.

After sitting there for a moment, trying to recover from his ordeal, he climbed off the bed to look in the mirror and was shocked to see how sweaty and red-faced he was. His clothes were stuck to him and his hair was a mess. He also felt light-headed and thirsty, but too sick to get himself a drink. So he lay back on the bed and stared at the ceiling. Moments later, he'd fallen asleep once more.

27

A deafening bang woke Oliver.

He sat up, looked around his bedroom and wondered if he was dreaming again, but he didn't think so. The noise still echoed in his ears. The bedroom seemed darker than it was earlier. When he woke up from the dream where he was in the supermarket – the dream he was sure he'd remember for the rest of his life – the sun was shining through the window. But now, it was dark. Not night-time dark, but winter dark.

He walked over to the window and looked out to the empty space where his mum's car would normally be. A sudden flash of light lit up the fields and the forest. A thunderstorm was on its way.

Another boom filled the air, shaking the bedroom window. It made him jump a little, but he was relieved that it was just a thunderstorm and nothing more horrifying. Especially after the dream he'd just had.

He went to get himself a glass of cordial from the kitchen, and a chocolate bar; the last one. There were still a few tins of food in the cupboard, but the excitement of looking after himself had worn off. The cuts on his fingers still hurt, his stomach ached for a decent meal, and his energy levels were lower than ever. He had to ask Mrs Wheaton to help him tomorrow at school. He knew he couldn't carry on like this.

The view through his bedroom window was now a scene of torrential rain and flashes of lightning, to a soundtrack of thunderclaps. He watched while eating the chocolate as he stared into the fields.

A sudden jolt of inspiration came to him as he decided he'd try to do another drawing.

He loved dark pictures and scenery, and the view over the farmer's fields during a thunderstorm would make a great picture.

He picked up a charcoal pencil from the desk. His head hurt as the noisy pencil sharpener did its job, but it only took a second to sharpen it to the fine point it always did. He then pulled out a new piece of paper. Even though he was scared, even though he felt ill and tired, he still felt the small skip of excitement in his belly as he looked at the blank sheet, trying to envisage what it was going to turn into.

His fingers were hurting, and they were hurting enough to make him think maybe he couldn't draw. But he tried to ignore the pain and decided to give it a try. He put charcoal to paper, and began to draw.

Oliver took his time with the drawing. Not just because of his wounds, but also because this picture was going to be what he referred to as a *three-day picture*. Most pictures were done within a day, or even within an hour, but when a picture had more meaning than usual, he would sometimes take much longer with it. *The Lost Boy* could've been a *three-day picture*. But as it was just a boy sitting under a tree, it didn't take too long. But there was definitely meaning behind it. That picture was one that came from the heart; a picture that was more of a story than just a drawing.

The picture he was working on now was a much more complicated scene. There were fields, the farmhouse, the outbuildings and vehicles. And he knew at some point he'd draw Kaiser in the distance somewhere. He'd even draw the bedroom window from which he was looking through as a frame to the scene. This picture, almost certainly a three-day picture, would hold a lot of meaning for him. They all did in some way or other. But certain pictures meant more to him than most.

He realised there was a story to be told in the drawing of him being alone, looking at the view, but also the feeling of being trapped. And nothing signified that more than a thunderstorm.

He hadn't figured out how to draw the storm and lightning yet; maybe he would finish the picture first and then use an eraser to create the flash of forked lightning across the page. But he wasn't sure. What he was sure about, thanks to the pain in his fingers, was that after only half an hour of drawing his creation, he'd finished for the day.

He decided the pain was too much, left the picture and went into the kitchen.

As he got there, before he could decide on what to find to eat, he heard a noise. And whatever it was, it wasn't thunder.

28

Oliver heard shouting. It was in the distance, but it grew louder as whoever it was came closer. The noise of the rain drowned out the words, but it sounded like a woman's voice.

He froze to the spot, just like he had in the dream at the supermarket. He wondered if in his dazed state when he came home from his trip to the school, whether he'd locked the door or not. The key was in the back of the door, so he presumed he must have. He certainly hoped so. He didn't want whoever it was to just walk in.

The indecipherable shouts continued. Oliver thought he heard his name, but he wasn't sure. He stood closer to the door and listened.

'*Oliver,*' the voice screamed. It was definitely female.

Oliver stood on his tiptoes and tried to see through the waterfall of rain cascading down the kitchen window. He saw a figure run past, heading towards the door. His heart felt as though it was trying to escape from his chest.

'*Oliver!*'

This time not only was he sure he'd heard his name, but he also recognised the voice.

'*Mum,*' he shouted, as he jumped towards the door and unlocked it.

No sooner had he managed to turn the key, the door burst open, almost sending him flying as his mum came rushing into the room. She turned and slammed the door shut, locking it rapidly with shaking hands, turning the key and sliding the bolt across.

His mum was soaking wet, her clothes dirty and torn and her face was covered in cuts and bruises.

She dragged him away from the kitchen door and crouched down before throwing her arms around him and holding him so tight that he couldn't breathe, but he didn't care. His mum was home. He didn't know where she'd been. He didn't know what had happened to her, but at that moment, he didn't care. He was over the moon to have her back where she belonged.

He couldn't stop smiling as the tears rolled down his face. Now, surely everything would be OK. Everything could get back to normal. He had a lot to tell her about; the bunker, the fox, the cuts on his fingers. But all he really wanted to do at that moment was hug her.

But his relief was short-lived as his mum released the hug and held him by the shoulders. Suddenly he felt scared again as he saw the look of fear on her face.

'Now, Oliver, you have to listen to me...'

As Oliver stood there in the kitchen, looking into his mum's eyes, her eyes that he'd never seen so wide, there was a sudden, deafeningly loud bang, a noise louder than any of the thunderclaps he'd heard so far.

The kitchen door flew open. But not in the same way it had minutes earlier when his mum came in. This time, it burst open, broken in half as bits of glass flew all over the kitchen floor.

He buried his face into his mum's shoulder as she threw her arms around him once more, gripping him tight, even more than she just had.

As he turned to look, he saw a man standing in the doorway with a metal pole in his hand. Not as long as the piece of wood the ghostly figure from his drawing was carrying, but long enough to do some damage. He was holding it in front of him almost like a sword. But then Oliver focused on the man holding the pole. The man who stood in the doorway of the bungalow; the man who seemed out of breath as his chest expanded and deflated with every lungful of air; the man who looked as though he was in a very bad mood. And above everything else, the man Oliver recognised.

Louise

1

Louise Derwent was applying her makeup at the dressing table mirror in her bedroom. She was wearing her bright red skirt and a white blouse. Although she was only going to the supermarket, she still liked to look her best. Not to attract any attention, just to help her to feel as good on the inside as she tried to look on the outside. She knew Oliver didn't like it when somebody wolf-whistled at her, or when men stared, and Louise didn't really like it either. She wasn't particularly flattered by moronic behaviour from the kind of man that did that sort of thing, but she did like knowing that although she was now the wrong side of forty, she still had her looks.

She'd recently considered going back into modelling. She'd made quite a healthy income in the past before giving it up to start a family. But she wasn't sure if she'd be able to claw her way back into the industry after being out of it for so long. Doing topless modelling again was definitely out of the question. Mainly because she now had Oliver. Although everything she did was always tasteful and never seedy, she couldn't bear the thought of Oliver's friends teasing him about it at school. She had considered contacting her old agent to see if she could get her any work. But she was worried that she'd only find her the kind of work she'd done before. She never regretted any of the photos, and she was lucky enough to always work with photographers with a higher-class reputation. But now she was forty-two, she thought she might be considered too old to be taken seriously again. If she did go back into modelling, she would only want fashion shoots or advertising projects. She had no intention of going down the road of glamour or erotic; even though she knew that was where the money was.

After losing Michael, she didn't really feel like smiling, certainly not in the way she used to when taking part in photo shoots. But as the last year or so went by, she slowly learned to smile again; on the outside at least. She hoped that one day soon, she'd be able to feel better on the inside too.

Michael was the love of her life, there was no doubt about that. He was handsome, intelligent, energetic and funny. But after they'd been together a few years, the darker side of Michael started to emerge. It became obvious that the reason he was so funny, and tried so hard to make Louise happy, and Oliver once he was born, was because he was trying very hard to hide the fact that he suffered badly with depression.

Michael's demeanour seemed to change when Oliver was four or five years old. Louise noticed that Michael would regularly drift away into deep thought. It could be when she was talking, or when he was playing with Oliver, or even when he was watching television. He would just stare into space. And whenever Louise would ask him what was wrong, he would just say he was tired or daydreaming.

It was during one of these episodes that Louise saw a tear roll down his face. She'd asked him if he was OK, but he just wiped the tear away and then acted like nothing had happened. After a week or so of her constantly asking him if he was OK, he finally opened up to her about how he really felt. He told her he'd been feeling depressed for a long time and for most of his life he'd struggled with bouts of feeling miserable and deflated, but he'd hidden how he felt from everyone; his friends, work colleagues, his parents, and Louise. He told her he'd tried extra hard to be funny and make people laugh, thinking that if he could make others smile, then in turn, that would make him happy. He admitted to Louise that it did, for a while. He explained to her once that he felt like an actor. A very good actor, Louise thought. He was always the life and soul of the party, or of any gathering for that matter. If Michael was in the room, no matter how big the room was, or how many people there were, you always knew he was there. Not in a boisterous or annoying way, he was just a big personality, and everybody loved him.

Louise tried to convince him to get help, but he refused. He said he could deal with it himself. She tried to comfort him as much as she could, but when he was in one of his quiet moods, she found it best just to leave him alone. Occasionally she would send Oliver to him, usually when

Michael was lying on the bed. She once popped her head around the door and saw Oliver cuddled up to him, fast asleep. Michael had his arm around him as he stared at the ceiling with tears running down his face. That was the moment Louise felt the most helpless.

Michael refused to go to the doctor, or to accept help from a mental health charity. Louise had contacted them without telling Michael and the agent on the other end of the phone convinced her to give him Michael's mobile number. The man had a soothing voice and he was obviously good at what he did, but when he rang Michael, Michael just thanked him for his time and ended the call. Louise thought Michael would be annoyed at what she'd done, but he never even mentioned it. He just carried on with his day as if nothing had happened.

Michael spoke to Louise about how he felt a few times. Usually when he'd had a couple of drinks. He didn't drink a lot, but he would usually have one or two cans of lager a night. It was during one of the rare nights when he'd had four or five cans – most likely at a weekend – when he'd opened up to her, and he even cried. But the next day he'd would act like nothing happened.

Louise spoke to her doctor, and even made appointments for Michael, but he never turned up. As time went by, she realised that she couldn't help somebody who wasn't prepared to help themselves.

Although Louise knew Michael was suffering with depression, very severe depression, she didn't think he'd ever do what he did. He told her he'd never go that far, and that he would never leave her, or Oliver. But eventually, after years of suffering, the illness got the better of him.

2

Louise went into Oliver's room. He was drawing as usual. He would spend hours drawing pictures, and they were very good, but they seemed to have taken a dark twist since Michael had died. He would draw dead bodies, creepy ghosts and graveyards. There had been many a time she'd leaned over his shoulder and seen a drawing that made her stop in her tracks. Some of them were so dark that she started to think there could be something wrong with him. Yes, he was an introvert, and yes, he preferred his own company to being with others, but the dark and creepy drawings would make any parent wonder if there was something going on in his brain that he needed help with. She also hoped to God that Oliver hadn't inherited his dad's illness. She'd hate to lose him like she had Michael. This was why she hadn't told Oliver his dad had taken his own life. She hadn't even told him his dad had died. She just couldn't bring herself to do so. She regretted her choice, not only because she was worried it would come out at school one day – parents at the school gates had a way of gossiping without checking behind them to see who's listening – but also because Oliver constantly talked about him; more often than not, asking when he was coming home. Louise knew she'd made a mistake, but she was finding the mistake a hard one to rectify. At some point she would have to tell Oliver that his dad had died, but she knew she wouldn't tell him how he'd died until Oliver was much older. If she told him his dad had died through an illness, she'd technically be telling the truth. Depression was an illness, and Michael had fought it his whole life until one day, it got the better of him. And that was the truth.

'OK, sweetheart, I'm off to the supermarket. Are you sure you don't want to come?' she said, resting her hand on his shoulder.

'I'll stay,' he said, still drawing.

Louise kissed him on the top of the head as she looked at the picture. 'That's nice, Ollie. You like the charcoal pencils then?'

He nodded, but carried on drawing.

'You're not going to...'

Oliver interrupted by sticking the charcoal pencil into the noisy pencil sharpener that was fastened to his desk. Louise hated it. Michael had brought it home from work when they were having an office refit, and fixed it to Oliver's desk. Although it worked very well, it made a ridiculously loud grinding noise.

Louise started her sentence again. 'You're not going to draw a dead body under the tractor, are you?'

Oliver shook his head before pointing to the tractor in the distance.

Louise looked over to Hunter's Farm and saw the tractor in the field that looked remarkably like the one in Oliver's picture. 'Excellent. It's very good.'

'Thanks.'

'You're getting better and better. One day you'll be a famous artist.'

Louise did believe that was possible. Especially if he carried on improving at the rate he had been over the last year or two. And nobody could fault his enthusiasm and effort.

'See, if you had a games console, that would distract you and you wouldn't be as good.'

Louise felt bad for not being able to afford a games console. Oliver had asked her for one, and she'd started to put money aside, hoping to have enough come Christmas time. But the fact that Michael died in the way he did, left her with nothing. Insurance companies don't always pay out for suicides, and Michael's certainly didn't, so Louise had to try to make ends meet herself. But it wasn't easy, especially as she needed a job that suited Oliver's school hours. She didn't mind him being on his own for an hour or so, but not for any longer. He was very sensible, and she knew he'd be OK. But she also knew he worried.

Louise picked up the unopened pack of coloured pencils from the corner of his desk. She'd bought them at the same time as the charcoal pencils, even though she'd doubted he'd ever use them. And she couldn't really afford to use what little money she had spent on them. 'I see these were a waste of money.'

Oliver smiled and carried on with his drawing.

'Right, I'm going. Is there anything else you want?' she said as she headed over to the door.

'Chocolate,' Oliver replied.

167

'I know that,' she answered, smiling. She then turned back to him. 'You be good.'

'OK.'

'I'll be back in twenty minutes,' she said as she left the room.

'Mum!' Oliver shouted.

She put her head back around the door.

'I heard voices this morning.'

This made her a little uncomfortable. 'Voices?'

'Yes. It was really early. The sun was up, but I think it was about six. It sounded like a man talking.'

'Oh... err... that was just the television. I fell asleep on the sofa last night so the TV was still on when I woke up.'

'OK,' Oliver said.

'Twenty minutes, OK?'

Louise felt guilty for lying to him. But it was too soon to tell him about Vanni. She wanted to get to know him a little more before allowing them to meet; even though she did feel as though she was falling for him.

Vanni was born in England, but had Italian parents. He was also a year younger than she was, but that didn't bother her. He was very handsome, with short dark hair and a thin, neatly trimmed beard. She always used to say she hated facial hair, but her opinion was beginning to change. Probably because of how neat he kept it.

Louise had met Vanni when she was shopping the previous Saturday. Being approached by men in the supermarket was something that happened now and then. But Vanni was clever. He'd picked up a pack of

168

chicken breasts and asked her what to do with them. She'd spent a couple of minutes explaining how to prepare, season and cook them, and even threw in a couple of serving suggestions. When she'd finished, he told her she was right. Louise asked what he meant by that, and it was at that point he admitted he was a chef and owned his own restaurant. She could've been annoyed, but she saw the funny side. And Vanni had a mischievous look in his eye – she couldn't help but be won over by his charms.

She felt guilty for being interested in another man. But Michael hadn't just died. He'd left her. He'd left her on her own with their son and no money. She couldn't stay faithful to him for the rest of her life. She had to move on sooner or later.

Vanni had asked her to join him in the supermarket cafe. They had sat and chatted for an hour. This was something she'd never done before. Any boyfriends she'd ever had, including Michael, she'd met either through work or friends. This was the first time she'd given in to someone trying to get to know her in a supermarket. But there was something warm about Vanni. She felt completely safe in his company. He wasn't pushy, he was relaxed and friendly. And he managed to keep his eyes on her face rather than the curves she was blessed with. It was a breath of fresh air to talk to a man whose eyes didn't keep falling south of where they should be. Louise was happy with her hourglass figure. And it had helped to pay the mortgage off on the bungalow, but she didn't always enjoy the attention it brought her. She was sick of feeling like an object. Most men struggled to keep their eyes on her face and sporadically shot them elsewhere when they thought she wasn't looking.

But Vanni was different. When he looked at her, his eyes danced all over her face as they spoke to each other. And when he looked into her eyes, he seemed to look so deeply, almost as though he was lost. He was different to all the others.

Louise counted the cup of coffee in the supermarket cafe as their first date. The second was a meal in his restaurant the following Tuesday night. Vanni had suggested this because it was one of the restaurant's quieter evenings.

Her first impressions of him being a nice person were confirmed when she saw the way his staff behaved around him. They were all smiling, helpful and very friendly as they served their boss and his date. He was obviously a good person to work for.

Even though she had only stayed for an hour, not wanting to leave Oliver on his own for too long, even though he was most likely asleep, it was still a magical evening.

Their third date had been the previous night. Oliver *had* heard voices that morning because Vanni came to the bungalow after he'd finished at the restaurant on Friday night. Louise offered to make him a late supper, and afterwards, they just sat on the sofa telling each other their life stories. She told him everything. All about her modelling career, Oliver and of course, Michael and how he'd died.

Vanni had had his fair share of tragedy too. His wife, who was also his childhood sweetheart, had passed away after a short battle with cancer. That was four years earlier, and he'd stayed single ever since.

They talked for hours. The clock on the living room wall said three-twenty when Vanni excused himself to go to the bathroom.

Louise closed her eyes just for a second, or so she'd thought, only to wake up at six-thirty with Vanni asleep at the other end of the sofa.

She woke him and asked him to leave. Although she could feel herself falling for him, and she felt a connection she'd not felt in a long time, it was still too early for Oliver to find out that his mum had another man in her life. She would have to speak to Oliver first before allowing the two of them to meet.

The only thing Louise had doubts about when it came to Vanni was the fact that he was so successful. He had his own restaurant, he drove a BMW, and he owned a house on West Chorley Road, which meant it would be a very nice house. Not quite as big as the houses on *Millionaire's Row* as the locals referred to it as, but they were still nice houses. She didn't want him, or anyone else, to think she was after him for his money. Louise had struggled financially ever since Michael had died. She had been successful in her modelling career, and that, along with Michael's wage meant they had been able to pay the mortgage off after only seven years. But the money she'd earned had all gone.

Michael had asked Louise to give up modelling to start a family. He wasn't an overly jealous man, but he didn't like men staring at her in public. In fact, he'd confronted men a few times when he'd seen them leering. He had certainly been protective of her. He said to her once, *I don't mind people looking. After all, you're beautiful. But they need to do it in a respectful way.* When he did ask her to give up modelling, it wasn't down to jealousy. It was for the same reason as Louise; neither of them wanted Oliver to be the subject of any jokes about his mum posing in her underwear, or less.

Once the mortgage was paid off, they lived comfortably on the wage Michael brought home from his job as a graphic designer for an advertising company. He never climbed the ladder within the company, mainly because he never truly enjoyed what he did for a living. His dream was to become an artist. But when he failed to become famous for the landscapes he painted, it steered him in the direction of graphic design. Although he was good at it, Louise knew it was always in the back of his mind that he was only doing that job because very few people bought his paintings.

Since Michael died, Louise hadn't worked. She'd recently applied for a job in the supermarket, and she'd asked in all the local shops about part-time work, but so far, nothing. It didn't help that she couldn't afford to pay for Wi-Fi at home. Most jobs insisted on filling in applications online, so she'd spent a long time standing outside the supermarket so she could apply for jobs while using their hotspot, with her second-hand smartphone that had a crack through the top corner.

At the time of Michael's death, the bank balance had already been depleting. His bonuses had stopped a long time before he'd died. Although the mortgage was paid off, for which she was relieved, there were still other bills to pay – gas, electric, her mobile phone, council tax, the car, and the ground rent to Hunter's Farm. There were also things like school uniforms and dinners, and all the class trips she refused to let Oliver miss out on, even though he didn't seem overly bothered about going on them. She was determined to make sure he didn't miss out on anything.

Times were hard in the Derwent household. But as much as she'd been struggling to make ends meet, she didn't want to get help from a man. As much as she liked Vanni, she really didn't want him to know how bad her finances were. All she needed was a job working twenty-four hours a week and she would be OK. But so far, she hadn't been able to find one. And she really didn't want Vanni or anyone else for that matter to think she was interested in him for his money. If anything, she was interested in him in spite of his money.

3

Louise always used the smaller trolleys in the supermarket. It was easy to get carried away while wandering up and down every aisle and buying much more than she needed. She also made a point of eating a decent breakfast before going shopping. If she shopped while hungry, everything looked much more appetising, and she would spend more money than she'd intended. Making sure her stomach was full, stopped her from doing that.

Her mobile rang. She took it from her handbag and her heart skipped a little as she looked at the screen. It was Vanni. But she decided not to answer it. She didn't want to appear too eager, and she thought it would be nicer to phone him from home later, maybe while sitting in the garden enjoying the sunshine.

She was sure she liked him, and she could really see their relationship going somewhere, but she didn't want to rush things. After all, he'd only left her house four or five hours ago.

After half an hour of filling the trolley with all the items from the list – all the cheapest brands of course – she decided to head to the stationery section to see if there was anything she could buy as a treat for Oliver.

As she turned the corner, she saw a man she recognised. And he saw her.

Hemal Kharti was in his early twenties. He still lived at home with his mum and dad, two brothers and two sisters.

Hemal was tall and skinny, and always dressed very smartly, although the clothes didn't hang on him well. Today he was dressed in black pants, shoes and a white patterned shirt, almost as though he was dressed for a night out rather than a trip to the supermarket. But as usual, his shirt wasn't tucked in properly, and his belt was too high, revealing his colourful socks. He was always polite and friendly to everyone he came across. But whenever he saw Louise, he would stare at her open-mouthed. If he was with his mum or dad, they would tell him to stop and he would. But if there was nobody around, he would just continue to stare, making Louise uncomfortable.

The phone calls went on for weeks. She hadn't realised her number was available to anyone on the online directory. Although she could remove her number, by then it was too late. He wouldn't say anything. Louise would just hear him breathing down the phone. She would usually hang up, but occasionally she would lose her temper and shout at him. As time went by, it happened more and more until eventually, she removed the landline. The phone calls were always from payphones, which made it harder for the police to prove who it was as – even though there were only three payphones in the town – they didn't have any cameras on them, unlike the payphones in supermarkets or shopping centres that would've made it easy to find footage of the caller.

One day, when Louise was raking up leaves in the garden, she saw Hemal hanging around the woods behind her house.

She phoned the police as soon as she saw him, and they came out straight away, and although they didn't arrest him, they took him home and spoke to him and his parents about what had happened, and about the phone calls.

Things went quiet after that.

Hemal's family hadn't spoken to Louise since the incident. She presumed it was because the news of what happened went around the town like wildfire. Louise never told anyone, but Len Hunter saw the police take Hemal away, and he enjoyed telling anyone who would listen about how the perverted young man had been caught spying on her. And of course, he embellished the story, telling everyone Hemal was under arrest, when the truth was, the police just gave him a verbal warning.

Louise wasn't annoyed with Hemal's family, and she would've kept it to herself. But because of Len, everybody in Whitford knew. It was a horrible time in her life. She really didn't need somebody stalking her, especially just after Michael had died. Living in a house that felt as though it was in the middle of nowhere made Louise feel a little isolated, especially in winter when the dark nights closed in. She was angry and upset with Hemal and had no interest in ever talking to him again.

After he was taken home by the police, that was the end of it. But occasionally Louise would pass him on the street, or, like now, in the supermarket.

His parents must've got through to him because his gaze shot straight to the floor and he awkwardly walked away from her at a fast pace.

Louise was still scared, but she was glad he didn't stare at her like he used to. She almost felt sorry for him in a way. She presumed he had learning difficulties of some kind. He still lived at home, and she didn't think he'd ever had a job, whereas all his siblings worked. But either way, whatever his problems, he'd still scared her with the phone calls, and she was terrified when she'd spotted him hiding in the woods. It was hard to have sympathy for him when it had gone on for so long.

After choosing a pack of white A4 card for Oliver, Louise made her way to the checkout. Once she'd paid, she went to the cigarette counter to put her last ten pounds onto the electricity card. After that, she went outside to load the car.

Once all the shopping was in the boot, she took the trolley back – not forgetting to retrieve her pound coin – and when she got back to the car, she sat in the driver's seat and put her key into the ignition. She waited until an old couple walked past in front of the bonnet. Her car made such a racket when it started it would've scared them to death. Once they'd passed by, Louise turned the key. Instead of the noisy clatter of the engine, there was a ticking sound and nothing more.

177

Her heart sank as she realised the car was dead. She presumed the battery must've died, but she wasn't sure. Although she knew a mechanic – one who was kind enough to let her pay weekly the last time the car had something wrong with it – it was Saturday, so she wouldn't be able to contact him until Tuesday with it being bank holiday weekend.

The car would have to stay put.

She was very tired from her late night with Vanni, and although she'd eaten breakfast before she'd set off to the supermarket, she was still lacking in energy. She had a long walk ahead of her, a walk she was dreading with four carrier bags full of food.

She knew Oliver would be OK. He was used to her being out for longer than this. And he would only be drawing anyway, and maybe taking the odd chocolate bar from the cupboard. She always told Oliver that she'd be twenty minutes. She knew she'd be longer and Oliver knew she'd be longer. But in the past when she'd said she'd be an hour, it seemed to scare him, almost as though he panicked a little at being on his own for so long. Whenever she told him twenty minutes, he wouldn't even look up from his drawing.

After nipping back inside the supermarket to tell the lady at Customer Services that her car would have to stay there until Tuesday, Louise went back to the car to get the carrier bags. She considered asking someone for a lift. She even thought about ringing Vanni back and asking him if he was free, but she didn't want to put on him just yet.

After just three dates, they weren't actually a couple as of yet, so it didn't feel right to ask him for help.

The bungalow was only a mile or so from the supermarket, so she decided to walk. It was warm and sunny, but not so hot that she couldn't manage a bit of exercise.

After taking the bags out of the car, and locking it, she set off over the carpark, two bags in each hand.

By the time she'd reached the edge of the carpark near the roundabout, she had to put the bags down and have a rest. Although they weren't overly heavy, they still dug into her fingers a little.

After she'd got her breath back, she negotiated all the crossings and made her way along the grass verge at the side of the carriageway, wishing she'd worn her flat shoes and not her heels.

Several cars beeped at her, all men of course. This annoyed her. Had any woman ever been flattered by a man beeping his horn as he leered through the window on the way past? It certainly didn't impress Louise.

The carriageway that felt very short when she drove along it now felt like miles as she walked along the grass, carrier bags still digging into her fingers.

After she'd managed around a hundred yards, a car pulled up in front of her, two wheels on the grass verge. It was an old, dark blue Fiesta.

Louise stopped for a second then put her head down and carried on walking. As she reached the car, the passenger window rolled down. 'Do you need a lift, love?'

Louise briefly looked up to see two young men in the front seats wearing baseball caps, and hoodies. They were both skinny and pale. Her immediate reaction was that they were nothing but a pair of scumbags. This was confirmed when the smell of cannabis hit her. She had no intentions of getting into a car with strangers, but when she realised that they were driving under the influence of drugs – even a drug that some people argue should be legalised – she decided that she wouldn't even bother to use manners with them.

'No,' she said, sternly, and continued walking.

They both laughed. The driver then started to move the car forwards along the verge so they were driving alongside her as she walked.

'Come on,' the driver said. 'We won't charge you.'

Then the passenger said, 'Yeah. I'm sure we can think of some other way of you paying us.'

Louise felt sick.

She then noticed another car pull up on the verge, twenty yards or so in front of the fiesta. A lady got out of the driver's side. She had dark hair tied back in a bun, and she was wearing a very colourful sari. It was Hemal's mother.

As Louise watched her, the passenger in the Fiesta grabbed her right wrist. His hand felt hot and sweaty as she pulled her arm away quickly, almost dropping the bags, and shouting, 'Get off!' at the top of her voice.

Mrs Kharti marched to the car and put both hands on the door of the passenger side. She bent down and looked

180

through the open window with her head almost reaching inside the car.

'Go! Now!' she shouted sternly in her strong Indian accent.

That was all she had to do. The boys laughed and threw some inaudible abuse her way as the window closed and they pulled out into moving traffic, causing a car to swerve and beep at them.

Louise felt relieved, but now she felt uncomfortable as she stood in front of her stalker's mum. As she looked up ahead at Mrs Kharti's car, she could see the shape of someone in the passenger seat and presumed it was Hemal.

She didn't quite know what to say to Mrs Kharti, so she started by thanking her. 'That was very kind of you. Thank you,' she said, still struggling for breath from walking so far with the grocery bags.

'Why didn't you go in your car, or take a taxi home?'

'I went in my car. It's broken down in the supermarket car park. And I can't afford to waste money on taxis.'

'Well, it's a long way on foot to your house, Mrs Derwent.'

'I'll be fine. Thanks for getting rid of those... idiots.'

'It's no problem. You just have to be stern. If their mothers had been stern with them, they wouldn't behave this way.'

'True,' she said, getting a better grip on the bags. 'Anyway, thanks again.'

'I will give you a lift.'

Louise suddenly felt even more uncomfortable. She would rather walk, even though there was still a long way to go.

'No, I couldn't. I don't want to put you out.'

Mrs Kharti stood up straight and folded her arms, looking Louise in the eye. 'Is that it, or do you not trust my family?'

Louise's shoulders dropped. 'Mrs Kharti, what happened in the past is exactly that; it's in the past.'

'Then why can't I give you a lift to your home?'

Louise didn't know what to say. But she certainly didn't want to get into a car with her stalker. Even if he was in the front seat and she was in the back. It just wouldn't feel right.

'Look, Mrs Kharti, I'm very grateful for you stopping and helping me, but I will walk from here. Thanks again.'

Louise walked past Mrs Kharti and the car where Hemal *was* sat in the passenger seat.

Mrs Kharti shouted over the noise of the traffic, 'He didn't do it, you know?'

Louise stopped in her tracks. Still holding the carrier bags, she turned to look at Mrs Kharti once more.

The lady – whose confidence and stern demeanour scared Louise a little – stepped towards her with her arms folded. She then spoke quietly, presumably so Hemal couldn't hear. 'My son is innocent.'

Louise didn't answer.

'He is... feeble-minded, Mrs Derwent. He can't help but stare at a beautiful woman like yourself. But he is not malicious in any way. He would not make phone calls. He doesn't like the telephone. He won't even answer our phone at home. He wouldn't ring you or anyone else.'

Louise thought for a moment.

'Then why was he in the woods near my house?'

'He wanders off sometimes. He loves wildlife. You should see his bedroom. It's full of books about animals and wildlife. When he goes missing, he is always found in a forest or woodland somewhere. He wasn't stalking you; I promise you that.'

Louise didn't know what to say. Maybe Mrs Kharti was right. But Hemal still had a creepy, leering look on his face when she saw him in the woods. He wasn't prosecuted for what he'd done, but Louise presumed his mum wanted everyone to think he wouldn't do such a thing. Any mother would defend their son, so Louise didn't think less of Mrs Kharti for doing so. But she still had no intentions of ever getting into a car with them.

'Well... like I say. It's all in the past.'

With that, Louise turned and walked away.

4

Louise's fingers were hurting, she was dripping with sweat, and by the time she'd reached the gravel road that led to her house, she felt as though she'd never wear heels ever again.

As she made her way along the lane, her mobile rang once more.

She put the bags down on the ground and rummaged through her handbag. It stopped ringing by the time she'd found it, but when she checked who it was, she couldn't help but smile. Even though she was in a bad mood from her long and uncomfortable walk, the fact that Vanni had tried ringing her gave her butterflies in her stomach.

She couldn't wait to unpack the shopping so she could phone him back. He must like her to have phoned twice already, so soon after leaving her that morning.

She put her phone back in her bag and carried on with her journey, smiling as she went.

'Mrs Derwent,' a voice said, almost causing her to drop her bags.

It was Len Hunter from the farm. He stepped out from the corner of the hedges at the bottom of his drive, Kaiser a few yards behind him.

'Sorry,' he said. 'I didn't mean to scare you.'

'It's OK,' she said, and carried on walking, but a little faster than before.

Louise couldn't stand Len Hunter. He was in his mid-thirties, and he'd inherited the farm from his dad who'd died four years earlier. Louise had got on well with his dad, Ronald. He was a gentleman. He was always polite and he always made Louise feel comfortable whenever she spoke to him. But dementia took hold of him fast, and Louise never actually saw him for the last year or so of his life. Since he'd died, Len seemed to become even more creepy. It was almost as though his dad kept him in line, but now, he was free to do as he pleased. Which more often than not, was staring at Louise whenever she passed his farm, or was doing something outside her house. Whenever they spoke, he would stand there, looking her up and down, and not even attempting to be discreet about it.

Len always wore scruffy blue overalls and dirty boots. He had messy, greasy hair, a thin, pale face and horrible eyes that seemed to be too close together. Louise knew he couldn't help that, but if he'd have been a nice person who smiled instead of ogled, he might not have looked so ugly. But he made her skin crawl whenever she saw him, she just couldn't help feeling that way. And today was no different.

'Where's your car?'

'Broken down,' she said, still walking.

'Hang on,' he said. 'I could tow it back for you.'

'It's fine thanks. I need to get back to Oliver.'

There was a brief moment of silence before he said, 'Oliver's not there.'

Louise stopped, her ankle almost buckling as her heel stomped into the gravel.

She turned to look at him.

'He's in my house.'

Her heart sank.

'He came and knocked on my door because he was wondering where you were.'

'Are you serious?' she asked.

'Yes. Come on. I've left him watching telly.'

She couldn't believe it. She'd told Oliver to stay away from Len Hunter. She was an hour or so later than she said she would be, but he still shouldn't have knocked on his door.

She set off towards the farm.

Len sprinted to try to keep up with her. 'He's fine; there's no need to worry.'

'I want him back home; now.'

Kaiser trotted alongside her. He growled a little, but Len told him to stop and he did as he was told. Although she would normally be fearful of Kaiser, nothing was going to stop her from getting her son back. She didn't even notice the pain in her fingers from the carrier bags anymore.

Louise reached the door before Len. After climbing the four or five steps leading up to the house, she opened the door with her elbow and walked inside. She put her bags down on the kitchen floor and looked around.

The kitchen was dark and dirty. There were plates and cups scattered across the counter tops. The wooden table in the centre was the only place that was tidy with nothing but an empty fruit bowl on top. And the room smelled musty and stale.

'Oliver!' she shouted, as she walked through to the living room. It was empty. Nobody on the sofa, and the television wasn't switched on.

'Oliver!' she shouted once more, but there was no answer.

Her heart sank even more.

She turned and walked back through to the kitchen.

Len Hunter was standing in front of the, now closed, kitchen door. His face held an expression she couldn't quite read, almost apologetic as he pursed his lips together in a fake smile. He then raised his hands, palms facing towards her.

'Now look...' he started.

Louise didn't wait for the rest of the sentence. 'Out of my way,' she said as she walked towards the door.

'Listen...'

'Move!' she shouted, barging him to the side to get to the door. But her fear grew as she turned the handle to find it locked.

'Now listen...'

'Give me the key,' she said in a low voice.

'All I want...'

'Give me the key!'

He stayed where he was, looking at her, palms still facing her.

'Listen,' he said calmly. 'All I want to do is talk.'

Louise stepped away from Len. She was disgusted by him. He was dirty, and he smelled. Not just a smell from working on a farm, but a smell of only showering once a week; if that.

'I have to get back to my son,' she said, looking him in the eye.

'And you will. But I just want to talk to you.'

Louise couldn't believe what was happening. She had to get back to Oliver, and this horrible excuse of a man wasn't going to stop her from doing so.

'Please,' he said, gesturing towards the kitchen table with his right hand.

Louise shook her head, refusing to sit down. She thought about her mobile phone. It was in her handbag, which she'd put inside one of the carrier bags.

'I just want to talk,' he said again.

Louise decided to try to be stern, just like Mrs Kharti had said. She took a step towards him. She could smell him even more, but she tried to ignore his odour and looked him straight in the eye.

'You,' she started, leaving a pause for dramatic effect, 'need to let me go, right now.'

He gave her another creepy smile and slowly shook his head.

'Now!' she screamed.

He just sniggered at this.

Louise didn't know what to do.

'All I want to do is talk. We'll sit down at the table and have a cup of coffee, and then you can go.'

Louise didn't answer. The two of them just stared at each other.

The staring contest was suddenly interrupted as her mobile phone started to ring from within the bags on the floor behind Len.

Without thinking, she leapt down onto her knees to get it. The cold, hard, stone floor hurt, but she ignored the pain as she reached for her handbag. As she pulled the phone from her bag, Len, leaned over and grabbed her by the wrist, snatching the phone from her hands.

Louise tried to get it back but he pushed her away as he looked at the screen.

'Vanni?' he asked. 'Is that the bloke you did last night?'

Louise suddenly felt dirty. Nothing happened last night with Vanni, they hadn't even kissed until that morning. But it was none of Len's business. And he certainly shouldn't be taking note of who visited her home. She felt violated.

Len cancelled the call, laughing. 'He'll think you've gone off him now. He'll think he wasn't very good in the sack.'

'Give me my phone.'

It began to ring again.

Len looked at the screen again. 'He won't take the hint, will he?'

Louise lost her temper and fought to get her phone back, grasping at him frantically.

Len cancelled the call again as he tried to keep the phone out of reach, like a school bully holding a smaller child's pencil case at arm's length.

She fought and fought to try and get to the phone. He turned away from her as she grabbed the back of his neck, digging her nails into his warm, sweaty flesh.

As she swung a hand, hitting him on the top of his head as he faced away from her, his elbow suddenly flew towards her, hitting her in the mouth and sending her falling backwards, over the carrier bags, where she landed hard on the cold kitchen floor.

She felt dazed, but she also felt even more scared. This wasn't a game to him anymore.

'You see!' he shouted. 'You had to go too far didn't you!'

Louise fought hard not to wet herself. Len Hunter wasn't just a stupid and pathetic man anymore. He was dangerous, and he was angry.

He paced up and down in front of her. 'All I wanted to do was talk to you, that's all! But no, that's not good enough. You had to push it didn't you?'

Louise didn't speak. She held the back of her hand to her mouth before pulling it away to see the blood. Things had suddenly become serious. She knew she had to get out.

The mobile rang again.

'For God's sake,' Len screamed, then threw the phone as hard as he could at the stone floor. It smashed into pieces, cutting off her only contact with the outside world. She knew her only chance of getting out was to overpower him somehow.

'Why couldn't you just sit and have a coffee, eh? It's not that hard, is it?'

He began to pace around again. 'You're just like all the others. You dress yourself up to get attention, but once you get any, you're suddenly not interested.'

Louise pulled herself up. Once standing, she wiped more blood away from her mouth then bent down and picked up the four carrier bags before looking directly at Len. 'Open the door,' she said.

He shook his head.

'Open it.'

'I can't. It's gone too far. I'm not going back to prison.'

This sentence made her feel sick. She didn't know he'd been in prison, or what he'd been in prison for. Now she knew this, she wondered how far he would go. Before, he was stupid and pathetic. Now, he was dangerous, maybe even deadly.

'Put the bags down,' he said.

She shook her head.

'Put them down!' he shrieked.

Although this made her heart jump, she stood her ground and didn't move.

He lunged at her, one hand on her throat, the other grabbing at the bags.

She tussled with him once more, fighting to hold onto the bags. Not that the bags mattered at that point, but she really needed to get to the door.

The bags hit the floor, groceries spilling out, and she fell backwards against the table. The wooden legs screamed as they scraped against the stone floor. Louise steadied herself and stared at her attacker, barely able to believe that the situation had grown to this. He looked truly evil as his jaw twitched from side to side.

Len took a step towards her. She watched him pull his right shoulder back and he clenched his teeth. Then suddenly, everything went black.

5

Louise woke up staring at the ceiling. A ceiling that was not only dirty and stained, but also covered in woodchip wallpaper. It took her back to her childhood when every room seemed to be covered in the stuff. She also remembered helping her parents strip the bedroom walls once, which had felt like an impossible task, scraping just a few small pieces off at a time, no matter how much water you poured onto it first.

After a few brief seconds of thinking about the paper, and her childhood, she suddenly remembered where she was and sat up quickly.

Her head hurt, and her face ached as she looked around the room. Her lip was tender from when Len Hunter had elbowed her. The left side of her face was sore, and pain bloomed when she touched it.

She remembered everything going black. He must've punched her hard for her not to even remember hitting the floor. She gently ran her fingers over the back of her head. There was definitely a lump, and it also hurt to touch.

The room she was now in was about the same size as her bedroom at home. But it was empty, apart from the bed she was sitting on.

In the corner there was what looked like a small en suite. The door was open and she could see a toilet and small sink through the gap. But the rest of the room was empty. It certainly wasn't big enough for a bath or even a shower.

In the main room, there was a single light bulb hanging from the ceiling with no shade. And the floor was bare, with uneven wooden floorboards.

The walls were covered in a horrible patterned brown wallpaper that she couldn't imagine anyone ever going into a shop and choosing, especially with the pattern of thin gold swirls that didn't seem to be in any particular order.

There were areas where the paper had torn or fallen away from the wall. And the room with the toilet still showed the bare plaster. Louise presumed it had been added later and nobody had bothered to decorate since.

The wooden door facing her was closed, and she presumed it was locked as she could see a lock above the handle. It was a Yale lock with the keyhole on the outside of the door, she presumed. But she could see, even from where she was sitting that the internal latch had been removed.

There was a window to her right, but no curtains. The glass was dirty and stained, but she could still see through it into the fields. It was at this point she realised she was on the ground floor.

She knew she was still inside Len Hunter's farmhouse. But the room she was in felt like a prison cell. There was a white sheet on the bed, but no cover. And the pillow was so flat it may as well have not been there.

Louise got up from the bed and almost fell forwards as her head spun. She made her way over to the window and leaned on the sill.

The dirty window was double glazed, and had a small section at the top that opened. But there was a lock on the handle.

As she leaned her head close to the glass, she could see over to her bungalow, but only the back end of the house was in view. She pressed her face against the glass so she could see more. But all she could see was several inches of the corner brickwork.

She went over to the door, knowing with all certainty that it would be locked, but that didn't stop her trying the handle. After examining the Yale lock, she could see the metal where Len must've sawn off the latch. She felt it with her fingers, if was rough where the metal had been cut. She tried the handle again, this time shaking it more violently. When the door didn't open, she began to bang on it as hard as she could with the base of her hand. When there was no answer, she began to scream, *'Let me out!'* over and over again. A sudden feeling of nausea came over her. She stopped shouting and ran to the cubicle in the corner of the room. When she saw the black ring of dirt around the toilet bowl, and smelled the stale water, that was enough for her to drop to her knees and throw up into the bowl, doing her best to hold her hair back as she did.

After flushing the toilet, and rinsing her mouth under the tap, she looked around the bathroom. It hardly qualified being called that. There was a sink, and a toilet.

The floorboards were bare, and some of the white paint had crumbled from the walls onto the floor, but nobody had bothered to vacuum or sweep it up. And although there was a small, round mirror nailed to the wall above the sink, Louise could barely see her reflection as it was so dirty.

She wet her hand before wiping her palm across the mirror. Once she'd done this, she was shocked to see how badly beaten she looked. Her top lip was swollen on the right side, and she had a bruise that looked as though it would be a black eye by the next day. The white of her left eyeball was red, almost purple. She knew there would be a nasty bruise there tomorrow.

She didn't quite know how she felt. She was in pain, and scared, but she was also angry; very angry. But she felt as though she had to be the negotiator in the situation. Len Hunter held all the cards, and she had to play the game if she was ever going to see Oliver again.

Shouting and screaming and even threatening Len wasn't going to bring the situation to a conclusion. She had to think of a way of getting the better of him.

She remembered reading about a young woman who got away from her kidnapper by coming on to him. But the thought of that made her feel even more sick. And she didn't really think he would fall for it. After all, she was a model, not an actress.

She pressed her ear against the door and listened. She couldn't hear anything. No TV, no radio, no sounds of him in the kitchen. Nothing.

She knocked on the door again, only gentler this time. She wondered if Len was waiting for her to calm down before he came back.

If she was right, then she had to fight all her urges to scream and shout. She couldn't put the thought of Oliver being alone in the house out of her mind and she didn't really want to. Oliver was her main priority. She had to be very clever if she was going to get out of this room and back to him.

'Len!' she shouted. She didn't scream his name, just shouted it in the same pleasant tone she would use when shouting to Oliver to get him up in time for school.

There was no answer.

'Len!' She called again, followed by a polite knock.

Again, no reply, and she didn't hear any movements.

Her stomach was telling her she was hungry, but the thought of food, especially in this filthy, smelly farmhouse made her feel even more sick. Her legs were weak, but they managed to take her back over to the bed where she sat down.

Louise tried her best to weigh up the options she had. If she shouted, nobody would hear. In fact, the only person likely to hear, other than Len, would be Oliver. And she really didn't want him coming over to the farm looking for her.

The door to the prison cell was made of solid wood. She couldn't imagine being able to break it down with her bare hands. And with the window being double-glazed, she didn't think she could break it, not without a heavy object and there was nothing in the room she could use. The mirror might come in handy if she could get close to Len. But there wasn't anything else in there.

She wasn't sure if she could bring herself to kill another human being. But she knew she had to do whatever was necessary if she was going to get back to Oliver. And if that meant killing Len Hunter, then she'd have to do that. If she could go through with it, that was. But other than the mirror, and the bed, there wasn't anything else in the room she thought she could use. And the thought of smashing the mirror to use a shard of it to stab someone sent her stomach swirling. Even if it was Len Hunter.

Was there another possible solution to bring an end to the situation? How long could he keep her there before someone noticed?

Maybe Oliver would walk into town and look for her. In which case, he might ask a stranger for help. Louise had drummed it into him not to talk to strangers, but maybe through fear and desperation, he would. Louise had also told him never to knock on Len Hunter's door. She hoped to God that nothing would push Oliver into doing that. She didn't want him anywhere near Len Hunter.

Oliver was a clever and creative young boy. She beamed with pride whenever she was with him. He was quiet, but when he did speak, he was always polite and very intelligent, and articulate. Yes, he was awkward around others, and didn't really know how to make friends. But in a strange way, Louise liked that, because it brought them closer together. She did hope that as he grew older, he'd manage to forge some friendships with others. Maybe even find a girlfriend who loved him as much as she did. After all, he couldn't live with her forever. Although at that particular moment, Louise didn't mind if he did. She never wanted to let him out of her sight again.

The teachers at the school had spoken to her several times about Oliver and his disposition. And they also showed concerns about his choice of drawings. Mrs Wheaton was obviously a little disturbed by them. But although a little concerned herself, Louise didn't want to stifle his creativity by stopping him from creating such pictures. And if drawing pictures with dark and twisted themes helped Oliver through the difficult times in his life, then that was fine. Although Louise did wonder to herself what kind of things Oliver would draw if he knew the truth about Michael.

Louise was also aware of what Mrs Wheaton was hinting at when she'd mentioned taking him to see a doctor. She suggested this during a conversation about his lack of ability to form friendships. It was obvious to Louise that she was hinting at the fact that Oliver might be on *the spectrum*. Although Mrs Wheaton didn't actually use words like autism, or Asperger's, Louise knew what she was getting at. Louise wasn't stupid. She knew full well that Oliver's brain worked differently to most. But he was polite, well-behaved, and very good at his school work, so Louise didn't feel the need to go down the road of diagnosis when Oliver seemed perfectly happy. If he was upset at not having any friends then that would be different. But that wasn't the case. He was perfectly happy spending most of his time on his own.

Louise still hoped that Oliver would learn to make friends as he grew older, if he wanted to. But she would only ask for outside help if she felt his happiness was at stake.

She wondered if his intelligence, and his ability to problem solve with a superb ability for lateral thinking would help him if he was on his own for a long time. Louise hoped this wouldn't have to be the case, and she'd be back with him very soon, but first she had to find a way out of this house.

Vanni. Louise realised that Vanni might be her one chance of getting out of this prison cell. He would keep ringing her, and... and maybe he'd get fed up trying and presume she'd lost interest. She really wished she'd answered the phone to him earlier.

Louise glanced at the window then got up from the bed and went over to inspect it. It was about a five-foot square. The panel that opened was only twelve inches or so, reaching across the top of the window.

Louise tried the handle, but it was locked. She wished she used hair grips. Not that she knew how to pick a lock, but she'd have certainly given it a good go. She pressed her hands on the glass, gently at first, but then a little harder. The glass moved and bowed a little as she leaned on it. She wasn't sure if she'd be able to break it with her bare hands, but it might be worth a try.

After wiping her hands on her skirt, she leaned on the glass and pushed again. She wasn't really trying to break it at that point, just testing its strength. But she was also worried that if it did break, she'd be left with broken glass embedded in her wrists. Just as she started to press a little harder, she heard footsteps.

6

Louise had never been in a situation like the one she was in now. Her life had been interesting so far, especially when she was a model. She'd travelled the world, met many different and interesting people. But even though she'd had an amazing life, she'd also suffered her fair share of grief.

Her mum died when Louise was sixteen after a short illness. When she was twenty, her dad died of heart failure. Having no siblings, Louise had to grow up fast and learn how to look after herself. Luckily, she was already earning decent money from modelling, so she managed to pay for her rented flat in Whitford town centre.

Her parents had lived in a council house, so there was nothing in the way of inheritance. Her dad had left just enough money to pay for the funeral.

Louise had already moved out of her family home by the time her dad had passed away, which was something she felt guilty about. Maybe if she'd stayed living with him, he might've looked after himself better, and maybe his heart would've seen him through to old age. But it wasn't to be. Bacon and sausage sandwiches were a nice treat, but they shouldn't be eaten every day. And when she cleared the house, she was shocked to see how many empty beer cans were in the recycle bin. She hoped he'd forgotten to put it out to be emptied and the cans had accumulated over a month or so, but she didn't think this was the case.

Louise felt as though she'd lost her whole family in a short space of time. Her grandparents had all gone by the time she was a toddler, and to lose her parents before they got to meet their grandchild – although it was many years later when Oliver was born – was something that always brought a tear to her eye.

She wondered if losing her parents was the reason why she'd wanted to get married and start a family so badly.

When she was younger, she always said she'd never get married. She was going to travel the world and live in as many different countries as possible. She'd certainly managed to visit many parts of the world, sometimes on holidays, but usually while working. She'd been to Spain several times, Italy, Portugal, and even the Bahamas. This was when her confidence grew. If the agencies were prepared to send her abroad for the photo shoots, then she must've been good at what she did; and she must've been considered beautiful by others. The agencies were certainly prepared to part with money for her.

People always told her how attractive she was. She wouldn't believe them at first. Of course, her mum and dad would say she was gorgeous, but she started to realise they might be right as she grew through her teenage years.

When Louise looked in the mirror, she would see all her faults. She was curvier than she would've liked. She considered her breasts too big compared to the other girls she knew, and the other models that she worked with. The other girls would feign jealousy of them, but she knew they were happy with their own petite breasts that suited their figures. Louise would also have preferred a smaller nose; to her, her nose was a miniature model of a ski jump. And she didn't like her ears. They were too big and stuck out a little at the top. Or that's what she thought whenever she looked in the mirror.

Michael had told her that she was being ridiculous whenever she mentioned these things. He would tell her he loved her nose, and her ears were fine, and he always commented on her beautiful smile and gorgeous brown eyes.

She realised that the business she was in meant she had to spend a lot of time in front of the mirror. And she understood that perhaps you are your own worst critic. But her self-esteem seemed much healthier once she'd quit the world of modelling.

She still spent a lot of time on her appearance; it was a hard habit to get out of. But she started to see herself differently. She was no longer the product with which she had to sell to earn money. Once she'd quit, she saw herself; Louise Derwent, wife and mother-to-be. And that was just fine. That was enough for her. But unfortunately, it wasn't enough for Michael.

7

The door opened before she got to it, and Len Hunter walked in.

Louise was furious when she saw him. She opened her mouth to shout as she stepped towards him, but stopped when she saw the huge knife in his hand, which on closer inspection, was actually a machete.

She froze as Len pointed it at her.

'On the bed,' he said softly.

As she saw the serious look on his face, and had a brief glance at the rusty blade of the machete, she thought she'd better do as she was told.

Louise perched on the edge of the bed as he continued to stare at her. Len lowered the weapon, then turned around and bent down to pick something up from the floor. As he turned back to her, he was holding a cup and the machete in one hand, and a small plate in the other.

He walked slowly towards the bed and rested the plate on top of the mattress. He switched the cup from one hand to the other so he could hold the machete properly, pointing it back towards Louise before offering the cup to her.

'Try anything, and you won't be so pretty once I've swung this at your face.'

Louise realised that she wasn't breathing. She inhaled deeply, still looking Len in the eye as he walked backwards away from her, still holding the weapon in her direction. As he got to the door, she realised he was about to leave, which meant he was going to lock the door again.

'Wait,' she said, shocked at her weak and croaky voice. 'I need to get back to Oliver.'

He stopped and looked straight at her. Louise could see on his face that he wasn't happy with what he'd done; there was confusion and guilt in his expression. He obviously knew he'd gone too far, and he was probably trying to work out how to put things right. She presumed he didn't want to kill her, but she also couldn't see a way out for him. First chance Louise got, she'd not only escape and go back to Oliver, but she'd also go to the police. She knew that, and she was sure Len knew that too.

'Please,' she said. 'Let me get back to my son. He's all alone and...'

Before she could finish her sentence, he stepped backwards through the door and slammed it shut.

Louise's sobbing quickly became a heart-wrenching cry as she sat on the edge of the bed. She placed the cup of tea on the floor, spilling some as she did. She saw through her teary eyes that the plate had a piece of toast and jam on it. She placed it onto the floor next to the cup, lifted her feet onto the bed and lay down on her side. She cried and cried as she lay there, feeling scared, frustrated and angry. She needed to get back to her son. She had to sort this, but she didn't know how. And she didn't know how long Len Hunter would be willing to keep her locked in this room for.

8

L en walked briskly to the other end of the farmhouse before climbing the staircase and heading for his parents' bedroom. There were two staircases in this house, the house that was far too big for one man to live in on his own. In fact, it was far too big when his mum and dad were alive. This staircase led only to one room; all the other bedrooms were accessed by the staircase near the kitchen.

After Len's mum died, his dad, stricken with grief at losing his wife, moved into another bedroom in the house, before he finally ended up needing full-time care, and eventually ending his days in the downstairs bedroom that was now occupied by Louise.

Len's mum and dad's room still lay untouched since she'd died, and Len would only ever go in there when he was upset about something, or if he needed some guidance.

Every other room in the house felt the decay and grime of being occupied only by men. Neither him nor his father were very good at housework or decorating. And the house had been allowed to fall into a state of uncleanliness and neglect. They had both been far too busy with the everyday jobs on the farm to care about the inside of the house. Len's mum kept the place spotless when she was alive, and even used to decorate without any help from either of them. But since she'd died, Len and his dad had spent most of their time outside anyway, and so never bothered with the upkeep of the inside.

The rooms were dark and dusty, and Len knew from the television programmes he'd occasionally slouched in front of after a hard day's graft, that the decor and the furniture was way behind the times. If he was ever to decorate, he would have to move all the clutter that had accumulated over the years. And now that he ran the farm on his own, he couldn't see that ever happening. Not while he lived there alone. He didn't see the point.

He still wondered if Louise and Oliver would move in with him.

Louise could look after the inside of the house, cooking and cleaning, and doing the odd bit of reorganising the place. And Oliver was growing up into a big boy. He was sure he would like to help out on the farm. Yes, he was skinny and a little weedy at the moment, but a few months of working on a farm would soon build him up. Len thought that Oliver could have his bedroom, and he and Louise would move into his parents' old room. He would have to pack away all the photos of his mum and dad first of course. He couldn't sleep in there with his parents' smiling faces watching over them, let alone do anything else.

This was the one room in the house that still looked as good as when his mum was alive. There was thick dust on all the surfaces, but everything was still in its place; all the photos, his mum's clothes, her makeup and jewellery on her dressing table. Apart from the dust, you wouldn't know she'd gone.

Len leaned his back against the wall as he stared at the photo frames on the drawers on each side of the double bed.

The bed still had the peach-coloured cover that hung down to the floor. It was a little messed up from when he'd sat on the bed the last time he'd been in the room. That occasion was when he'd asked his parents for their blessing for him to try to speak to Louise and get to know her a little more.

He'd told them that he liked her and wanted to see if she would feel the same way, and that he hoped that one day she could be his wife. He was sure they would've approved. His dad had always liked Louise, and Louise had seemed to like his dad. Len was always a little annoyed or maybe even jealous that she would smile at his dad and stand talking to him, but she wouldn't even give Len the time of day. That was why he had to get her into the house. So she could see that he too was a nice person. But things hadn't gone according to plan.

Tears rolled down his cheeks as he stared at the photos. He then banged the back of his head on the wall, giving himself an instant headache. He did this several times before shouting in frustration.

'I don't know what to do,' he said as he wiped his eyes. 'She wouldn't talk to me, so I got her to come in the house, and she just flipped out for no reason.'

He started to pace back and forth.

'Why did she have to do that?' he shouted. 'I wasn't going to hurt her. I just wanted to talk to her, and now look what's happened.'

He stopped pacing and slammed his back against the wall once more.

'I... I don't know what to do,' he said as he started to cry uncontrollably. He slid down the wall until he was sitting on the carpet and buried his head in his arms as he cried, wishing with all his heart that his mum and dad could offer some advice to help him out of this situation. But no advice came. He just sat there crying on the floor of his late parents' bedroom, loathing himself for his actions, but hating Louise even more for hers.

9

Louise began to feel as though she was all cried out, almost as though she couldn't cry even if she wanted to. Once she realised that she felt this way, she sat up on the bed and dried her face with the shoulder of her blouse.

She picked up the cup and took a sip. The tea had far too much sugar in it but she didn't care. She needed the energy so she drank it all at once. She felt a little sick at the sight of the dirty and tea-stained cup so tried her best not to focus on it.

The now-cold toast would also give her some energy. She knew it was made in that dirty kitchen, where this nightmare had begun, but again, she tried to put that out of her mind and ate it as fast as she could.

As soon as the tea and the toast were gone, she got up from the bed. Louise kicked off her heels and paced back and forth barefoot as she tried to focus on the problem in hand. That's all it was, a problem that needed solving. She had to get back to Oliver, and in order to do that, she had to either escape, or convince Len to let her go.

She still thought that breaking the window was a possibility.

She went over to it and pressed against it once more. The glass moved a little, just as it had done before.

She examined the edges, wondering if she could dislodge the frame somehow. But it didn't look as though it would budge. Not without a lot of force, and she had neither the strength nor the tools needed.

She walked over to the door and knocked, just giving a polite tap as though she was knocking on the front door of a friend's house.

'Len,' she called. 'Len... I've finished my tea and toast. Are you there?'

She tried not to embellish her niceness. If she was too nice to him, he would realise straight away that she was up to something.

'Len,' she called again.

Moments later she heard footsteps.

'On the bed,' he snapped from the other side of the door.

She did as he said and sat down, picking up the plate and the cup.

The door opened.

In walked the man who Louise had never liked since she first met him. Now she detested him. But even though she felt this way, she had to push the thoughts of hatred to the back of her mind.

She almost smiled, but not quite.

Len still held the machete as he walked over to her and took the cup and plate. Without thinking about it, Louise grabbed his wrist. If she had thought about it, she might've hesitated because he could have easily swung the rusty machete in her direction. But he didn't. He just froze and stared.

'Please sit down,' she said.

He looked taken aback.

She spoke in a soft tone, but she didn't want him to think of her as being flirtatious and cause him any excitement that could trigger a sexual assault of any kind. And she knew he could take off her hand with one swing of the machete.

He stood there for a moment gazing at her, obviously pondering her request to sit down.

'No,' he finally said and turned as if to walk away.

Louise held onto his warm and sweaty wrist.

'Please,' she said. 'I just want to talk. I'm not going to try anything, am I? Not with that in your hand. I just want to talk.'

She let go of his wrist and patted the bed at the side of her.

He looked her up and down. He made no secret of looking at her legs and cleavage. But then again, he never did.

'Talk,' he said. 'But I'm not sitting down. And try anything, and I will cut you.'

The sentence sickened her to her very soul.

She was suddenly very aware of needing the bathroom. But she focused on the conversation. She had to convince him to let her go. She also noticed the key in the outside of the door as it was now wide open. But she didn't think she could get to it, and if she did, it would be of no use to her. Not unless she could go through the door and trap Len inside.

'Look,' she started. 'I can see now that you didn't mean any harm. You just wanted to talk to me and I panicked and it all got out of hand.'

'That was all I wanted,' he said, raising his voice a little. 'Just to talk to you. But no. You had to react like that, fighting to get past me.'

'I can see that now. But I was scared,' she said. 'I just wanted to get back to Oliver. Surely you can understand that?'

He paused for a moment. Then he nodded, closing his lips together.

'I understand that I caused the situation in the kitchen. And I'm quite happy to keep what happened to myself. I know you're not a violent man. And I know you wouldn't normally behave that way. It just got out of hand really quickly and you panicked. But nobody has to know.'

She didn't know if she was a good enough actress to convince him. But she almost convinced herself.

He started fidgeting as he stood in front of her, waving the machete a little with a flick of his wrist.

'No,' he said. 'I don't believe you.'

'What do you mean?' she said.

'As soon as you get out of here, you'll go straight to the police.'

She shook her head. 'I promise, I won't. I just want to get back to Oliver. He'll be scared on his own. He's only ten.'

Len stroked his chin, as he shook his head slightly.

Louise watched him with bated breath, hoping she'd convinced him. But his eyes widened as his anger grew, she started to see that he wasn't convinced.

She stood up and moved closer to him.

'Please,' she said.

He stepped back, lifting the machete and pointing it at her.

'I need to go to him.'

His jaw twitched, his breathing became a little heavier as the seconds passed.

Louise kept her gaze on him.

Len paused, as though he was thinking about it, but then he shook his head. His expression then turned to a snarl as he pushed her backwards onto the bed and then left the room, slamming the door behind him, causing the room to shake.

Louise briefly felt as though she was getting through to him. She could see him thinking as she spoke. But now, as she saw her plan fail with the door slammed shut and locked once more, the floodgates opened again as she began to cry.

10

Louise was surprised to realise she'd fallen asleep. She didn't know how long for. It could've been five minutes, it could've been five hours; she had no idea.

It was still reasonably light outside, although inside the room was no longer as bright as it was earlier. In fact, it was quite dark. Partly because the sun was now at the opposite side of the sky, and partly because of how dirty the glass was.

After yawning, and stretching, her thoughts returned to the window, so she got up from the bed and walked over to press on the glass once more, still wondering if she could break it with her bare hands.

She looked around the room, hoping to spot something she could use to break the glass, but there was nothing in there.

Suddenly, she remembered her red heels, the shoes that now sat on the floor next to the bed. She picked one up and felt the heel. It was metal at the bottom, but she didn't know if it was strong or hard enough to break the glass.

Len would probably hear the noise if she tried to break the window, if he was in the house, but he was a farmer. There was a good chance he was out in the fields somewhere. Unless he'd abandoned all his responsibilities to keep guard of her.

She tapped the glass gently with the heel of her shoe, just to get a feel for it. She'd have to swing hard to break it, but it was worth a try. She didn't know where to hit to get the most chance of the window breaking – the middle, or if it would be better to aim for the corners? She opted to try the middle first.

She held the shoe high above her head, took a deep breath, and then swung hard at the glass. It made a deafening noise as the steel connected with the window, but it didn't break.

She swung again. This time, it left a tiny dent in the middle of the window. This gave her a little confidence so she swung again.

Nothing happened.

She stood back and took a deep breath. She pictured martial artists breaking bricks with their bare hands, like she'd seen many times on television. If they could do that, then surely, she could do this.

She took another deep breath before pulling her arm back and swinging hard and fast, screaming out loud as she swung.

The heel hit the glass harder this time, and the impact created a diagonal crack across the centre of the window, about two feet long.

A wave of euphoria swept through her body – it might actually be possible to escape. But Louise knew she had a long way to go.

She swung again. The crack in the window grew another four or five inches.

As she pulled her arm back ready to swing again, she froze.

Through the dirty, broken window, Len Hunter was staring back at her. He clenched his teeth together, but he didn't speak, and he didn't shout.

Louise dropped her shoe to the floor as she stared back at him.

The seconds felt like hours as they remained there, just looking at each other. Then he turned and walked away.

Louise started to panic. Was he going to beat her? Was he going to tie her up? He almost certainly was going to take her shoes away, which would leave her with no chance of breaking free.

She sat down on the bed and awaited her punishment.

As the minutes went by, she started to feel more and more scared. Her heart was pounding hard, and she felt weak and nauseated. Len had had more than enough time to walk around the house and get to the room. So, the fact that he hadn't got there yet meant he was possibly looking for a weapon, or maybe even a length of rope.

A sudden loud bang made her jump. It was accompanied by a sudden loss of some of the daylight that was making its way through the broken window.

Louise turned to look, and saw a large panel of wood covering the lower half of the window.

Len Hunter was holding it in place as he hammered nails into it from the outside.

Louise jumped up to look through the window. Although she couldn't quite see over the top of the wood.

The banging was relentless. He was working fast to make sure she stayed his prisoner.

Louise banged on the glass over and over again.

She screamed at him. 'Please... please don't... I won't break it anymore.'

Len didn't stop hammering the nails into the board long enough to listen to her screams. He didn't even look at her as she pleaded with him. He just carried on with what he was doing.

Moments later she heard the sound of metal being dragged on concrete. She then saw him climb the stepladder he'd put in place and hammer a second board over the top part of the window, making the room completely void of daylight; now only the low wattage bulb hanging from the ceiling allowed her to see what she was doing.

'No,' she shouted. 'I can't see.'

Again, her screams were ignored as he continued to bang the nails in.

Once the banging stopped, Louise stood in silence, devastated at what had just happened. She then went over to the bed, climbed on top and lay down, her head resting on the uncomfortably flat pillow. She began to cry as she wondered if Len would be coming to speak to her. Possibly to reprimand her for breaking his window. She had no idea, but what she did know was that this room – the prison cell – was even more terrifying in the dark.

11

Louise could see through the tiny gaps in the wood that it was now dark outside, and not much brighter inside. The bulb which hanged from the ceiling couldn't have been more than fifteen watts, if that.

She felt ill, with different emotions shooting through her mind and body; fear, anger, hatred, frustration, helplessness. She also felt as though she could be sick, but lacked the energy to go and throw up into the toilet again. So she just lay there on her side, breathing deeply while staring at the door. How dare he do this to her. How dare he do this to Oliver. She felt as though she could kill him. This was an emotion she'd never felt before. But if she was going to survive this, and get back to Oliver, she had to be prepared to do whatever necessary. If Len had to die then so be it.

She jumped up from the bed and tried the door again, on the off chance he'd not closed it properly. But it was still locked.

She walked around the small room in her bare feet, trying to think of what options remained. Breaking the window had been a good idea, but she should've waited until she knew Len was out of the house, watching until she had seen him in the distance working in one of the fields. But it was too late for that now. Even if she could smash the glass into pieces, she wouldn't have the strength to push the wooden panels off; she'd heard how many nails he'd hammered in to hold them firmly to the wall.

She was trapped. Suddenly she froze. There were footsteps outside of the door.

She went to it and banged on the wood with the heel of her hand. 'Len... Len please.'

The footsteps stopped, making her think he was standing outside of the door.

'Please, Len... You have to let me get home to Oliver. I can't stay overnight. He's only ten years old, he'll be terrified on his own.'

She couldn't hear him, but she knew he was there.

'Len,' she said, a little softer. 'Think back to when you were ten years old.' She paused before saying, 'You wouldn't be happy, would you? Can you imagine not knowing where your mum was?'

She thought she heard him breathe, or maybe it was a sigh. But either way, she felt as though she might be getting somewhere.

'If you just unlock the door, I can go and check on him, and this will all be over.'

Silence.

Louise felt as though she'd said everything she could say. She'd been polite, and spoken to him with respect. She'd tried to appeal to the good in him, if there was any. But even horrible people – murderers, kidnappers and even paedophiles, surely, they still loved their mums.

Surely he understood what he was doing to Oliver by keeping her there.

'Len,' she said again.

Nothing.

She waited.

Suddenly, the door shook as a deafening bang filled her ears, causing her to jump backwards. He'd either kicked or punched it, but whichever it was, it was hard. Then, at the top of his voice, he shouted, *'What the hell do you want me to do?'*

Louise stood back from the door, starting to regret her actions.

'If I let you out,' he said, no longer shouting, but still talking loudly, 'you'll go straight to the police. I'm not stupid, you know.'

With that, she heard his footsteps as he briskly walked away.

Louise heard a door slam somewhere in the house. Wherever it was, it was far enough away for him not to hear her. She knew it was pointless pleading with him. So she walked over to the bed and sat down. All out of ideas, she resigned herself to the fact that she was spending the night there.

12

Sunday 2nd May

Vanni didn't know whether to be angry or upset with Louise. He'd spent a magical evening with her, connecting to her in a way he hadn't felt since his wife was alive, and then she'd ignored all his calls. The first three calls just rang out before going to answerphone, but the last two, she'd either switched her phone off or the battery had died. But that was yesterday, and surely, she would've charged her phone by now. Especially by ten-thirty in the morning. She was definitely avoiding him, and he didn't understand why. They'd both shared their life stories that night. He'd been careful not to just talk about the loss of his wife four years earlier. He'd made sure he was empathetic to Louise. He even let her talk more than he did. He could've easily rambled on about his own problems. Finally, after four years of struggling to cope with Nadia's death, he'd found someone who understood what he'd been going through. Louise's situation, although in the same league when it came to pain, was a little different. Losing a partner to suicide must have been an unbelievably difficult thing to come to terms with. Although Nadia had passed away, Vanni knew she still loved him. But Louise didn't really know that her husband still loved her. He'd obviously been suffering, but how could he leave the woman he loved, and his son. Vanni didn't understand it, and he knew Louise didn't either.

That night, Vanni and Louise had been there for each other. He'd listened to every word she'd said, and felt a closeness he hadn't felt since Nadia was alive. So why would she blank him after such an amazing evening? He hadn't forced himself on her. They hadn't even kissed before the goodbye kiss the next morning, and she'd initiated that. Why would she ignore him? What had he done wrong?

He pulled his car up outside her house. He knew she didn't want to introduce him to her son yet, which is why he'd had to sneak out of her house the previous morning. He fully understood that. It wasn't fair to let her son meet, and possibly become attached to, a man who she didn't know was a permanent fixture or not.

Vanni already felt as though Louise was the one for him. He knew it sounded ridiculous, even in his head, but she was something special. Not only was she incredibly beautiful, and had curves that would no doubt turn heads wherever she went, there was also something about her he couldn't explain. He felt at ease with her. He felt as though he could tell her anything. He also felt as though they were meant for each other. They've both been touched by tragedy, and both had to continue with their lives even though they could have easily given up.

Louise had to carry on because of her son, Oliver. Vanni had to carry on because of his restaurant. Although the two weren't the same, Vanni had built the business from the ground up, and it wasn't just bricks and mortar to him. It was a living and breathing entity with fourteen members of staff, most of whom had all stayed with him and helped him through the difficult times. He couldn't let the restaurant die. Too many people depended on it. And more importantly, it had been a joint venture between him and Nadia. It was both of their dreams to open a restaurant, and they had succeeded. She'd made him promise to keep it going, and he intended to keep that promise.

As he parked up at the side of Louise's bungalow, he saw that her car wasn't there. But he still climbed out of the BMW, leaving the engine running, and knocked on the door.

For a moment, he thought he heard movement inside, but he wasn't sure.

He waited.

There was no answer, so he knocked again.

After waiting for another minute or so, he gave up and walked back to his car.

He took out his mobile and tried her number again. It went straight to voicemail, just as it had before.

'Look, Louise, can you please give me a call. I just want to talk to you.'

He didn't know what was wrong. Had she gone off him already? He hadn't felt rejected the previous morning, when she'd hugged him tightly. And that kiss wasn't fake. She had meant it.

There was nothing else he could do, so he decided he'd head off to the restaurant to make an early start, hoping she'd phone him back soon. At least at work he'd be busy instead of just staring at his phone, waiting for it to ring.

He got back in the car, turned around and headed off down the track.

13

Louise had no idea what time it was. She was starving hungry, and other than the water from the tap in the cubicle, she hadn't had anything else to drink all night. She liked her caffeine in the morning, but since Len had kicked or punched the door the previous night, she hadn't heard from him. Although she was repulsed at the thought of anything from that kitchen touching her lips, she really wanted a cup of tea or coffee. Her head was pounding and she felt queasy. She had slept a little, but not much. The thought of Oliver being alone all night in the bungalow was terribly worrying. She didn't think he would do anything stupid, like burn the place down. But she was still worried. He was a sensible boy, more sensible than most boys his age. And she was pretty sure he could keep himself safe, but she also knew he would've been terrified on his own, especially at night-time.

She heard a noise; it was a car.

She jumped up and ran to the window. She couldn't see anything through the tiny gap in the boards, other than daylight peeking through, but she could hear a car on the gravelled track near her house.

Could it be Vanni? He would be wondering why she wasn't answering his calls. But she also knew that Oliver wouldn't answer the door to him. At that moment she regretted teaching him not to answer the door when he was home alone. She knew he'd be safe with Vanni – although she hadn't known him very long – and he would definitely phone the police. But no, she knew Oliver would be hiding behind the sofa or in his bedroom as soon as he heard a knock at the door.

She listened carefully.

A few seconds later she could hear the faint sound of knocking in the distance.

'Vanni!' she screamed over and over again as she thumped hard at the glass.

When she stopped to listen, all she could hear was the gentle hum of the car engine running.

'Vanni! Vanni!' she shouted again.

'That's enough!'

Her heart almost stopped as the deafening voice bounced around the walls of the small room. She turned to see Len standing in the now open doorway, again holding the machete. She momentarily considered carrying on with her screams, but when she saw the look of anger on her captor's face, she decided against it.

'I'm not going to keep letting you get away with this sort of thing,' he said quietly through closed teeth. With a tilt of his head, he gestured towards the bed. Louise obliged and slowly walked over to it, not lowering her gaze from his face as she did. She sat on the bed, and listened to the faint sound of a car making its way along the gravelled track until eventually, there was silence.

Len lowered the machete and backed out of the room before slamming the door shut.

14

Len had been sitting in his living room for over an hour since the last episode with Louise. He hoped she would fall asleep so he could leave the house. He guessed she wouldn't have slept well so it might be a possibility.

There was enough food in the bags that Louise had brought in but he still needed coffee, and lager. He was also running low on tinned food. The shopping bags only had fresh food that needed a certain amount of cooking knowledge to prepare. Len knew how to cook sausages and bacon, and he knew how to fry eggs, but that was about it. His dad had been quite a good cook, before the dementia set in at least. But Len never showed an interest. Which was why he now lived on a diet of fried food, microwave ready meals and pizza.

He crept down the hall and edged slowly towards the door to the room where Louise was.

He listened for any movement, but there was nothing. He hadn't given her any food or drink that morning, thinking she might be easier to control with an empty stomach, and if she wanted a drink, there was the tap. Louise clearly had a feisty side, so he didn't want to give her energy by feeding her too much. And he'd realised that if she was a coffee drinker, caffeine withdrawals could make her angry at first, but the sickly feeling should take over, maybe even give her the shakes at some point.

He put the key in the yale lock and turned it, trying hard not to make a sound. As he pushed the door open, he peered around to see her lying on her side. He felt a little relieved that she was asleep, and began to close the door so he could leave the house, knowing now that she wasn't going to cause any more commotion while he was gone. But then he stopped. Instead of closing the door, he walked inside.

She was on her side with the pillow folded over to make it thicker to support her head. Her skirt had ridden high above her knees, revealing her thighs. And her large breasts had fallen forwards as if trying to escape above the top button of her blouse.

He walked closer to the bed and knelt down in front of her, drinking in her scent. Although she'd been there for almost twenty-four hours, he could still smell a faint trace of her perfume. It was now mixed with a sweet sweat smell that he found intoxicating as he breathed deeply, closing his eyes.

He opened them and looked at her closely, first starting at her feet and then making his way slowly to the top of her body, and then stopping at her face.

He wanted to feel her soft white skin, but it wouldn't take much to wake her. He couldn't resist holding out his hand and moving it gradually over her face, caressing the space in front of her, moving his fingers as though he could feel her. Her warm breath touched the ends of his fingers as he kept them there for five or six breaths. He then moved his hand past her face and neck, stopping at her breasts, holding his hand only a few millimetres away from the flesh above her blouse. He slowly grasped with his fingers, still not touching her, but imagining what she felt like as he stroked the air in front of her. He continued like this along her abdomen, over her right hip and down the curve of her thigh.

There was nothing he wouldn't do to this woman, but at that moment, he was still trying to think of a way out of the situation she'd caused. He knew once he'd touched her, there would be no going back. There was no doubt in his mind that she would report him, so he would have no choice but to kill her. And he didn't want to do that; not unless he had to.

She gave a sudden cough that made him jump backwards. He was crouched in front of her, one hand on the ground, but she didn't open her eyes, so he stood up and slowly backed out of the room, trying hard not to disturb the sleeping beauty as he closed the door.

Still feeling dizzy, and a little weak at the knees after being so close to Louise, he left the house and walked to his car and climbed inside. How could he get himself out of this mess? He'd done nothing but go over everything in his mind ever since he'd locked her in the bedroom. He was still angry with her. All he wanted to do was talk. Why couldn't she have just done that? Was he not good enough for her? He was a businessman with his own farm, and his own house. She could do a lot worse than him. Why couldn't she sit and talk for five minutes? He just wanted to show her what he was really like.

Before he started the engine, he got back out of his car and walked along the track towards Louise's bungalow. He knew Oliver would be inside, wondering where his mum was, so Len thought he'd better go and check on him.

He thought about telling him not to worry and that she'd be home soon. But Len didn't want to say anything that would put Oliver in the picture should the police come sniffing around. Len knew the only way to resolve this would be to kill Louise, but he didn't think he could kill Oliver. He quite liked him and had tried talking to him many times, but usually his mum shouted him away. She would be polite and say something like, *Come on, Oliver. Don't bother Mr Hunter, he's busy.*

That always infuriated Len. Why would she be so paranoid about her son talking to his next-door neighbour? Len wasn't going to hurt him, he just liked talking to him.

At Louise's house, Len stopped and listened with his head towards the glass of the kitchen door. He thought he heard some movement inside. After a moment or two of standing there in silence, Len looked through the kitchen window.

The kitchen led through to the living room. It was almost open-plan, apart from the archway separating the two rooms. In the living room he saw what he presumed was a den. A large blanket draped over something – probably dining chairs judging from the height of it – and lots of branches stood up against the structure, as if to camouflage it. This obviously had the opposite effect as it

232

was up against the wall in the living room. You couldn't miss it.

He saw the blanket twitch a little, which meant Oliver was definitely inside.

Len smiled to himself at the boy's attempt at surviving on his own. It was a relief that this was what he was doing, and not out looking for help. At least he'd been making himself comfortable, as though he was preparing for life on his own. Len didn't want him to go looking for help, although he thought it unlikely, given how shy and quiet Oliver was. Len had wondered if there was something wrong with him before now. Oliver spoke in a very direct manner, usually without looking at him. He didn't behave like any other kid that age that Len had ever known. So maybe he had some time to think of a way to sort things out and possibly find a way to resolve the situation before Oliver went blabbing to the police.

Len walked around to the front of the bungalow and looked through the living room window. The blanket twitched again. Len smiled and walked back towards his farm, climbed into his car and headed to the supermarket, hoping that neither Louise or Oliver would do anything stupid in his absence.

15

Once again, Louise had no idea how long she'd slept for. She couldn't believe she'd slept at all, especially as she was worried sick about Oliver. She was angry with herself – how could she allow herself to sleep when Oliver was on his own? She felt exhausted, but she was also so stressed that she didn't think sleep was a possibility.

She walked over to the window. There was still daylight poking through the gaps in the wood, but it could be morning, afternoon or evening, or even the next day. She doubted that, but the way she felt, it was possible. Tiredness and a lack of food was starting to have an effect on her.

In the bathroom, after using the toilet and washing her hands, she leaned forward and took several large gulps of water before turning off the tap and wiping her mouth with the back of her hand.

The face looking back at her in the dirty mirror above the sink looked different somehow. She would normally force a smile, or try to look her best. She knew most people – consciously or unconsciously – adjusted their faces a little when looking into a mirror, trying to create the best version of themselves. Whether this was a widening of the eyes, a forced smile, or even a head tilt, she knew this was something she was guilty of, along with many other people. But not this time.

She hardly recognised the person looking back at her, with a tired looking face, and heavy eyes with bags beneath them. The bruises on her eye and mouth were almost black, and her hair looked as though it was beyond help. She couldn't see a modelling agency signing her up with how she looked at that moment. If she sat on a street corner, she imagined people would stop and give her the change from their pockets, or maybe bring her a cup of coffee. After what Len had done to her, she looked anything but beautiful.

Her heart jumped as she heard the door unlock so she walked back into the bedroom, just as Len came through the now open door.

'Stay there,' he said, pointing the rusty machete at her again.

She did as she was told.

With his left hand, he threw a pre-packed sandwich and a bottle of cola onto the bed and gesturing with the machete that she should make her way over to it.

She did as he wished and without waiting for him to walk away, she tore the box open and took as big of a bite as she could manage to try and tame the growl from her empty stomach. It was cheese and pickle, which wasn't her favourite thing to eat, but she didn't care. This much-needed sustenance for survival would give her energy to keep going. If it wasn't for Oliver, she would've already given up. But she had to stay focused, for his sake. It was also a relief to eat something that hadn't come from Len Hunter's filthy kitchen.

Len stood watching as she ate. She was used to him backing out of the room, so when he didn't, she wondered if he had something to say.

Eventually, when she'd wolfed down both sandwiches from the torn box, he spoke. 'So... How do you feel?'

Louise felt the anger build up inside her. She wanted to shout and scream at him. *How do I feel? How do you think I feel?* But she didn't. She'd already thought beforehand that if he came and spoke to her, she had to keep him talking. If she lost her temper and shouted at him, he would either be violent or he'd just slam the door shut, both physically and metaphorically.

'I'm OK,' she replied.

He nodded.

After a moment of silence, he said, 'I checked on Oliver.'

Her stomach flipped, almost rejecting the food she'd just eaten.

'I didn't knock on the door, but I saw him through the window.'

This made her feel a little better, but not much.

'He's built a fort in the living room,' he said, smiling a little.

She thought once more of the night before, wondering if her son had managed get to sleep. And if he had, was it in the fort Len had just informed her of? But she knew he would need a night-light of some kind because he didn't like to...

It suddenly occurred to Louise that the electricity would've run out by now. The card was in her purse, but the last time she'd had her purse was when she was in the kitchen.

'The electricity,' she said.

Len looked confused.

She stood up from the bed.

'I have a pre-payment meter...' she started, but he cut her off by raising his hands – both the one with the machete and the empty one – and gestured for her to sit.

She sat back on the bed, trying to calm herself.

'He won't have any electricity. The power will have run out by now. The card is in my purse.'

Len seemed to think for a moment.

'OK,' he said, finally. 'I'll get it and take it to him.'

'No,' she said with a slightly raised voice. Although she wanted him to have the power on, she didn't want Len anywhere near her son.

'I'll just post it,' he said, as if he'd read her thoughts. Or he'd already thought it through and knew he shouldn't be seen taking the card, or anything else, to Oliver, especially if the police turned up at some point.

'Does he know how to use it?'

'Yes,' Louise said, thankful that Oliver was inquisitive enough to get her to show him what to do. Luckily, the power had gone off several times since the electricity company insisted on her having a pre-payment meter after falling behind with payments. And Oliver always offered to insert the card and get the power back on, almost as if he enjoyed doing it.

'I'll sort it,' Len said.

He stood and left the room.

After making sure the door was locked, Len went to the kitchen and searched Louise's handbag for her purse. He'd already looked inside the purse earlier. There was no money, just a few credit and debit cards.

He found the electric card, although he'd never seen one before. It looked like a credit card, only it had the electricity company's logo on it.

As he went to leave the house, Kaiser appeared at the top of the steps, whining for food. Len thought he'd better feed him first, so he took the metal bowl from the kitchen top, grabbed a tin of food from the cupboard, and with a fork, emptied the food into the bowl.

He stepped through the door again, where Kaiser stood waiting patiently for his dinner. But before he descended the steps to put the bowl down for the dog, Len saw Oliver walking along the track away from the bungalow. This worried him; Len wondered where he was going, and whether he was looking for someone to help him.

As he walked by, Oliver sporadically glanced over to the farm, obviously struggling to keep his head down and pretend he hadn't seen him.

Len put the bowl onto the ground then stood with his hands on his hips and watched the boy walk by.

He couldn't help but smile to himself at the fact that this ten-year-old boy was embarking on a mission. Whether it was to get help, or to just go to the shops for food, he couldn't help but admire his courage.

Len hoped he wasn't going to the police. If he did, he imagined his house would be the first place they would check. He'd already thought that if he saw a police car approaching, he'd have to come outside and meet them as far away from the house as possible, just in case Louise was shouting or knocking.

The other option was to run into the bedroom and put Louise in a chokehold until she passed out, hoping he could get rid of the police before she came around and started shouting again. He really hoped he wouldn't have to do either. But he knew one way or another, this situation had to come to an end. He just didn't know how yet.

Once Oliver was out of view, Len set off on foot in the direction of the bungalow with the electric card in his pocket.

Once there, he tried the door handle. It was locked, so he posted the card through the letter box and walked away.

He hadn't made it ten metres from the house when he suddenly realised what he'd done. At some point, the police could turn up, and the card posted through the door would be a huge clue for them. If Louise had been killed, kidnapped or run away, she wouldn't have managed to get the electric card back to Oliver. And Len had just left his prints all over the card and the door handle.

He started to panic. He couldn't believe he'd been so stupid. Pulling his sleeve over his hand, he went back and wiped the door handle, but there was nothing he could do about the card.

What could he do? Maybe he should petrol bomb the bungalow. But although it would remove the finger prints, it would mean the authorities would investigate.

He regretted keeping Louise in the house, and he badly wanted it all to end. But he still couldn't see a way out of it.

He considered going after Oliver and keeping him in the house too, but kidnapping a woman and a child seemed a much worse crime than just holding the woman captive. He briefly wondered whether to come clean. Or maybe it would be best to kill her and dispose of the body.

The more time went by, the worse he felt. He knew he was capable of killing her, but just wasn't sure if that was the best option. He didn't think he could kill the boy though. Louise deserved it for the way she'd treated him, and the way she dressed, trying to get everyone's attention and then pushing away any interest she got from him. But Oliver hadn't done anything wrong. He hoped he wouldn't have to kill either of them, but he especially felt this way about Oliver. But he had to be prepared to do whatever necessary. He wasn't going back to prison.

Len strode around the back of the house, hoping a window was open so he could climb through and get the card back. But they were all closed. He noticed a watering can next to the wall beside a few empty plant pots, some garden shears and gloves.

An idea came to him. He grabbed the watering can and filled it from the outside tap and then took it to the kitchen door. With his sleeve over his hand again, he pulled the letter box open and pushed the spout of the watering can through, then tipped the can, pouring all the water through into the house.

Maybe the water would stop the card from working, but he was pretty sure it would wash away his finger prints. He cared more about removing the evidence than he did Oliver being able to watch TV or use the microwave.

He took the can back and put it where he'd found it. It wasn't the perfect crime, but he hoped it would deter the police from knocking on his door. The next hour or two would be spent watching for Oliver's return. And hoping that he came back alone.

16

Louise spent the next couple of hours marching around the room she was now calling *the cell* in her mind. At least, it could've been a couple of hours; it could have been longer. Or it might have only been twenty minutes. She was losing all concept of time. With nothing to do but worry, she was oblivious to what time of day it was. Small beads of light were still showing through the gaps in the wood, so she knew the sun hadn't set. But she still struggled to place the time of day, and even the actual day itself. She thought it was still Sunday, but she wasn't sure. It was a bank holiday weekend, which went against her. Any other weekend, by Monday the school would try to contact her to see why Oliver hadn't turned up. This gave Len Hunter and extra twenty-four hours. She wondered if Oliver would make his own way to school on Tuesday. Or maybe he was already out looking for an adult to tell them his mum had not come home. Louise knew that it was most likely he was just staying at home, hiding in the fort he'd apparently built, and probably still drawing pictures. But how long could a ten-year-old survive on their own for? What would he have eaten? There were a few chocolate bars left and some cereal. But she didn't think there was much milk left. She'd bought some from the supermarket, but that was most likely in Len's fridge by now. At least the power would be back on soon, if it wasn't already. It wasn't cold enough for him to come to any harm without the power on. And although he'd helped her in the kitchen a few times, he didn't really know how to prepare hot food; not unsupervised, anyway.

At least now he had electricity – that made her feel a little better. Maybe he could watch some television to pass the time.

The door opened again.

'On the bed,' Len said, as he came into view.

She did as she was told, even before she saw the machete.

He walked back and forth in front of her. He clenched his fists and had started to sweat. He wasn't scowling at her, but she could tell by the fast, short breaths that he wasn't happy.

'What's happened?' she asked.

'Nothing,' he snapped. 'We just have to decide what we're doing.'

'What do you mean?' she asked.

He stopped and looked her in the eye. 'What d'you think I mean?'

She recoiled as he shouted.

'This can't carry on,' he said, still moving around the room. 'One way or another, this has to come to an end.'

Louise took a deep breath. 'You could just let me go.'

He shook his head as he continued the laps of the floor. 'You would go straight to the police.'

'No, I wouldn't. I promise.'

She then grabbed his hand – the one without the machete – and looked at him. He stood still and returned her gaze.

'I promise,' she repeated.

He stared at her, and Louise thought she might just be getting through to him.

But then he shook his head. 'Bollocks,' he shouted. 'Do you think I'm stupid?'

She stared at the door that was still ajar and wondered if she could make a break for it as he reached the other side of the room.

'As soon as I let you go, you'll go home to your son, and then you'll phone the police. I'll be arrested within the hour. I'll get sent back to prison, I'll lose my farm, I'll lose my house, and when I get out of prison, I'll have to move away because I'll be known as the person who kidnapped you, and then...'

Louise stopped listening to him. The rant continued as he walked back and forth holding the machete out in front of him.

'... and I'll never get a job, and I'll have to...'

As she watched him, she made a mental note of the floorboard furthest away from the door that his boot landed on. It was the same one every time.

She made the decision that she'd jump up and bolt for the door after his boot landed there. But fear and dread made her stomach twist in agony. She was terrified, but she had to try something. She didn't know how long it could be before she got another chance like this.

She decided she'd make a run for it once his boot hit that floorboard just three more times.

She watched.

One.

He turned back.

Two.

He turned again, still ranting.

She then held her breath.

As his boot landed on the floorboard a third time, she leapt up from the bed and ran for the door.

Just before she reached it, he tackled her from behind and threw her to the floor like a wrestler.

She screamed and writhed to try to get free. But a hand landed over her mouth; a hand that smelled of dirt and oil. She bit it hard, and he shouted in pain, then pulled his hand away and slapped her hard on the mouth before covering her lips once more.

Louise thought of biting him again, but decided against it.

His face was next to hers as they lay on the ground, his legs wrapped around her. He shushed into her ear softly. The smell of dirt and oil was now accompanied by the smell of his stale breath.

Louise felt sick. She lay still, hoping he would get off her and leave the room without any more verbal abuse or violence. She felt like crying; another attempt at escape faltered.

He took his stinking hand away from her mouth, but he didn't move.

'Why did you have to do that?' he said quietly in her ear.

'Get... off... me,' she said, keeping her voice low, but, she hoped, stern. Mrs Kharti would've been proud of her.

Within a few seconds, Len released his arm from around her, and slowly climbed off of her before standing up.

Louise dusted herself off and then also got to her feet.

She watched him look at his hand. She could taste the oil and blood in her mouth. She then spat onto the floor.

As he wiped his hand on his overalls, she realised the door behind him was still open.

Without thinking, she made another run for it, bolting past him and heading for freedom.

He grabbed her again, shouting *'No,'* as he tackled her.

Louise reached forward and managed to get a hand on the door, but Len swung a foot and kicked it shut as they both fell backwards to the floor.

As the door slammed closed, they both froze, lying on the hard wooden floor completely still.

'No!' Len shouted as he pushed her away before jumping up from the floor. He pounced towards the closed door and began frantically pulling at the handle.

'No!' he screamed again, this time kicking hard at the wood.

After he finished what seemed to Louise like an uncontrollable temper tantrum, he turned to look at her, an expression of anger and disbelief on his face, his eyes wider than she'd ever seen them before.

Louise couldn't believe it either. Of all the things that could've happened to make the situation worse, this was one she could've really done without. From that moment onwards, Louise had a new cell mate.

17

Once he'd picked up the machete from the floor, called her a *stupid bitch* at the top of his voice, and spent a minute or two kicking and shoulder-barging the door, Len turned and slid his back down the door until he was sitting on the floor, holding his shoulder. He looked as though he could burst into tears, but he didn't. He just sat there with a pitiful expression on his face, almost as though *he* was the victim.

Louise was just as devastated. She couldn't believe Len was now trapped inside the room with her. But she couldn't help but take a little pleasure from that fact that his plans were going awry. She did, however, wonder how they were going to get out now, and above anything else, she feared for her own safety as she now had to share a room with her captor; someone who had been in prison. What for, she didn't know, but what she did know, was that he was creepy and perverted. She felt more scared now than she had at any point so far during this whole ordeal. The only comfort she took was the fact that while Len was locked in the cell with her, he couldn't get to Oliver. She hoped Oliver would go to the police and get help. But if he did, how long would it be before they checked the farm? With Kaiser outside they couldn't get into the property, not without a dog handler. They could be locked away for days before that happened.

She looked at Len with utter contempt. She'd never before felt so much hatred for a human being. She'd never in all of her life had a bad thought towards anything or anyone. But now, she wished him dead.

She had to keep her cool though. The only way they were getting out was if they could work together somehow. She had to keep calm and focused if they were going to get free.

'So, what now?' she asked him, quietly.

Len lifted his head and stared at her, his beady eyes piercing through her as if he considered everything that had happened her fault and not his.

'What d'you mean?' he snapped. 'What can we do? We're trapped.'

'We must be able to get out somehow,' she said.

Still holding the machete, he pulled his knees up and folded his arms over them before resting his head. He looked like a child that'd been sent to his room for not eating his dinner.

Louise was beginning to get more and more angry.

'So, you're just going to give up?'

He lifted his head.

'Is that it?' she continued. 'You find yourself in a predicament, and you just give up?'

He stared at her. 'I'd keep quiet if I was you.'

She could feel her pulse racing and her body tensing. But she didn't want to prompt another attack, so she stayed quiet.

After a few minutes, Len got up and walked over to the window. He looked at it in silence, obviously weighing up his options.

The window had the crack across the middle of the pane, but even if he could get through the glass, there were the two large panels of wood he'd nailed across it from the outside. Louise thought he might be strong enough to push them off from the inside, but she remembered the sound of him knocking the nails into the panels, and there were lots of them. Something he was no doubt regretting at that very moment.

He wasn't doing anything. He wasn't trying to break the glass further, or trying to kick the door in again. He just stood there in deep thought.

Louise guessed he was weighing everything up. After all, he had a lot to lose. She wondered why he couldn't just break the window and try to knock the boards off from the inside? But she knew he must've been thinking of what would happen after that. If he got them out, what would he do then? Tie her up? Gag her? Knock her unconscious? Kill her? If he was to get them out, then he'd have to decide what to do with her afterwards.

'Can I ask you something?' Louise said.

He turned to look at her, still without speaking.

She felt nervous, but she still asked her question. 'Why have you built a prison cell in your house?'

His eyes widened. 'A prison cell?' he shouted. 'You think this is a prison cell?'

'Isn't it?' she answered.

'This was my...' he didn't finish his sentence. He looked as though he was trying to hold back tears.

He then leapt forward and grabbed her by the throat with his right hand, still holding the machete in his left.

Louise felt as though she was about to wet herself, but she fought hard not to let that happen. Partly because she didn't want to wet the bed, the only place she could sit comfortably, but also because she didn't want to give him the satisfaction of knowing how scared she was.

'Is that what you think of me? You think I'm the kind of man that builds a prison in his house to keep people captive?'

She struggled to breathe as he tightened his grip on her throat.

'This was my dad's bedroom,' he shouted before throwing her onto her side.

He started walking around the room, only this time, he kept his eyes on her as she sat herself up on the bed.

'He had dementia. He used to walk off and disappear in the night.'

She held her hands up as if to show an apology.

'I had to keep him in here sometimes because I couldn't watch him twenty-four hours a day.'

She nodded, still keeping her hands up.

'He would spend daytime with me, but if I didn't keep an eye on him...'

'OK,' she said. 'I understand.'

She didn't fully understand. This room was horrible. It was dark and dingy. She really hoped that Len's dad wasn't locked in here for too long. She understood how difficult it must've been looking after someone with dementia, especially on their own. But even though she could imagine how hard it was, surely, he could've taken the time to make the room a little nicer for him; a few pictures on the wall, a lick of paint, a few ornaments even. To Louise the room was a prison cell, it didn't feel any better than that. Even if she hadn't been trapped in there, she would still feel that way about it. She felt sorry for Len's father; but also, she felt a little sorry for Len.

18

'Two veal, one salmon, one sirloin,' a voice said. Only Vanni was looking at his phone again, and not really paying attention.

'Vanni,' Sarah shouted.

He stood up from leaning against the wall and put his phone on the shelf in the kitchen.

'Vanni, you need to get focused. She'll ring you back; don't worry.'

'OK,' he snapped.

Sarah ran the restaurant, even though Vanni was the owner and head chef. Sarah was somebody who'd worked for him when Nadia was alive, and she'd promised Nadia she'd look after him, and the restaurant, after she'd gone.

Vanni didn't always like the harsh way Sarah spoke to him. Most of the time she would be respectful, and she always knew how to keep the staff in line. But if ever Vanni wasn't firing on all cylinders, Sarah would make sure he got back on track. Some people might consider this behaviour as her not knowing her place, or even overstepping her bounds, but Vanni knew that finding a member of staff as committed as Sarah was a once in a lifetime thing. He certainly didn't want to manage the place without her. And he couldn't be annoyed with her for telling him off. After all, she was right. He had to get his mind focused on the busy Sunday afternoon shift. He couldn't keep stopping to check his phone, as tempting as it was.

Many of the customers presumed that Vanni and Sarah were a couple, even before Nadia had died. Vanni had a special relationship with Sarah. She was slim, blonde, and had a beautiful smile. But he never thought about her in any other way than as a friend and colleague.

Sarah shared an apartment with her partner, Rachel, a couple of doors down from the restaurant. So even on her nights off, she would still call in and check that everything was running smoothly. She and Rachel would sometimes have a meal there too, which Vanni knew was only so she could sample the food and service from a customer's point of view. Sarah definitely had the restaurant's best interests as her number one priority. And Vanni felt like a close second.

There had to be a reason why Louise was ignoring his calls. Perhaps she was worried at how quickly they seemed to be falling for each other. It scared him a little too. But that was OK. If she wanted to ease off, he understood completely. He didn't want to take things too fast anyway. It felt strange to him, the thought of being in a relationship with someone other than Nadia. He felt guilty, even though he knew he had no reason to feel this way. But the least she could do was to be honest with him. He'd bared his soul to her, and this was how she repaid him. He couldn't help but feel hurt.

'I'll say again; two veal, one salmon, one sirloin,' Sarah barked.

He jumped into action, grabbed a pan from the top of the cooker. But as he did, he lost his grip on it and it hit the floor with an almighty crash.

Vanni didn't look up from the floor, but he knew the rest of the kitchen staff were looking at him.

Sarah came around from the service side and took him gently by the shoulders.

As she walked him through the back door of the kitchen, she shouted 'Dave,' indicating that he should pick up the pan and carry on with the order.

As they got outside to the alley, Sarah gestured for Vanni to sit on the wall. This was where the staff who smoked would spend their breaks.

The back of the restaurant was just an alleyway where all the deliveries were made. There was nothing there but the bins, and a few empty crates from the bottle deliveries, and it was where Vanni parked his car.

Although it'd been a busy afternoon, the light was starting to fade so he knew the evening rush was about to start.

Sarah stood facing him.

He was in charge, and Sarah knew that. But that didn't mean he wasn't about to get it from her both barrels.

Sarah was only twenty-nine, but she'd learned fast and with her hospitality qualifications behind her, she knew the business well enough to run the restaurant, with or without Vanni.

'What's the problem?' she asked.

'Nothing,' he replied.

'It's not nothing,' she snapped. 'Your head's been in the clouds all day.'

'I'm just having an off day, that's all.'

He went to stand, but she put her hands on his shoulders and gently pushed him back down.

'Dave and Sunni can manage the service if you're not feeling good.'

'I'm feeling fine,' he said.

'Is this something to do with Louise?'

He looked at her. Nobody knew him better than Sarah. He didn't want to insult her by lying.

'What's the problem? She seemed like a really nice person. She was very friendly when you brought her here for a meal.'

'I know.'

'If you're feeling guilty...'

'It's not that,' he said, cutting her off.

'Well, what is it then?'

He took a deep breath as he wondered how much to tell her. But she wasn't just his member of staff, she was his friend too. He decided to tell her the truth.

'I spent the night with her,' he said. He then held his hand up as if to wave away any misinterpretation. 'Not in that way.'

She nodded, looking a little confused.

'She made us some supper on Friday. We stayed up all night talking. I fell asleep on her sofa and left early the next day. We kissed on the doorstep as I left, and she meant it.'

'OK,' Sarah said. 'So, what's the problem?'

'She won't answer my calls.'

'Maybe she's been busy,' Sarah said.

'She's kicking me into touch,' he answered.

'Well, look... if she's having second thoughts, just leave her and see if she contacts you. Don't chase her, because you'll push her away.'

Vanni rubbed his eyes with his finger and thumb.

'I know you're right, it's just...'

'It's just what?'

'We had an amazing night. We spoke for hours. I opened up to her in a way I haven't been able to with anyone since Nadia died.'

Sarah looked as though she was trying not to look offended, but then she gave a little smirk.

'Don't get me wrong, Sarah, you've been amazing. I couldn't have got through this without you. It's just that... it's easier talking to someone who didn't know Nadia; someone outside of the circle, you know?'

'I know what you mean,' Sarah said as she sat next to him on the wall.

'And she opened up to me. She's had her own tragedy. She lost her husband and she told me all about him, and everything she's gone through. She said she'd not been able to speak about those things with anyone else. We really had a connection. I don't know why she's ignoring me.'

'How many times have you texted her?'

'About four or five,' he said.

He then saw that Sarah was looking at him, waiting for the truth.

'Six or seven,' he said, smiling.

She smiled back.

'Nine or ten phone calls... and one visit to her house.'

Sarah laughed a little.

'I've blown it, haven't I?'

'Not necessarily,' she said. 'But don't try again tonight. She might be having second thoughts about being close with someone, and that's understandable, especially after everything she's been through. But if that is the case then chasing her won't help. Let her figure things out and she'll contact you. You just need to give her some space, that's all.'

'Really?'

'I bet you my week's wages against yours,' she said, holding out her hand.

Vanni smiled, and then shook it.

19

The light through the gaps in the wooden panels was fading. This frustrated Louise more as she realised the day was getting closer to ending, which meant another night for Oliver on his own. She guessed it was mid-evening. Maybe eight or eight-thirty.

Louise didn't think she could feel any more uncomfortable than she already did, but when Len sat on the bed, she felt a sudden rush of repulsion.

He didn't sit too close to her, and she moved closer to the wall to be as far away from him as possible, but she still felt as though she shouldn't be on the same bed as this man; or any man. Even though there was no chance of her falling asleep again, she still felt as though this was invading her personal space. A bed was somewhere you went to sleep, or to be on your own and escape the worries of the day. Who you shared your bed with wasn't a decision you took lightly. Until meeting Vanni, she couldn't have imagined sitting on a bed with anyone other than Michael or Oliver. But she would never have chosen to share a bed with Len Hunter; not if he was the last man on earth. And now he was there, only two or three feet away. The smell of his sweat and body odour made its way across the uncomfortable bed towards her. The bed that now suddenly seemed even more uncomfortable. She would rather sleep on the hard wooden floor than next to him. But she hoped to God that one way or another, she could get out of this cell before nightfall.

Len didn't look at her, he just sat there, staring at the floor, still holding the machete. Louise wondered if she could be ruthless enough to use it should he fall asleep. She hoped she would. In her mind, she had to do whatever necessary to get back to Oliver. But there was a problem with her plan. Even if she could get the machete from him, and slice his throat from ear to ear, it wouldn't change the fact that she was trapped. She had to work with him to get out of the cell first.

'I need to get back to my son,' Louise said.

He turned his head to look at her. After staring for a few seconds, he said, 'I know.'

She waited for more.

Finally, he said, 'There's nothing I can do.'

'We can't just give up. I broke the window with my heel. Maybe we should try to break it further.'

'I've boarded the outside. It isn't going to budge.'

'Is that it?' she asked.

'What do you mean?'

'Do you not think you can break through it, or do you not want to?'

He shook his head.

'If you're wondering about what happens next, we can make a deal.'

'Not interested,' he said.

'You might like it. And we've nothing else to do.'

He took a deep breath before saying, 'Shoot.'

260

'My house is on your land, isn't it? I pay you ground rent.'

'So?'

'So, I don't want to leave my house. How about, we make a deal that you don't charge me the fifteen pounds a year fee anymore? And you let me live my life there as I was before, and I won't say anything to anyone about... about what's happened.'

'And fifteen pounds a year is worth keeping quiet for? You must think I'm stupid.'

'It's not just that. If I go to the police and you get arrested, I might have to leave the house. Especially if you end up selling up. I want to stay there. This deal means I can.'

She didn't think that was true, and she didn't think he'd fall for it, but she had to start negotiations somewhere. And he was right. The first thing she would do once she was back with Oliver was to go to the police.

He didn't answer her and looked away.

'Well, how about this? We get out of here somehow, and I go back to Oliver while you make a run for it. You smashed my phone and I got rid of the landline after...' She stopped herself after realising she really didn't want to talk to him about Hemal. 'After I realised that I never used it.'

He stared at her now and she could see he was pondering.

'Even if I did go to the police, it would take me an hour to get there. I've no car, remember?'

He shook his head. After a moment of silence he said, 'I can't go back to prison.'

It scared her every time he mentioned that he'd been in prison before. She wasn't sure if she wanted to know why, but she did feel as though keeping the conversation going was the best plan. She had to try to connect with him if they were going to get out.

'What were you in for?' she asked.

The look on his face made her regret asking.

He didn't answer.

The silence seemed to go on forever. His head moved slowly from side to side. His jaw was twitching and he breathed heavily through his nose.

Louise was tempted to break the silence by telling him he didn't have to answer, but she didn't. She left him seething with anger. She didn't know if he was angry with her, or with himself, or maybe even with whoever put him away. But the temperature in the room definitely seemed to change.

Len stood and began to walk back and forth again, only this time he slapped the metal blade of the machete on his thigh as he moved.

'You're all the same,' he muttered.

'Excuse me?' she said.

'Women,' he yelled. 'You're all the same.'

He started to move faster.

Louise could see he was going into another rant so she pulled her legs up onto the bed and moved as far back towards the wall as she could.

'You all dress in that way, showing off your curves and your smooth skin. You plaster yourselves in makeup, you leave nothing to the imagination with your short skirts and low tops that barely cover anything. And the minute a man shows an interest, you turn away. You lead us on, but throw a hand in our face whenever we so much as look at you.'

Louise was terrified.

'You want to know why I was in prison?'

'No,' she said, doing her best to look away from him. 'I don't.'

'Well, I'll tell you!' he screamed. 'Because a tart like you pushed me away, that's why.'

Louise's heart was beating hard in her chest.

'Just because I tried it on with her, I was sent to prison. She was gagging for it and then when I tried to take things to the next level, she tried stopping me. Well, I'm a man. I have needs, and when it's gone that far you've no right to say no. And I'm the one who goes to prison.'

Louise wanted to be out of the room more than ever before. There was nothing she could do but stay on the bed and listen to his tirade.

'Who does she think she is? And who do you think you are?'

She looked up to see him throw the machete across the room before lunging towards her. He grabbed both her wrists and dragged her up off the bed. His hands were hot as his fingers dug into her. He held his face close to hers as he stared into her eyes.

263

'This is all your fault. You walk around over there in your house, you constantly look over here, you wear your slutty outfits and then... then when I just want to talk to you, you make this happen. Fucking women. You're all the same.'

He let go of her wrists and hit her hard on the side of her head, sending her flying to the floor. Before she could control her dizzying vision, he was on top of her, sitting on her hips as he grabbed her arms and flung them above her head.

Louise felt helpless. She didn't know what he was going to do. She now knew that this man was not only violent, but he was also a convicted rapist.

He stared at her, teeth clenched and lips parted, his breaths short and rapid. His eyes then slowly moved down her face towards her body.

Once his eyes were on her chest, Louise briefly glanced down to see her right breast had all but escaped from her blouse.

She shook her head quickly.

He looked back at her face and gave an evil grin. His face and eyes didn't look as though he was smiling, but his mouth was.

He then pulled both of her arms together and slammed them to the wooden floor, overlapping each other this time. He then pulled his left hand away, forcing extra weight down with his right hand to trap her wrists.

His left hand was now free as he continued to look her up and down. Louise could hardly breathe with the weight of him on her stomach. Even though he was skinny, he was strong, and heavy.

Louise felt another wave of sickness come over her. This disgusting man on top of her, looking her up and down like a delicious meal he wanted to devour. And his awful breath and body odour repulsed her. She could feel her stomach turning.

He rested a hand on her stomach, just below her breasts and slid his fingers towards her navel. But suddenly he stopped and fixed his eyes back on her face.

He removed his hand from her belly and sat back a little. This put more weight onto her hips, but she didn't mind because it meant his face was a little further away from hers.

'You'd like that wouldn't you?'

She didn't understand.

'You'd like it if I touched you so you could tell everyone. You could go to the police, tell them you've been assaulted or raped. That's what you want isn't it?'

He released the grip on her wrists, climbed off her and took a step back.

Louise sat up and pushed her chest back into her blouse.

'I'm not going to do it,' he shouted. 'You can tell people I asked you to come here, you can tell them I kept you here, but I didn't touch you. You're just like that other bitch. She wanted me to carry on. I did nothing wrong.'

He then leaned over her and yelled again, 'I did nothing wrong!'

She held her hands up as if to agree with him, but turned her head away. She certainly didn't agree with him, and she didn't want to know any more about what he'd done. Even though he protested his innocence, she was pretty sure he was guilty and deserved to go to prison.

'*You're all the same,*' he screamed once more, before turning to the door and kicking it as hard as he could, over and over again.

As he continued with this enraged outburst, Louise looked over to the machete that was lying on the floor next to the room with the toilet.

A torrent of expletives continued to pour from Len's mouth as he repeatedly kicked the door. But the door didn't budge.

With a rush of blood to her head, Louise stood and ran over to the machete.

She picked it up with both hands and held it out in front of her, and pointed it towards the crazed, raging madman.

After several more kicks, and the door not budging, he stopped and turned back towards the bed. Only he stopped halfway as he saw Louise standing in front of him with the large, rusty machete.

Although Louise was now the one in control, she felt more scared than she had been throughout the whole ordeal. Len just stood there breathing hard as if he'd been under water for the last three minutes. Louise expected him to look angry, or maybe even afraid.

She certainly wasn't expecting him to smile.

20

The machete didn't feel right in her hand. Especially now that Len was laughing at her. Louise suddenly felt weak, as though her legs were about to give way. But she knew she had to stand her ground. He was stronger, quicker and possibly much more merciless than her. But she had the weapon. She also had the desperation to get back to her son. Surely he knew that she'd be prepared to do whatever necessary to get back to Oliver. Although she felt weak, she would do whatever she had to, including bringing Len Hunter's life to an end. But the machete seemed to gain in weight as she held it out in front of her. She felt as though she could hardly hold it up. She knew it was down to the fear and sickness of what was happening to her, as well as her empty stomach.

Len feigned a step forward.

Louise waved the machete wildly at the space in front of her.

He smirked again.

She knew he was testing her, wondering how far she would go. She wasn't even sure of that herself. But she had to be strong.

He jumped forward again, this time bending down a little as he did.

She quickly moved her feet back, swinging the machete once more. Only this time, she almost caught his hand.

The evil smirk on Len's face changed to one of surprise. He obviously hadn't thought she would have the guts to use the machete. But now he knew. The first time she'd swung it, it was a reaction. The second time was to try and hurt him.

He jumped forwards once more, only this time, Louise bit her lip and swung the blade towards him more aggressively.

'Shit!' he shouted as the blade caught the back of his hand. He turned around and pushed his hands between his legs as he hopped up and down.

Louise felt a rush of euphoria at the fact that she'd summoned the courage to hurt him. Partly because she had managed to defend herself, but also because she felt that she might be gaining the upper hand.

'You bitch!' he screamed.

He stood up straight and stepped towards her.

'Don't even think about it,' Louise said, holding the blade up at his face.

He stopped. He wasn't laughing any more.

'I'm through with this,' she said. 'Take one more step towards me and I'll bring your life to an end.'

She didn't feel as though that was the best line she'd ever delivered, but she said it with enough conviction that it stopped him in his tracks.

Louise had to think fast. She needed to be out of here as quickly as possible. The longer they were in there, the more chance there was of Len finding a way of getting the machete from her.

'Right,' she started. 'Here's what's going to happen. You're going to get us out of this room, or I'm going to do you some real damage.'

Len was looking at his hand, which was bleeding quite badly. He stepped back and reached for the bedsheet. Still facing her, he lifted it and wrapped the corner around his hand. The dirty, white fabric instantly turned a dark shade of red.

'How do you expect me to get us out? We're locked in.'

'The window,' she said. 'You need to break it and knock the panels off.'

Thinking quickly, she continued. 'Drag the bed over to that side.'

He looked confused.

'Now!' she shouted.

He rolled his eyes.

'I'm not messing about,' she said.

Still holding the bedsheet in his fist, moving slowly, he grabbed the metal bedframe and pulled it hard. The metal legs of the bed scraped along the wooden floorboards. The noise was as torturous to Louise as the sound of fingernails scratching a blackboard, but she didn't stop him.

'Right in front of the window,' she said.

Once he'd finished, a breathless Len Hunter turned to her and said, 'Now what?'

'Climb onto the bed, and kick that window as hard as you were kicking the door.'

He shook his head. 'I won't be able to break the glass by doing that. And even if I could, I could slice my leg open.'

She took a step towards him, aware that she could be becoming too confident, which would no doubt suddenly change if he got the machete back from her.

She spoke quietly. 'Either you risk cutting your leg, or I'll cut the rest of you.'

He seemed to consider his options for a moment before giving in.

He climbed onto the bed, still grasping the bloody bedsheet with his hand. He then unravelled the sheet and let it fall to the bed. After balancing himself on the unsteady mattress, he lifted his right boot and thrust it at the window while holding onto the metal headboard of the bed. The glass panel, already cracked diagonally by Louise's heel, didn't move.

He kicked again. The crack stretched a little further, but the panel still didn't give way.

Len kicked over and over again, not quite with the same rage he'd attacked the door with, but it still looked as if he was trying as hard as he could while attempting to stay on the bed.

The crack had finally made its way to each corner of the panel, but it still didn't give way. Out of breath, Len jumped down and sat on the edge of the bed. 'It's no good. It isn't budging.'

Louise was annoyed, but she could see how hard it was to kick the window with full force.

'You can't just give up,' she said. 'We're going to die in here.'

That sentence sounded a little far-fetched as it left her lips, but it was possible. They had no food. And although they had water from the sink in the tiny bathroom to keep them alive, it was only a matter of time before one of them killed the other.

'I have a delivery coming on Tuesday. We can shout and hope the driver comes to let us out.'

'Tuesday is ages away. And don't forget your dog is on the loose. He wouldn't get past him.'

Len didn't answer.

Louise moved a little closer to him.

'Get up and try again,' she said.

'I'm losing blood here,' he shouted, showing her his hand.

The gash did look painful, but it shouldn't have been enough to slow him down.

'I don't care. We're getting out of this room now.'

He shook his head as he gave a short laugh.

'You think this is funny?' she snapped.

He smiled, showing his horrible, dirty teeth.

'You trick me into coming into your house, you assault me, you keep me prisoner, and you think it's fucking funny?'

He wrapped his hand in the sheet again then moved back onto the bed as if to get himself more comfortable.

This infuriated her. 'Stand up,' she shouted.

He held out his uninjured hand. 'OK,' he shouted back. 'I will in a minute. I'm just feeling a little light-headed.'

'The cut isn't that bad.'

'It's not just that. I'm hungry. And I haven't had a drink for ages.'

She understood what he was saying. She felt that way herself. But she had to keep control. If she let him just sit there relaxing, then he'd continue to disobey her.

'I don't care. You need to do as I say, when I say it. Do you understand me?'

'I understand you. But it doesn't make a difference. We *are* going to die in here.'

Even though she was fully aware of their predicament, hearing someone say it, even a monster like Len Hunter, made her feel weak at the knees.

It momentarily crossed her mind to give up, even pass the machete back to him and sit there waiting for death. But she had to keep going, for Oliver, and also for herself.

'So you just give up?'

'I feel like that's the best option.'

'Well, I'm not giving up.'

He smirked again. 'You will.'

'What?' she asked.

'You will give up. I can see the energy draining from you. You're trying to act tough with the blade in your hand. But you haven't got much left.'

'You don't know that,' she said, shaking her head, feeling more and more anger at this pathetic man, who didn't even deserve to be referred to as a man.

'I do.'

'I've got a lot more fight left in me,' she said.

'Who are you trying to convince, me or yourself?'

'I'm not done by a long shot.'

'You are,' he said.

Louise didn't know what the point of his argument was, but she felt herself getting more and more angry. Her chest rose as she took deep breaths through her nose. She didn't understand why he was trying to bait her.

She could picture herself jumping onto the bed and swinging the machete at him over and over again, like a scene from a horror movie. But she resisted the urge to do so. Possibly because she didn't want to become a murderer. Or maybe because she wasn't sure if she had the strength to succeed before he took the machete off of her.

'I'm not done,' she said through clenched teeth. 'And you aren't either, so get up, now.'

'We will be trapped in here until we die.'

'No,' she said.

He jumped forwards and perched on the edge of the bed, as if he was testing her reactions, but she stood firm.

'You were right before,' he said. 'The delivery man won't get past Kaiser. And the human body can survive for weeks without food as long as there's water. But you know what it can't survive for long without?'

'What?'

He leaned closer towards her.

'Sleep.'

21

The silence in the room was deafening to Louise. After Len had pointed out to her that at some point, she would have to sleep, that was all she could think about.

She was exhausted. She'd never felt so tired, and weak. Although she'd slept a little, she knew her body and her mind needed much more than she'd had so far. Not only had she missed out on sleep once she'd become Len's prisoner, but she'd also missed out on most of Friday night's quota when Vanni came to spend the evening with her; the evening that went onto Saturday morning.

Although it was a magical night, Louise knew she would have to catch up, and she would've most likely done so Saturday night. But now, as Sunday evening drew to a close and the darkness showed through the gaps in the wooden panels, she could feel herself losing the battle.

She'd jumped up from the bed several times to walk around the room, trying to fight the urge to drift off. And the thought of her sleeping in the same room as Len Hunter both scared and repulsed her.

Len seemed to be settling down for the night himself as he lay slumped against the wall at the other end of the bed.

Louise wondered if Len had maybe struggled to sleep the previous night. She wondered if the stress of keeping somebody in a home-made prison cell was quite tiresome.

As well as him having to keep an eye out for any police officers turning up, and making sure nobody came snooping around the property.

Louise knew this was typical of her. Even in an extreme situation like this, she still put herself in other people's shoes. Not that she cared what happened to Len, or what stress or torment he was experiencing. But she did still see things from his point of view, and she knew he would've been on edge all night, possibly even causing him to have a bout of insomnia.

She could see him fighting the urge to fall asleep. Even though he was the one that pointed out to her that sleep was essential – no doubt revelling in the joy of causing more nervousness and fear for her – he must've been getting tired himself. He was obviously hinting that she wouldn't be safe if she fell asleep, and that was how she felt. He would certainly take the machete back from her if he could. But after an hour or two of uncomfortable silence, and him sporadically jumping as he momentarily fell asleep, his head finally slumped to one side as his breathing changed into long deep breaths.

Louise wondered if him being asleep was a good time to try and escape somehow, but she knew he would wake up if she even got up from her end of the bed.

After a few minutes of listening to him breathing, Louise decided to close her eyes, just for a second. That's all she needed, just to rest her eyes.

Within seconds, she'd drifted off to sleep.

22

Monday 3rd May

As Louise woke up, her stomach flipped as she looked quickly around the room. Waking up in the cell wasn't too much of a surprise as she'd dreamt about the situation. And she was pretty sure she'd had a dream where she was trying to find Oliver.

Amazingly, the machete was still in her grip, so even though she'd slept, she must've still been aware of where she was.

As she looked over to her left, she saw that Len was already awake, and was stretching while sat on the edge of the bed. When she looked to the right, she could see light making its way through the gaps in the boards. She must've slept for at least six hours she thought. But she wasn't sure. She wasn't even certain what day it was, but she guessed it was Monday.

Louise got up from the bed and went into the toilet room to drink some water straight from the tap, scooping it towards her mouth with her left hand as she held the machete in her right. She then walked back into the room.

It crossed Louise's mind that she could bring Len's life to a sudden end by swinging the machete across his neck as he sat there perched on the end of the bed. That would take the smug look off his face. It would also solve the problem of being stuck in the room with this horrible excuse of a man. The only problem was, she didn't think she could get out of the room without his help, and she also didn't like the thought of not only witnessing, but causing a horrific wound to another human being, even if he did deserve it.

She continued to hold the blade out in front of her, pointing it towards him. It felt heavier than it had before, but she still held it up.

She felt repulsed at the thought of sleeping in a room with such a disgusting man, a man who'd been in prison for rape. She couldn't believe she had slept, but she had, and amazingly, Len hadn't woken up in the time she was asleep. But now she had to start thinking about getting out of the room once more, and getting back to Oliver.

She was ready to get things moving.

'You are going to stand up now,' she said, calmly, maintaining eye contact at all times. 'Then you are going to kick that window until it shatters.'

'Or what?' he asked.

'Or I'm going to slit your throat from ear to ear.' She'd previously heard this sentence in her head, but it sickened her to say it out loud. And she didn't know if she'd said it with enough conviction for him to believe her. There was a huge difference between catching the back of his hand in self-defence and making a deliberate attempt at killing him by aiming for his throat.

He smiled again, which made her feel sick, as it did every time he smiled, or grinned.

'You wouldn't,' he said, before looking down at his hand that still looked wet with blood, and adjusting the bedsheet.

'You don't know what I'm capable of,' she said, doing her best to convince him she was serious. 'And you haven't considered how far a mother would go to protect her child. Believe me, you don't want to try me on this. You really don't know me at all.'

Louise held the machete higher, but stepped back a little to keep a distance between them. She knew the weapon was shaking, but she still looked him in the eye, trying her best to keep control.

There was a rattling noise outside she thought was rain. Her first thought was how she longed to be able to go outside and stand in it.

'That's where you're wrong,' he shouted, jumping up from the bed, still smiling.

'I do know you, Louise,' he said, taking another step towards her.

She tried her best not to, but she couldn't help but swallow.

'I know you very well. In fact, I even know your phone number off by heart.'

Louise was confused at this. She took another step away from him as he slowly said each number of her landline.

Once he'd finished reciting the number, she said, 'How do you know that?'

'How do you think I know?' he snapped.

He took another step closer to her.

'How do you think I'm able to say your phone number out loud, without having to read it? How do you think that number has stayed in my head so easily?'

It suddenly hit her. She knew why Len Hunter knew her number by heart. Suddenly, everything fell into place.

'Because you've rang it lots of times,' she said, quietly.

He nodded. 'I have.'

Louise couldn't believe what she was hearing.

'I know your number because I dialled it over... and over... and over again; from three different phone boxes.'

She shook her head as she took another step away from him, only for him to move towards her. She was very aware that her back was getting closer to the wall.

He stopped. After a moment of silence, he burst out laughing. Still holding the bedsheet around his hand that draped from the bed and onto the floor, he moved back and forth as he laughed, sporadically bending over as he did.

'And you blamed the stupid Paki boy,' he said, in between laughs.

Louise shuddered at his ignorance and bigotry, but was too shocked to scold him for it.

'It was perfect. I'd been phoning you for months, and you got the village idiot arrested. It was brilliant.'

She couldn't believe it. She remembered thinking at the time that it could've been Len. But every time she saw Hemal Kharti, he stared at her in the way he always did, and when she saw him in the woods behind her house, she presumed she'd caught her stalker in the act. Mrs Kharti said he was innocent. Louise hadn't believed her, even after she'd helped her by chasing away the idiots that had pulled their car up next to her. Louise not only felt guilty for blaming Hemal, but she now felt even more disgusted at the fact that she was trapped in the room with the man who held her captive, but also the man who'd constantly phoned her. He rang all hours of the day and night, breathing heavily and making disgusting noises, to the point where she had to remove the landline and get the police involved. Another feeling of nausea came over her when she remembered that Oliver answered the phone once. The caller she now knew was Len, had shouted at him to *put that bitch on the phone.* Oliver was far too young to be shouted at viciously like that. Yes, he was resilient, and he'd put it out of his mind a day or so after the phone call, but it was still something he shouldn't have experienced.

Louise was livid. She also owed Hemal Kharti and his family a huge apology. But first she had to deal with Len Hunter, who she now knew was not only her captor, but also her stalker.

She held out the machete towards him. She was frozen with anger as the silence – other than Len still sniggering – went on for a good few minutes.

She could feel her temper taking over her and she pulled the machete above her head.

'You bastard,' she shouted. She was raging, not caring where it hit him as long as it did hit him, when a sudden

loud bang scared her, stopping her before she swung. It was so loud and booming that the room shook.

She dropped the machete. It landed on the floor in between them.

As the seconds went by, she realised it must've been thunder.

Len then obviously realised the same thing as he shot his gaze down to the floor.

They then both leapt towards the machete at the same time.

Her hands gripped the handle just before Len's did. They struggled back and forth as they fought for the weapon. Louise was on her knees as Len crouched over her, trying hard to get her to release the machete from her hands.

He swung her around, partly lifting her from the floor. She landed on her back as he knelt on her stomach. The pain was excruciating as the breath left her lungs. She couldn't breathe, and she was in agony, but she refused to let go of the handle, still holding it with both hands.

He slammed her hands against the solid wood of the floor, over and over as she kicked her legs and tried to twist her hips as he was sat on top of her. The pain was almost unbearable, but it was nothing compared to the pain in her stomach as he knelt on top of her with his full weight pressing down.

Eventually, it was too much to bear, and she loosened her grip. The machete spun away, but Len hadn't realised as he slammed her empty hands down to the floor. As soon as he did realise, he leaned over and grabbed it. He then held the blade against Louise's throat.

She instantly went from violently kicking her legs and writhing her body, to staying perfectly still as she felt the cold metal dig into her neck.

She couldn't breathe. Not just with the weight of him on top of her, but also because she didn't want her skin to press onto the blade any more than necessary.

After a moment of lying there completely frozen, she gave a small cough, and started to breathe short gasping breaths.

'I could end this right now,' he hissed. 'One quick move and your boy would never see you again.'

That was the worst thing Louise had heard him say so far. She didn't respond; she couldn't if she tried. Feeling the rusty, metal blade, and knowing he could stop her ever being reunited with Oliver with one quick motion, sickened her to her very soul.

Another loud thunderclap shook the room, but this time neither of them flinched. But then, Len lifted the machete and to Louise's relief, he climbed off her and sat on the floor by her side. He still looked angry, but he just sat there.

Louise lay still. Her chest rose and fell as her lungs tried hard to make up for the lack of oxygen.

After a minute or so, she sat up on the floor, facing away from Len. She adjusted her clothes to make sure she was still all in place. She'd survived another ordeal, but she was also aware that she was still trapped in the cell.

The floor was uncomfortable, so she slowly got up and walked over to the bed and sat down. The bloodied bedsheet that lay crumpled on the floor gave her a small amount of satisfaction – that he'd lost so much blood, and was still bleeding.

Although she needed him to help get out of the room, she started to feel as though she'd be better off without him. Maybe if he did collapse through loss of blood, she'd be able to concentrate on the job in hand without having to keep one eye on him all the time.

'I've had enough of this,' he said.

Louise looked at him. His gaze was fixed on the floor as he shook his head slowly from side to side.

'I never meant for this to happen. And I never wanted to be like this.'

Louise didn't want to get into any more conversations, but she felt as though she was about to be dragged into one.

'I was a good boy when I was younger,' he said, looking up at her. 'Just like your boy... Oliver.'

Louise wanted to jump up and hit him just at the thought of him comparing himself to Oliver. They were nothing like each other. There was no way that Len Hunter hadn't shown signs of being a problem child at age ten. He must've had some weird predispositions or attributes that would lead him to be the person he was today. He must've picked on other children at school, or teased the girls, pushing or pinching them. He must've pulled the wings off flies or broken birds' eggs by throwing stones at them, or even climbed trees to dislodge their nests. He must've laughed when he saw an old person fall over, or have had a penchant for watching violence, or maybe even taking part in the violence. Or he must've thought it was funny when a school pet died, or maybe he'd even indirectly killed the pet himself by sneaking it some food that he knew would cause its demise.

Louise didn't believe a person could just turn evil later in life. Evil could possibly be taught or trained, but a person like Len Hunter must've been born that way. He must possess the evil gene possibly inherited from other members of his family.

His father was a decent man. Surely there was no way he'd abused or beaten Len. Of course, Louise didn't know this for sure, but she would be surprised if she found out that Len's father wasn't the perfect parent to him. He had always come across like a calm and patient gentleman; quite the opposite of Len.

'I never wanted this to happen,' Len said. 'I just wanted to be happy; have a nice wife to share my life with, help me on the farm, enjoy evenings together in front of the telly.' He then looked up from the floor. 'Is that too much to ask?' he bellowed.

Louise didn't answer him, and she wasn't really listening. She had no interest in getting drawn into this discussion, and she had no interest in trying to make him feel better. But while he was talking, and as she lay recovering from the pain and torment he'd caused, she'd come up with a plan to try and get out of the room. But she would almost certainly need Len's help.

23

Bank holiday Mondays were usually very busy in the restaurant, but Vanni knew that because the nice weather was coming to an end, and Sunday was very busy, today might not be as successful. People seemed to be in more of a rush to leave the house when the weather was brighter. Sunday afternoons were a good moneymaker when the sun was shining. But on a bank holiday where the weather wasn't good, he could never predict how the day was going to be.

He was a little embarrassed about how he'd behaved the previous day, but Sarah's pep talk got him back on track. He was still upset about being blanked by Louise, but he'd tried his best to switch his mind off from it and concentrate on his livelihood.

He stopped preparing for a second just to check his phone; after all, he hadn't looked at it for an hour or so. But there were no messages or missed calls, so he put it back on the shelf.

'I saw that,' Sarah said, walking into the room with an espresso.

He smiled. 'Just checking.'

She handed him the cup and said, 'Do you want to get some fresh air?'

'I do,' he said. He then turned to the rest of the staff and said, 'Won't be a minute.'

They would always get in early and start the preparations way before the restaurant opened, so he knew they had plenty of time. In some ways Vanni enjoyed that time of day more than once they were open. *Setting the stall out,* Nadia used to say. He also found it a little more relaxing before the service would start. And there would be more time to chat to the staff, and maybe even have a laugh before the seriousness of looking after the customers began.

Once outside, they both sat on the wall as he drank his coffee.

'So,' Sarah started. 'You pulled it together well yesterday.'

'Thanks. And thanks for giving me a kick. I think I needed it.'

She smiled and squeezed his forearm gently. She then said, 'Do me a favour.'

'What's that?'

'Tell me again what happened with you and Louise.'

He was confused. 'Why?'

'Something's been bugging me, and I was thinking about it last night. Just tell me what happened.'

He took another sip of his drink. 'She made us both some supper on Friday night, which was the third time I'd seen her. We ate at her house with a glass of wine; only one because I was planning on driving home. And we stayed up most of the night talking. The next day she never answered her phone.'

'Was it switched off?'

'Not at first. It kept going to answerphone. Then as the day went on, she switched it off. I think she switched it off mid-ring at one point.'

'And did you say you went there?'

'Yes. Yesterday. Her car wasn't there, and there was nobody home.'

'And you said that Friday night felt like... I don't know... a special night?'

He bowed his head and looked at the ground. 'It really was. We told each other everything. We didn't sleep together, but it was a really special night. She hung on my every word, and I did the same when she told her story.'

'And what about in the morning?'

'She wanted me out of the house before Oliver woke up, which I understood. Although we both admitted to feeling close to each other, it was still too soon for me to meet her son.'

Sarah turned to face him, and looked a little more serious. 'This is important.'

'OK,' Vanni said.

'Did she kiss you goodbye?'

'Yes. Quite a delicate kiss. I'd even go so far as to say a loving kiss. Obviously, we're a long way off using the word love, but that was how it felt. She wanted me through the door, but once we were outside, she didn't seem to want to let go.'

'What I mean is, did she initiate the kiss?'

Vanni pictured it clearly in his mind. At first when she was rushing him out of the house, he thought she was having second thoughts about them. But the way she kissed him outside, he knew that wasn't the case. 'She did. She kissed me.'

Vanni could see Sarah thinking, but he didn't know what she was getting at.

'Why are you asking?'

'It was in my mind for most of the shift, and last night. It doesn't make sense.'

'I'm as baffled as you are. I thought we had something special. I know it's early days, but still. It certainly felt special.'

'Look, don't take this the wrong way,' she started.

'OK,' he said.

'But you are a real catch.'

He couldn't help but be flattered.

'You are unbelievably handsome, you own your own restaurant, and you are always a perfect gentleman.'

'Thank you,' he said, blushing a little.

'From what you told me about that night, and how I saw her when she was here in the restaurant with you, something isn't right.'

'What d'you mean?'

'She never took her eyes off you. Believe me, I know when a woman is falling for someone, and that's what I saw that night. And she shouldn't have cold feet just because you spent all night talking. And if she did have second thoughts, you'd have known that morning. She wouldn't have kissed you when you left the house.'

'Really?'

'Really. I've witnessed morning-after regrets, and that's not what you're describing.'

'So, what are you saying?'

She bit her lip and looked away for a second, as though she wasn't sure whether to say what was in her mind or not.

After a few seconds, she looked him in the eye again before saying, 'I think something might've happened.'

24

Louise walked away from the bed and made her way over to the wall opposite from Len.

He was still talking to her, but she'd stopped listening. The idea that had jumped into her mind could be a good one, but she had to back up to the wall so she could see the bed in full view to try to see if it would work or not. She really hoped it would.

'I just want to be happy...' Len continued, but Louise didn't care.

She began to examine the metal-framed bed.

The bars at the head end of the bed rose up from the mattress by about two feet. At the opposite end, the bars only reached above by about a foot. At the head end, there were three bars going from side to side, but the upright bars at each corner stretched above the cross bars by a few inches.

The bed frame was metal, probably steel, as were the bars, which were the same all the way around the bed, and they were a good three inches thick at least. The top of each side-bar was domed, but it still looked strong, strong enough to break the glass, she thought.

She looked at the length of the bed as Len continued to talk about himself. If they stood the bed on its end and swung it towards the window, it would almost certainly break the glass, and possibly even the wooden boards.

She didn't know whether to tell him her idea and see if he would help, or to concentrate on getting the machete back and making him do it on his own.

'My friends... they never stayed in touch...' he rambled. His speech seemed to be slurring a little, possibly through tiredness, she thought, or maybe through the loss of blood.

'And... and I never had many anyway, living this far from the town.'

Louise shook her head. She was starting to get even more angry with him. He'd tricked her, and kept her prisoner, and now he wanted her sympathy. That wasn't going to happen.

'So my best friend was my dad really...'

'Shut your fucking mouth,' Louise said, softly. It scared her as the words left her lips. It was almost like she had Tourette's as the sentence slipped subconsciously from her. These were words she wouldn't normally use, and she certainly wouldn't assert her dominance in such a way, not before now. She felt her anger taking over her.

Len stopped and looked at her. He looked both hurt and surprised at what she'd said.

'What did you say?' he said.

She took a step towards him. He was in charge, and he had the machete, but she could either apologise and retreat into her shell, or she could stand up for herself. She felt the blood rush to her head.

'I said, shut your fucking mouth, you pathetic piece of shit.'

He started to get up from the floor, but she put her hands on his shoulders and pushed him onto the bed before he could stand up straight, ignoring the machete in his grip.

His confused expression looked almost comical as he stared up at her.

'Don't you dare get up,' she said a little louder. 'You trick me into coming into your house, you attack me, you keep me prisoner here...' Her voice was getting louder and louder. 'You leave my son on his own, and then you sit there like a snivelling child expecting me to feel sorry for you.'

'I wasn't expecting you to...'

'Shut up!' she shouted. 'I'm talking and you will listen.'

He sat like a child being scolded by his mother, his mouth wide open in disbelief.

'You expect me to listen to you moaning and complaining at how bad your life is, but it's all down to you. It's you that didn't learn how to get on with other people. It's you that raped that girl. It's you that stalked me, and it's you that caused this situation.' She leaned over him as she shouted. 'So, don't sit there complaining to me about how badly the world has treated you when it's *all your fault.*'

He was silent. Louise thought he'd accepted his scolding. But then, his head started to move from side to side. His hands were shaking, blood seemed to be dripping from the cut once more. His jaw twitched. But Louise didn't care. She was in the middle of her own maniacal outburst and was too angry to calm down, and too angry to be scared.

'You bitch,' he whispered.

He leapt up, but as he got to his feet his skin turned completely white.

Louise stepped back and watched as the machete fell from his hand and bounced on the wooden floor. Within seconds of it landing, Len's eyes rolled backwards in his head, and his body collapsed like a puppet that'd had its strings cut.

He lay on the floor in a heap with his arms spread out, and his legs folded in what looked like an uncomfortable position.

This was Louise's chance to take back control.

She picked up the machete. She then leaned over Len with the idea of tying him up with his own belt. But unfortunately, he wasn't wearing one. So she undid one of his boot laces. They were tattered and torn, and probably ten years old, but she still went ahead with her plan. After unthreading them, she pulled his hands together and wrapped the lace around his wrists and quickly tied it in a knot. She would've tied it over and over, but he started to stir and groan, so once would have to do.

She kicked the machete across the room towards the toilet door. Next, she then dragged the bed by the head end and pulled it into line with the window. It was heavy, but she managed to move it.

Another groan came from Len, but she didn't look. She just concentrated on what she was doing.

She grabbed the bed by the bottom bar and lifted it from the floor.

It took all her strength to lift it above her head. She screamed as she pushed it into the air like a weightlifter. But as she held it above her head, she couldn't go any further.

Her legs shook and her knees turned to jelly. She knew she had to move her hands further down the underside of the bed to lift it onto its end, but she was neither tall enough, nor strong enough, to do so. So, she stepped back and let it crash to the floor.

The metal legs made a deafening sound as they landed. But Len remained unconscious.

Louise didn't know what to do. She couldn't lift the bed on her own, not high enough for it to topple over and fall onto the window. She needed Len's help, but she knew he didn't really want them to get out. As tired and as hungry as he was, he knew that if they managed to get out, then she'd be free to tell the police what he'd done.

Louise slowly walked around the room wondering what to do next. Even though she'd tied Len's wrists together, she knew he'd still be trouble once he'd woken up. He'd lost enough blood to cause him to lose consciousness, but maybe not enough to disable him completely.

As this thought entered her head, she decided to give it another try and grabbed the bed by the bottom bar again.

This time she put all her anger into it, screaming as she dragged it up from the floor. Once she held it above her head, she paused, taking several quick, deep breaths. She felt her cheeks expanding as she sucked air in and out of her lungs.

She could see the wooden slats of the underside of the bed above her head. She knew she had to transfer her hands one at a time to try to work her hands down the bed, which in turn would lift the bed more vertically until it fell in the opposite direction. But this meant she'd be holding the ridiculously heavy bed in one hand. It would only be for a millisecond, but that could be long enough for her to lose her grip, and she really didn't want the bed landing on top of her.

'What... what the hell you doin'?' she heard Len murmur.

As she stood there with one end of the bed held above her head, she couldn't stop from shaking. She turned her head to look over her shoulder and saw Len sitting up on the floor, looking down at his wrists.

'Help me,' she said.

'What's that?' he muttered.

'Help me,' she said, louder this time.

She couldn't focus on him fully, but from the corner of her eye, she saw the shape of him stand up and stagger closer towards her.

'You want me to help you?' he asked.

'Yes,' she said. 'I can't do it on my own.'

Her legs were shaking more and more. She felt as though she could pass out at any moment. Len didn't look as though he was about to help.

'Are you really trying to flip the bed over so it crashes through the window?' he said, a little more coherently this time.

'Yes. Now help me.'

'No,' he said. 'You're on your own.'

An overwhelming sense of rage flowed through her veins. She'd never felt as angry as she did at that moment.

'You piece of shit,' she shouted.

As she heard him laugh, she put all her fury into pushing the bed higher. She screamed as she began to move her hands one at a time onto the wooden slats.

The bed gradually became more and more upright. She pushed again and the bed rose further.

As she reached six or seven slats in, she lowered her head beneath the metal bar of the bed frame. As she did this, a creaking came from the wooden slats, which then turned into a loud cracking sound. The bed crashed down to the floor. Louise was almost knocked over by the force, but as she steadied herself, she realised that the wooden slats, which were bound to each other by cotton strips, had broken away from the frame.

She stood there with the strips of wood held above her head, the mattress falling against her and the bed frame back on the floor. She felt relief that she was no longer supporting the heavy, metal bed, but she could've cried at the fact that she'd failed to tip it over and break the window.

The loud crash of the metal legs hitting the floor was overtaken by the sound of Len Hunter laughing.

Standing inside the bedframe, still holding the slats and the mattress above her head, she turned to shout at him, intending to tell him exactly what she thought of him. But then she saw, with his wrists still tied together in front of him, he was holding the machete once more.

25

It was time. Louise had had enough. She almost didn't care anymore. She did care. She wanted to be back with Oliver. But everything she'd tried had failed. And yet again, Len Hunter seemed to have the upper hand. Even though he was weak from his injured hand and loss of blood. Even though he had his wrists bound together with his own boot lace, he still stood there holding the machete, taking control of her once more. Louise just wanted it all to end. Even if that meant her being hurt or even killed. One way or another, it had to stop.

'I'm done,' she said, dropping the mattress and the wooden slats as she climbed out from the bed frame.

Len tilted his head to one side and frowned.

'This ends now,' she said and walked over to him, trying her best show an air of confidence. She thought she was succeeding, by the look of bewilderment on his face and the way he was pointing the machete at her. But this time she wasn't acting, this was how she really felt. She'd had enough.

Once there, she stood in front of him, so close that the weapon's sharp point was touching her stomach. She kept her eyes on his, the smell of him in her nostrils once more.

She saw him swallow.

'You are going to put the knife down, and help me lift the bed and drop it through the window.'

She knew it was a machete and not a knife. But she also knew that the shorter the sentence, the more impact it would have.

He swallowed again and shook his head, then took a step back and said, 'I can't.'

'What?' she asked.

After a second or two of silence, he finally said, 'I can't because...'

She lifted her head as if to tell him to continue.

He took a deep breath. 'Because this can't end well for me.'

Louise didn't care how it ended for him. She didn't care about him at all. She just had to get out of the cell and home to Oliver.

'Whatever happens, however we get out, I'm finished.'

'I don't care,' she said.

'It's OK for you. You can go back to your life and your son. But I can't. You know I made the phone calls, and you'll tell the police about being kept here. I either kill you and try my best to not get caught, or I let you go and I spend the rest of my life in prison.'

Louise shook her head. 'You snivelling piece of shit.'

He looked offended as she continued.

'You pathetic waste of life. You pitiful excuse for a human being.'

Her anger was building. She'd given him a verbal attack before, but the gloves were coming off this time, even though he still held the blade close to her.

'You are the most pathetic, disgusting useless creature I've ever met. And before, you had the nerve to start pouring your heart out to me.'

'I was just stating the facts,' he snapped.

'No, you weren't,' she shouted. 'You've painted yourself into a corner and you don't know how to get out.'

He looked angry again, but she didn't care. The gloves were definitely off.

'Well, I don't care how you feel and I don't care what happens to you, I'm getting out of here right now.'

She stomped over to the head of the bed and lifted it again, only this time she held it at her waist as she looked over to Len.

'Help me,' she said.

He shook his head.

'Help me,' she said a little louder.

He still didn't move. She wasn't used to asserting herself, but she wasn't prepared to give up.

'Come and help me,' she screamed at him, but he still didn't move.

Louise lost her temper and dropped the bed, letting it slam hard like it had before.

As she stepped towards him to continue the onslaught, she heard a noise close to where the bed had crashed down. It sounded like a coin landing and rolling across the floor.

Louise turned back to the bed to see what it was. A bolt was rolling back and forth on the floorboards.

She walked around to the head of the bed and saw the hole where it had come from. Not only that, but the other bolts that held the bed together looked a little loose. She'd either not noticed this before or they'd slackened loose when she'd dropped the bed to the floor, which she realised she done three or four times by now.

She crouched down and started to undo all the bolts. She didn't need any tools to do this, she could do it by hand as they were all loose.

'What are you doing?' she heard Len ask, but she didn't reply, she just carried on undoing them.

Once she'd taken the bolts out, the metal bar that reached across the back of the bed fell down to the floor. It was the same length as the width of the bed, about three feet.

Louise picked it up. It was heavy, but not too heavy to swing. She placed it on the floor and began to drag the rest of the bed frame away from the window, with the wooden slats and mattress trailing on the floor.

Once there was a gap of around four feet or so between the bed and the window, she picked up the bar and took it over to the window.

'Listen, I can't let you...'

'Shut up!' she snapped. The look on her face must've shown she meant business because he stopped talking mid-sentence.

It momentarily entered her mind that even though he was the man and she the woman, and even though he still held the machete in his grip, suddenly she was the more dominant one, and he the submissive. She hoped it would stay that way. His wrists were still tied together, but she really wished she'd tied them behind his back and not in front. Not that that was possible the way he'd fallen when he'd passed out. But she knew the laces wouldn't hold him if he went into another rant, or a fit of rage.

She held the bar, one hand at the bottom and one half way up. She could almost taste freedom. She thought about Oliver, still hoping to God that he was OK.

The rain still poured down outside, but there hadn't been any more thunder or lightning for a while. The storm or the rain didn't bother her. She partly hoped it would be still raining when she finally got out of the room. She'd be happy to let the rain wash away what had been happening to her for the last two days.

She took a deep breath and then swung the metal bar at the window creating a deafeningly loud bang.

The single crack that already ran across the pane was suddenly joined by others. Confidence boosted by this, she swung again and again. By the time the bar had hit the window five times, the whole panel of glass was completely covered by cracks. Although the window still remained in its place.

She stopped and took a deep breath, the last few days' events still shooting through her mind. Almost like her life was flashing before her eyes, she pictured Oliver in the bungalow on his own, shivering with fear in the corner of his bedroom. She closed her eyes and put everything she had into the force of the swing.

The bar felt different this time. It didn't bounce back off the window, but instead went straight through, shattering the glass into a million pieces.

Without pausing to take in what had just happened, she held her hand over the end of the bar and slammed the opposite end against the wooden panels that Len had nailed to the outside of the window.

After hitting the board four times, one side came away, and a couple of hits at the opposite side knocked it off altogether. She did the same with the top panel and after several hits at each side, that panel flew off the frame too and landed on the wet ground outside.

She stood for a few seconds, the feeling of freedom rushing throughout her body as she watched the rain fall down hard outside.

She felt the cool breeze hit her, but more importantly, she took in the view of the bungalow to the right.

It felt as though she'd just reached the top of a mountain. She was overcome with relief, but she still couldn't allow herself to feel any level of euphoria until she knew Oliver was OK.

After dropping the bar to the floor, which was now covered by broken glass, she turned and pulled the bed back to the window.

Still barefoot, and wishing for shoes or trainers, she picked up the bar, stood on the bed frame and then climbed up onto the sill after brushing the broken glass away with her hand. But just before she hopped through the window, something caught her eye.

It was Len. He was crouched down and at first, she thought he'd passed out again, but then she realised what he was doing. He was kneeling down on the floor with the handle of the machete trapped between his knees, rubbing the lace that bound his wrists together against the upturned blade. Within seconds, the lace gave way.

Louise could tell by the look on his face that his episode of feeling sorry for himself had come to an end. His jaw was clenched and his chest moved up and down as he stood and took a step towards her.

She didn't wait to see the second step, she just leapt through the window and onto the wet ground, still grasping onto the bar.

Broken glass digging into the soles of her feet, but this wasn't going to stop her, as painful as it was.

She ran away from the house as fast as she could, but she only managed to run ten feet or so when she saw something that caused her to stop. Her feet slid forwards on the wet grass as she landed on her back, like a footballer doing a sliding tackle.

In front of her, soaking wet from the rain, with a confused look on his face, was the last thing Louise was hoping to see.

Kaiser.

26

Vanni thought about phoning the police. The fact that he and Sarah both thought something was wrong made him feel as though something might've happened. But if he phoned the police and they investigated, only to find out Louise was ignoring him, his pride would never recover.

The storm must've caused an accident on the carriageway heading into Whitford, because he'd been sitting in his car for almost an hour. The traffic was moving now, but only creeping along at a couple of miles an hour. It was times like these when he was thankful he'd chosen a car with an automatic gearbox. This was something he'd never thought of before, but now he was used to driving a car with his left leg tucked away and completely redundant from use, he had no intentions of ever going back to a manual.

He never fully relaxed when he wasn't at the restaurant while it was still open. But he did trust his staff, especially Sarah, to keep the place going. And he decided to let them cope after Sarah had convinced him to go and check on Louise. And his sous chef knew the menu well enough to cope. He'd left the restaurant in good hands.

He'd been feeling frustrated that he couldn't get hold of Louise. But he had given up trying to phone her until Sarah pointed out to him that something might've happened. He tried once more before he left the restaurant, and again on hands-free as he pulled out of his parking space, but it was still switched off.

The traffic jam added to his frustration.

Better behind it than in it, Nadia used to say. She'd always had a way of saying the right thing at the right time. He wondered what she would've said about Louise. He was sure she'd have been happy for him to move on at some point, and he was pretty sure she'd have liked Louise. Four years had passed now since she'd died, so Vanni knew he had no reason to feel guilt of any kind. But he did wonder what Nadia would have thought about Louise not answering her phone. At first, she'd probably have told him not to chase her. She'd have said something like, *If it's meant to be, she'll ring you.* But after her not answering for so long and with the phone still being switched off, surely Nadia would've told him to go to her too, just as Sarah had.

Saturday morning, everything was perfect. It was Monday now, and her phone was still switched off. If Louise was ignoring him, she must be very controlled to leave her phone off for that amount of time. Most people these days can't go two minutes without checking them.

Something was wrong. What it was, he didn't know. And his stomach was doing somersaults as he thought about it. He wanted the traffic to get moving so he could get there quicker. If it turned out she was ignoring him, then fine. At least he'd know the truth. But if not, and something had happened, he needed to help her. What it could be, he didn't know. Her car wasn't there and she wasn't home when he'd called at her bungalow. But surely by now she'd be home.

He knew Louise didn't want him to meet Oliver just yet, so he thought that if Oliver answered the door, he'd pretend to be a salesman, or maybe say he was lost, and ask to speak to his mother. She couldn't be annoyed at that.

As the car slowly moved along the carriageway towards Whitford. Vanni could see blue flashing lights up ahead.

The cars in front of him started to indicate right. The cars in the right-hand lane each slowed a little more to let one car at a time in, before they moved on.

As he got closer, he had to do the same. As he moved into the right-hand lane, he saw an ambulance, two highway patrol cars, and three cars that had all suffered damage of some kind. One was damaged so badly it reminded him of an accordion. One was squashed in at the side, and the last one, which was facing the wrong way had obviously been hit from behind.

He hoped that everyone involved was OK. He couldn't see anyone who looked injured, but six or seven people were standing around at the verge, including some police officers. It was a bad accident, but the demeanour of the people there made him think that everyone was OK.

As soon as Vanni's BMW passed the wreckage, he was able to put his foot down as the traffic jam seemed to instantly clear.

He was relieved now he was finally able to take the car up to the speed limit. He was hoping that within the next twenty minutes or so, he would be feeling even more relieved after hearing Louise's explanation as to why she hadn't answered his calls, and why her phone was still switched off. He couldn't think of a good reason himself, but he really hoped that Louise had one.

27

Kaiser had never really bothered Louise before. She'd found that if she stopped and stood still, he would stop running at her and just sniff around then walk away. She knew Oliver was scared of him. She'd told him many times that he just needed to stand still if the dog ever ran towards him, even if he was barking. But she knew he wouldn't have been able to. The sight of a huge, hairy and slavering German Shepherd heading towards you at top speed was enough to scare anyone, let alone a ten-year-old. Louise had spoken to Len in the past about how he shouldn't be allowed to roam free if that was how he behaved, and all Len said was something like *Don't worry, he won't bite. Not unless you're a burglar.* Not very helpful really.

Kaiser didn't look happy now as he'd watched Louise slide to the ground while running away from the farmhouse. This obviously confused him. Louise was on his land, and Kaiser couldn't have been fed since Len was locked in the room with her. She didn't know if hunger would play a part in whatever Kaiser was about to do, but she didn't think it would help.

She had to think fast.

No doubt Len was climbing through the window behind her. So she got to her feet, still with the metal bar in her right hand, and holding her empty left hand out towards the dog. She shouted, 'Stay,' as sternly as she could and then started to walk past him.

He looked confused, but he let her pass, and once she was a few feet from him, she shot into a sprint and ran as fast as her bare feet would take her on the muddy wet grass. She headed towards the bungalow. Although the road leading up to her house was lined by hedges, at the top of the lane, the hedges came to an end leaving a gap from the field belonging to the farm, and her back garden which led onto the forest.

She ran and ran as fast as she could, but her feet slipped and sank with every footstep. Her legs hurt and her knees shook, partly through fear, partly through a lack of food.

The rain had already soaked her through in the short time she'd been outside. She ran and ran, aware that she wasn't really heading in a straight line as she dodged the rubbish, scattered bricks and even a barrel lying on its side, along with all the other stuff that was always scattered around the farmhouse.

As she reached the gap in the hedges, she knew she was almost home. But suddenly, something heavy hit her on the back, pushing her forwards to the wet ground. She tried to keep a grip on the bar but to no avail as she felt it slip from her hand. She was suddenly aware that that something was now on her back. Within a second or two, she realised it was Len Hunter. Even in the rain she could smell him.

His face appeared next to hers as she faced the ground and he spoke into her ear. 'You bitch,' he said.

Louise could sense the anger in his voice, more so than what she'd witnessed during the last two days.

'You thought you was going home, didn't you?'

She had, but now she wasn't so sure.

'Well, you're wrong. I'm not finished with you yet.'

He released his weight from her back and grabbed her arm, dragging her over so she was now facing him. Jaw twitching, he pulled his arm back and slapped her hard across the face.

Before Louise could focus, another slap landed on the other side of her face. Even in the cold rain it felt like fire on her skin. She closed her eyes waiting for the next one, but instead of another strike, she felt the weight of him lighten a little, and he started screaming at the top of his voice. As she opened her eyes to see what was happening, she heard the growling.

It was Kaiser.

Obviously confused by the situation, instead of helping his owner, he'd grabbed him by his upper arm and was shaking him like a rag doll.

Len screamed and shouted, *'It's me. Kaiser; it's me!'*

But Kaiser, was in no mood for letting go.

The growling and snarling was deafening as he shook his owner's arm. It reminded Louise of the documentaries she'd seen when police dogs grabbed onto their suspects and didn't let go. But she didn't want to stay around to see him either eaten alive, or somehow break free to continue his attempt at halting her freedom.

'Kaiser... stop... Back... Kaiser.'

Louise got up from the ground and backed away from the scene of horror in front of her.

As she moved, she spotted the metal bar on the floor.

Len had seen it too and was trying to reach it with his free hand, the other arm still in Kaiser's powerful jaws. He didn't have the machete with him. She presumed he'd left it in the house when he climbed through the window, or maybe he dropped it as he'd landed outside. Even if he did have it, she didn't know if he would have used it on his own pet, but nothing this man did would surprise her ever again.

She considered moving the metal bar closer to him, as it was just out of his reach, but she didn't. The idea of being killed by a dog was horrific, and Kaiser didn't seem to be giving up his attack. But she couldn't bring herself to help Len. The only thing she could focus on was getting back to Oliver.

She turned and ran towards the house.

'Oliver!' she shouted. 'Oliver!' She shouted his name again and again.

Finally, she arrived at the door.

She tried the handle to find it locked, so she banged like hell, still shouting his name over and over. 'Oliver... Oliver.'

'Mum!' Louise heard him shout as he unlocked the door.

Relief shot through her from head to toe. She didn't know if he was OK, but he was well enough to call her name and unlock the door.

She forced the door open as soon as it was unlocked, which sent Oliver flying as she rushed into the room.

She turned and slammed the door shut, locking it as quickly as she could with shaking hands. She then pulled Oliver away from the door and into the centre of the kitchen.

Louise then crouched down in front of him, throwing her arms around him and squeezing him as tightly as she could.

After a few seconds, she lightened her grip and took him by the shoulders. There were tears rolling down his face, but other than that, he seemed fine.

'Now, Oliver, you have to listen to me…'

Before she could finish her sentence, there was a loud bang as the door burst open, broken in half as bits of glass flew all over the kitchen floor.

Louise and Oliver lifted their heads.

Standing in the doorway, with a metal bar in his hands, was Len Hunter.

Home

1

Life can be very cruel sometimes. You feel as though your life is just starting to get on track, and then something out of the blue comes along to ruin it. You get the job you've always wanted, only to find the people you work with are bullies. You find someone you love, only for them not to love you back. Or when you do find that one true love, you lose them through illness or mental health. The house of your dreams can end up being nothing but trouble with repairs or maybe even problem neighbours. The car you've saved up for what seemed like forever, breaks down and costs you more money than it's worth. Or you book a holiday that you think is going to be the trip of a lifetime, only to have it ruined through food poisoning, or bad weather.

Life had a habit of giving you with one hand and then taking away with the other.

Nobody knew that more than Louise Derwent.

She'd had her fair share of disappointment throughout her lifetime. And now, after spending almost two full days in what can only be described as a home-made prison cell, she'd managed to get free and get back to her house to find her son alive and well, only to have Len Hunter, her abductor, kick the door in.

The relief at finding Oliver OK was overwhelming. Anything could've happened during the time she'd been locked away in the farmhouse. But somehow, he'd managed to keep himself safe.

He was clean and fresh, so she presumed he'd had a bath or shower. And he was wearing clean clothes. Unlike Louise who'd been wearing the same clothes for the last two days. She felt dirty. She wanted to shower, especially as she'd been in contact with that disgusting creature, Len Hunter. She wanted to wash away his touch from where he'd hit her, and from where he'd grabbed her and sat on her. She was repulsed at the thought of this man being anywhere near her. A very long shower was needed, or maybe a bath with water so hot she could barely climb into it.

Although the thought of everything he'd done would stay with her forever, at that moment she had no idea how long her life was going to be. He'd already attacked her, and now that she'd escaped, what options did he have? Len either had to take her and Oliver back to his house and imprison both of them, or he had to kill them. But Louise was going to do her best to make sure neither of those things transpired.

She grabbed Oliver's hand and ran through the hall and into the bathroom, slamming the door shut and locking it. Len had already kicked the door in which was the main entrance to the house. The bathroom door wasn't anywhere near as strong, so it wouldn't take him long to do the same to that one.

Oliver ran over and sat on the toilet seat, looking more terrified than Louise had ever seen him before. His hands were shaking and the expression on his face was one of utter fear.

'Mum,' Oliver said.

'It's OK,' she said, leaning her back against the door.

Louise quickly looked around the bathroom, trying to think of a way of getting the better of Len.

The cup next to the sink which held the toothbrushes and toothpaste was plastic, as were the shower gel and shampoo bottles. She briefly considered trying to escape through the window, but even if the gap was big enough, which it wasn't, Len could break in before they had the chance to climb through it.

A loud bang made her scream as the door shook, sending her flying towards the centre of the small room.

The door hadn't broken, so she put her back against it once more, knowing she could get hurt, but hoping it would make a difference, possibly slowing him down a little.

Len kicked the door again.

The jolt shook through her to her bones as she tried hard to keep him out of the room. She was terrified, but there was no way she was going to give in. She had to protect her son no matter what.

'What's going on?'

She heard another man's voice from the other side of the bathroom door.

317

The attack stopped, as she stood there in silence, listening. She glanced over at Oliver, still trembling on the toilet seat. He also looked confused.

'Louise!' the man shouted.

Within seconds of hearing her name leaving his lips, and even though his voice was slightly muffled by the bathroom door, she knew who it was.

'Vanni!' she shouted.

Suddenly an array of noises came from outside the door told Louise that the two of them were fighting. Len Hunter hadn't graced Vanni with any kind of greeting, he didn't even answer his question. Louise knew he'd just gone for him.

She heard both men groaning as they struggled. A dull sound shook the floor. Louise presumed Len had dropped the metal bar, or Vanni had knocked it from his hand.

The noise seemed to move along the hallway towards the kitchen. She wondered if Len might be getting the better of him, even though Vanni was several inches taller. Vanni was big enough to protect himself. But he spent his working life in a kitchen whereas Len had to use his muscles every day while working on the farm. This had to give him the advantage.

Louise stepped away from the door and grabbed Oliver's hand, pulling him up from the toilet lid.

She unlocked the door and opened it slightly. She knew her only escape from the house was blocked by the scuffle between Vanni and Len as she had to go through the kitchen and then the living room before they could get to the patio doors at the back of the house. So she led Oliver through to his bedroom. Like she had in the bathroom, she scanned the room for a weapon. The pencil sharpener might've been heavy enough to do some damage. It was made of steel. But unfortunately, Michael had screwed it to the desk.

She rummaged through Oliver's toys, but the only thing she could find that would be remotely useful was a plastic baseball bat. She couldn't imagine it would be strong enough to bring a halt to the fight.

After giving up the hunt for a weapon, she knew she had no choice but to try to help Vanni overpower Len. Surely two against one would put the odds in their favour.

'Stay here,' she said to Oliver.

He nodded frantically.

As she opened the bedroom door, she saw that Vanni had Len in a bear-hug from behind, at the other end of the hall.

Blood poured from Len's nose; she hoped that meant Vanni might be winning the battle. But just as she was starting to feel a little relief, Len threw himself backwards, banging Vanni hard against the door frame.

Vanni's head hit the corner of the wood. Almost as if someone had pressed the *off* button, his body collapsed to the floor.

Louise's stomach sank as she stood watching Len wipe the blood from his nose, his arm also dripping from the disagreement with Kaiser. He stopped and turned his head until his evil eyes fixed on her. He seemed to snarl like a feral animal before he leapt forward with his hands held out in front of him.

Louise stepped back into Oliver's bedroom, screaming as she tried to slam the door shut. But before the door sank into the frame, it was propelled open by his boot, and Louise fell as the force of the door sent her flying across the room.

She'd been here with Len before, even if it was in a different house and a different room. This time she had Oliver in the room with her, and she was prepared to do anything necessary to make sure they survived. If that meant jamming her fingers into his eyes, or biting his face, she would do it.

Louise jumped up from the floor as quickly as she could. As she got to her feet, she swung her right hand in Len's direction as hard as her tired body would let her.

His head briefly fell to one side as the heel of her hand met his cheek. And he stumbled against the chest of drawers, wide-eyed from the blow.

As he steadied himself, she swung her right hand again. This hit didn't land as hard; just her fingers caught his face rather than the base of her hand, but it still shook his head.

She took a quick breath as she adjusted her stance ready to swing another haymaker, only this one didn't get the chance to land. Her arm had barely started to swing towards him when a backhander from Len hit her in the nose, sending her falling backwards, her eyes instantly filling with tears.

Her back had just hit the soft carpet of Oliver's bedroom floor when Len landed on top of her, both hands fixed firmly around her throat.

She was struggling for breath from the fight and now her oxygen supply was being cut off by Len's dirty and bloodied hands.

The tears from the impact to her nose were dispersing and her vision came back into focus. The evil expression on his face, and the grimace as he put all his strength into squeezing her throat, told her he meant business. This attack was non-negotiable. Even if she could speak, he wasn't going to listen. It was all about to come to an end. She tried to kick and fight but she couldn't lift her hips from the ground like before. He was about to win.

Her vision started to blur again as her body gave up the fight. She had no more strength left in her. She had no more effort. She wanted to beg for her life as she gazed into his eyes, but he wasn't going to abandon this attack. He was going to kill her. All Louise could think was if he was doing this to her, what was he going to do to Oliver?

Just before she faded away into unconsciousness, there was a loud noise from somewhere within the room. It was a noise she hated, but she couldn't place what it was.

Seconds after the horrible grinding sound had stopped, Len loosened his grip around her throat.

An uncontrollable gasp of air entered her lungs as he let go of her. She could feel her chest expand as her body was suddenly allowed to breathe.

Len jumped up off her and stepped backwards.

As Louise's vision recovered, she sat up on the floor to see Len staring, with his mouth wide open and his hands shaking in front of him.

Oliver was behind him, and a little to the side. Last she knew he was behind her. He must've shot past them as Len had her pinned to the floor. She couldn't make out Oliver's expression. He normally had a very straight, emotionless look on his face, but now his mouth was open. But he didn't look scared or upset. It was the same expression he had when he'd finished a job in the house, like washing the dishes or hoovering his bedroom.

Louise then looked back at Len and instantly realised what had happened.

There was a charcoal pencil sticking out of the side of Len's neck. Judging by the length of pencil on the outside, there were a good three or four inches embedded into his throat.

That was the noise she'd heard. It was the pencil sharpener. Oliver must've sharpened the pencil to as fine a point as possible before thrusting it into Len's neck.

Len was still on his feet, his mouth wide open in shock. Louise watched as he felt around with both hands until he found the pencil. After grasping his fingers around the end, he pulled it out.

It came out slowly, almost causing Louise to be sick as she saw it slide out of his flesh. As soon as the sharpened end was free, it was followed by a flow of blood which poured out in a small jet like a hole in a water bed. Len dropped the pencil to the floor.

Oliver ran in front of him to where his mum sat on the floor. She wrapped her arms around him, pulling him tightly towards her.

Len moved towards them. The jet of blood had stopped squirting, but it was still flowing down his neck, soaking his shirt all down the left side of his body.

Louise begged for it to end. He surely couldn't survive any more blood loss. His life had to be coming to an end.

As he came closer, his bloody hands held out in front of him like something from a zombie movie.

Louise and Oliver shuffled away, trying to get away from the evil creature that was in front of them.

But suddenly, the metal bar hit him on the side of the head, sending him crashing to the floor.

Vanni stood behind him, his face cut and bruised, and his eyes squinting in obvious pain. He dropped the bar to the floor and stepped over Len then knelt next to Louise and Oliver. He put one arm around Louise as he spoke into his mobile phone. She heard him ask for the police as Len Hunter writhed in pain on the bedroom floor. He was barely conscious as he rolled back and forth.

Louise could see the wound to his head and was sickened. A flap of skin, and possibly a chunk of scalp had fallen open as more blood emptied out of him.

She pulled Oliver even tighter towards her, not wanting him to see the scene of horror in front of them.

Once Vanni had finished the call, he put his arms around them both. They didn't speak, they just hugged each other as Louise watched Len turn himself over and struggle into a crawling position. He then sluggishly crawled from the bedroom and through the hall towards the kitchen. Neither Louise nor Vanni felt the need to go and hit him again. It was obvious he wasn't going to get very far, and it was quite clear his life, and not Louise's, was almost over.

2

Louise took a little persuading to go to hospital. But she agreed in the end. All three of them had been through a terrible ordeal. All of their experiences had been different, but they were all caused by the same man. A man whose body was found on the stone floor of his kitchen where the whole torrid ordeal had begun. Louise couldn't believe he'd made it that far before he'd died, but somehow, he had.

In the time it took for the police to arrive, and for them to find Len's body, Louise, Oliver and Vanni still hadn't moved from the bedroom floor. It crossed Louise's mind that Len Hunter could've disappeared, somehow managing to escape and begin a new life somewhere else. But with the stab wound to his neck and the laceration to his head, it was only a matter of time before his body gave up the fight. Even though she would never wish death on another person, she couldn't help but feel relieved.

Louise didn't want to go to hospital because at that moment, she felt as though she never wanted to leave her bungalow again, and she certainly never wanted to let Oliver out of her sight ever again. But she eventually agreed, as long as Oliver could go in the ambulance with her.

At the hospital, Louise was treated for dehydration. She was put on a drip and also given antibiotics to help avoid infection. Oliver was surprisingly healthy considering he'd spent the weekend by himself.

The cuts on his fingers were quite badly infected, but after being cleaned up by the nurses and given a tetanus injection and a course of antibiotics, he was told they should heal reasonably quickly. And Vanni just had a few cuts and bruises, plus a lump to the back of his head.

Louise was back home after just two nights. By then the crime scene investigators had finished their examination of her bungalow, and of the farmhouse, so Louise and Oliver could try their best to get back to normal. Although Louise wouldn't let Oliver sleep in his own bedroom, partly because the carpet needed replacing after the amount of blood spilled, and partly because she wanted him at her side as she slept.

The nightmares stayed with Louise for a few weeks. There were several times she'd awoken to find Oliver stroking her hair and shushing her gently. Louise wondered what effect the events would have on him, but he seemed to get back to normal within a day or so. He'd even sketched several more drawings, none of them creepy, almost as if he didn't want to worry her while she recovered from the horror she'd endured. But she was sure he'd get back to his eerie, ghostly pictures at some point. He was offered counselling; after all, he had contributed towards the death of another human being. But it really didn't seem to bother him. Oliver knew right from wrong and in his mind, Len Hunter was a very bad man. If he hadn't stabbed him with the pencil, Len would

326

have most likely killed his mum. So he had nothing to be sorry for.

As the weeks went by, her relationship with Vanni grew. She hadn't used the word 'love' as of yet, but she felt as though it was almost time to say it. He was everything she could have hoped for. He understood her, he was the perfect gentleman, and more importantly, he was really good with Oliver, and Oliver liked him.

Louise also felt ready to tell Oliver about his dad. She didn't think she would tell him how he'd died until he was much older. But he needed to know his dad wasn't coming back. It wasn't fair to keep him wondering. He needed to know he'd died. Louise knew he would cope. Oliver seemed to have a lateral way of thinking. Things were black and white to him. They just seemed to roll off his back. He'd showed amazing resilience during the time he was alone, and he'd looked after himself just fine. There was no doubt he'd be distraught at hearing his dad had died. But Louise knew it would be better in the long run. He'd already asked about the box. Maybe once he'd accepted that his dad wasn't coming back, they could bury Michael's ashes in the garden, maybe even have a small service of some kind. This would hopefully help Oliver draw a line under the grief. He would still miss his dad, but the waiting, wondering, and the hope he felt every time someone knocked on the door would all come to an end. She felt guilty for not being honest with him. But at the time it felt like the right thing to do. Now, she knew she had to tell him the truth.

3

Vanni pulled the car up onto the curb outside the huge, detached house on the road referred to by most as *Millionaire's row.* Louise took a deep breath as she sat in the passenger seat. Oliver was in the back.

A warm hand grasped hers as she fidgeted.

'It'll be fine,' Vanni said.

She turned to look at him. He smiled a smile that could convince her of anything. And although she was nervous, she knew she had Vanni's support.

Louise got out of the car and walked slowly to the front door. The house must've had, six bedrooms at least, she thought. There was a large, grassed area either side of the path that led up to the front door. As she stepped towards the red-bricked building she realised it was actually a three-storey house. It couldn't have been further from the bungalow she was used to living in. As impressed as she was at such a beautiful house, she couldn't imagine her and Oliver living there. It would take a full day just to run the vacuum cleaner around. But that wasn't at the front of her mind at that moment. She was too nervous to think of anything else other than the reason for her visit to this house.

As the butterflies flew around her stomach, she turned to look at Vanni. She could see Oliver watching from the back seat, but he didn't move.

Vanni just gave a slight nod to tell her everything would be OK.

Louise took a deep breath, and then knocked on the door.

After a minute or so, the door opened. She was shocked to see Hemal Kharti had answered. She'd been so worried about facing Mrs Kharti that she never imagined that Hemal might answer.

His face changed from a pleasant smile to a look of utter dread. He then stood back as the door swung wide open, seeming to struggle for breath as he sporadically turned and looked behind him, obviously panicking and hoping for support from his family.

Louise held her hands up and took a step closer to him. 'Hemal, it's OK. I'm not here to upset you.'

He moved further back into the house, looking uncomfortable.

'Who is it, Hemal?' the voice from behind him said.

Mrs Kharti appeared and her face changed too, from a pleasant and welcoming expression, to one of confusion.

'Mrs Derwent,' she said. 'I heard about what happened a couple of weeks ago. Are you OK?'

Louise couldn't believe how nice Mrs Kharti was. She already knew how strict and stern she could be. After all, she'd seen it first-hand. But after everything Louise had put her and her family through, she still showed concern for her, wanting to make sure she was all right before anything else. This made her want to cry. But she tried hard to fight back the tears.

'Yes, Mrs Kharti... I'm fine, thank you.'

'Terrible business that. I never liked that man, but I never thought he would do such a thing.'

She stepped forwards and gently held Louise's chin as she scrutinised the bruises on her face. They had faded to the point where they'd almost gone. But even though she'd covered them with her makeup, they were still partly visible.

'He was a very bad man,' Louise said, tilting her head as she was being examined.

Mrs Kharti gently let go of her and dropped her hand to her side. 'He was not a man. A man would not treat a woman in that way.'

'You're right, but I'm OK now. Just trying to get on with things.'

Mrs Kharti stepped back a little from the doorway and held out her hand. 'Would you like to come in, Mrs Derwent?'

'No, thank you. I won't take too much of your time. I just wanted to tell you...' the tears got the better of her and started to roll down her face.

'Mrs Derwent,' she said, stepping towards Louise and taking her by both hands.

Hemal was still standing behind his mother, but he didn't look quite as nervous as he did when he'd opened the door.

Louise swallowed as she tried to stop crying.

'What is it?'

'I owe you and Hemal, and all your family, an apology.'

'Why's that?'

Louise sniffed before she continued. 'Len Hunter told me... he told me when we were trapped in the house together...'

'Yes?' Mrs Kharti asked, eyes fixed on Louise with a look of concern on her face.

'It was him. It was him that made the phone calls. Not Hemal.'

She then fell into uncontrollable sobbing.

Mrs Kharti gently wrapped her arms around Louise as she cried.

Louise was embarrassed. She shouldn't be being comforted by the person she had wronged. But that was Mrs Kharti. For some reason or other she held no grudge for what had happened. She seemed to understand the mistake, and instead of being angry, which she had every right to be, she offered comfort to Louise. In her mind maybe she saw the situation as both her and Hemal having been wronged by the man she'd previously lambasted. And she probably felt a little relief that her son's name had finally been cleared.

After thanking Mrs Kharti for being so understanding, and giving a shy and nervous Hemal a hug of apology, she said goodbye and headed back to the car, where she was greeted by another warm and tender hand on hers.

4

It had now been four weeks since Oliver was left alone because of Len Hunter holding his mum hostage in the farmhouse. Oliver was much happier now that Mr Hunter and Kaiser were gone. His mum said that a dog handler came and took Kaiser to a dog pound. He hoped that Kaiser would get a nice new home living with someone better than Mr Hunter. Although Kaiser had scared Oliver, he wanted him to be OK. He didn't care about Mr Hunter, but Kaiser hadn't done anything wrong.

Oliver felt very sad at what his mum had told him the night before.

Hearing the news of his dad dying had started a flow of tears that didn't stop until he'd fallen asleep. But the next day he felt different. He knew he'd always miss his dad, but he felt a little better knowing that he'd died and not run away from them, which was something he couldn't understand. His mum said he would understand more when he was older. He could never figure out why his dad would just walk out one day and not come back. But the fact that he had been ill and then died meant that his dad had still loved him and his mum, and not just left. Oliver would always be sad about losing his dad, but at least he could talk about him now, and at least he knew they would be together again one day. He wasn't sure how heaven worked, and he'd wondered if when he died, whether his dad wouldn't have been there waiting for him because he'd left them? But now Oliver knew his dad had died, he thought that surely now his dad should be the first person he'd meet when it was his turn to step through the gates of heaven.

He felt better for knowing the truth. And he wasn't angry with his mum for keeping it from him. He understood her reasons. And now he could stop worrying about where he was.

Vanni had made a picnic at work and brought it to the bungalow.

Oliver liked Vanni. He especially liked how much his mum smiled when he was around. Oliver hadn't realised that his mum never smiled much before. She did when she was out shopping, but he could see a difference in her eyes when she smiled at strangers. When she smiled at Vanni, her face lit up and she looked truly happy, which, in turn, made Oliver happy. Vanni was very nice to Oliver. He always sat and spoke to him, and he would take an interest in his drawings. He never complained about them like his teachers did. Vanni would just say he liked them, or he'd ask questions about them like, *When did you draw this one?* and, *What made you draw a ghost?* and occasionally, *Where did you get the inspiration for this one?* This pleased Oliver. He started to draw pictures with Vanni in mind, hoping he'd like the finished product and say something nice about it. The three of them left the bungalow and walked through the back garden towards the woods. They'd decided they would have a picnic while sitting next to the bucket. Oliver hadn't been there since his dad had left... died. But now he knew the truth, he wanted to go there.

As they made their way through the forest, Oliver holding his mum's hand while Vanni held her other one, something caught his eye in the distance.

He stopped and shushed them both.

'What is it?' Vanni whispered.

Oliver pointed.

As his mum and Vanni looked ahead up the track, Oliver saw an old friend making his way towards them.

It was Franky.

'Oh wow,' his mum said.

Oliver let go of her hand and stepped towards Vanni. 'Can I have a piece of meat?' he asked.

'Of course,' Vanni said, putting the basket to the ground and taking a piece of ham from one of the sandwiches.

As the fox came closer, his mum asked, 'Is this Franky?'

'Yes,' he answered.

Franky was still trotting towards them, but he slowed down and then stopped in front of Oliver.

'I didn't...' his mum began then stopped mid-sentence.

'It's OK, mum. I know you didn't believe me.' Oliver held his hand out as he crouched down a little.

'Careful, Oliver,' Vanni said.

'It's fine,' he answered, then he spoke to the fox. 'Come on, Franky. You like ham.'

The fox gently reached up and took the meat from his hand. After chewing and swallowing it, he licked his lips, had a quick sniff around the ground in front of them, then turned and wandered off into the woods.

'You're welcome,' Oliver said, sarcastically, then turned and smiled at his mum and Vanni.

'I don't believe it,' Vanni said. 'I've never seen a wild fox come so close to people before. Aren't they usually nocturnal?'

'That was amazing,' his mum said. 'Oliver said he might've been rescued in the past. It might explain why he's not scared to wander around through the daytime.'

Vanni nodded. 'That would certainly explain his confidence around people. Unless he just likes you, Ollie.'

Oliver smiled. 'Maybe.'

The three of them then carried on with their walk.

Oliver knew his mum hadn't really believed him about Franky, which didn't bother him too much. But now she'd seen him, he wondered if she would begin to like him too, maybe even feed him. He hoped so.

5

Louise was lost in quiet reflection as Vanni and Oliver sat at the side of the pond trying to spot fish in the shallows.

The blanket felt comfortable on the soft grass as she soaked up the sunshine and ran through the events that had brought her to where she was right now. Her modelling career had ended a long time ago – even though Vanni had tried to convince her to give it another go – and from trying to help Michael through his depression, to losing him and then to the most traumatic event she'd ever had to endure, to right now, sitting in the sunshine feeling as though life couldn't get any better.

Vanni had offered her some part-time work in his restaurant, which she appreciated, after making sure he did actually need another member of staff and it wasn't just a nice gesture, which he'd assured her it wasn't. He said they could plan her hours around Oliver and his school. Vanni said it was only temporary though, as he was going to help her look for an agent and get her modelling career going once more. She wouldn't do glamour modelling again, or even anything that showed too much flesh. But Vanni had convinced her that it was worth trying as he told her how beautiful she was, which was something he did a lot. She hoped he was right. But at that point, she didn't really care. If she could get some modelling work then that would be great. However, as she looked at Vanni with his hand on Oliver's shoulder as they stood on the bank at the side of the pond, or *the bucket,* as it was known as, she felt as though she had everything she needed in life right there in front of her.

She'd wondered what would happen to Hunter's Farm, and if someone else, maybe a distant relative would inherit the property. But just now she didn't care.

Although she loved her bungalow, if things continued to go well with Vanni and they eventually ended up moving in together, they would most likely move in with him. Louise couldn't see Vanni giving his house up to move in with her, even though it felt like a house in the countryside. But that was way in the future.

At that moment, she wanted everything to stay exactly as it was. Everything in her life was perfect. And she hoped it would stay that way.

THE END

Acknowledgements

If you've ever wondered where the idea for a novel comes from, even the author might struggle to tell you.

Occasionally I remember when an idea jumped into my brain. But I can honestly say I don't know where the idea for All Alone came from.

What I can tell you is that it came to me during the 2020 lockdown. I know this because I was half way through another novel when it happened. When an idea appears, I usually write the first chapter, just to lay the groundwork so I can return to it at a later date.

However, this story, and especially Oliver and Louise, would insist on spending most of their time bouncing around the inner workings of my mind. When this happens, I know I have no choice but to keep going, even if it means putting other works on hold.

I have to thank quite a few people for their help: my lovely wife, Maggi, for reading the story, and for telling me the truth whenever I needed to hear it. My grandson, Joe, my nephews, Callum and Alex, and my friend, Matthew Vaughan for telling me what they'd get up to if they were left alone as ten-year-old boys. And some very helpful assistance from my friends, Vicky Gregory, Shimmi Munshi, and fellow authors, Bea Green, Neal James, and my very talented editor, Marie Campbell, as well as all my family and friends for their continuing support.

And finally, a heartfelt thank you to you, the readers; the people who follow my work, send me nice messages, and constantly tell me to hurry up with my next book. Without you, this would all be for nothing.

Printed in Great Britain
by Amazon